COVER UP

KC Burn

Dreamspinner Press

Published by
Dreamspinner Press
5032 Capital Circle SW
Ste 2, PMB# 279
Tallahassee, FL 32305-7886
USA
http://www.dreamspinnerpress.com/

Cover Up

Cover Art by L.C. Chase
http://www.lcchase.com

ISBN: 978-1-62380-238-7

Printed in the United States of America
First Edition
December 2012

eBook edition available
eBook ISBN: 978-1-62380-239-4

This is for everyone who isn't perfect.

ACKNOWLEDGMENTS

Thanks as always to my super support group—Alex, Dottie and Chudney. A special thanks to Dolorianne, who pulled my fat out of the fire on this one.

I also need to thank the Canadian Identity Theft Support Centre, especially Heather, who was super helpful and answered all my questions. If I got anything wrong, it's all on me.

CHAPTER
One

DETECTIVE Ivan Bekker limped into police headquarters. The taskforce had been a clusterfuck from word one. Both the Organized Crime Enforcement supervisor and his boss on the Drug Squad had butted heads from the beginning. The amazing thing was that they'd managed to succeed in pulling down several major players in the Russian mafia's drug trafficking ring. The supposedly surgical sting had devolved into a messy shootout in the middle of the warehouse district.

There had been a number of injuries and bullet wounds, but somehow, none of the good guys died.

Not yet.

Ivan stared across the floor, past the detectives busy on computers, on the phone, scribbling on paper, to the empty desks by Inspector Nadar's office. His friend, Kurt, had been loaded onto an ambulance, blood everywhere, and Kurt's partner, Simon, had accompanied. Hadn't taken long to figure out one of their own had been the hardest hit, and there was as yet no word on his status. It wasn't fair; Kurt and Simon had been on loan from Homicide, and a fluke shot had taken Kurt down.

He trudged into the locker room and peeled off his gear. Before he could shed his blood-splattered clothes, Inspector Sergio Martelli, head of the Drug Squad, rushed in.

"Bekker, my office. Now."

Always curt, today his boss sounded pissed off as well. Great. Just what Ivan was hoping for. All he wanted was a hot shower and the chance to go to the hospital, check on Kurt personally. Ivan had been drawn to Kurt after the man's previous partner, Ben, had been killed on the job nearly a year ago. Not attracted, but something about Kurt changed after Ben's death, making Ivan take note. A few weeks ago they'd gone out for drinks, and Kurt had come out to him. Most gay cops kept that information real close to the vest, and Kurt was no different, but Ivan was already out.

They'd managed drinks or dinner all of three times before today's shit storm, but Ivan considered the man a friend. He couldn't fucking die now.

With a baleful look at the showers, Ivan plucked the clammy, bloody shirt away from his body.

"Now, Bekker!" His boss's voice reverberated through the room, like the drill sergeant everyone likened him to. In fact, he'd heard it hadn't taken long for Martelli's fellow cadets in the police academy to shorten Sergio to Serge and then to Sarge. Most people thought it was his rank, and he seemed to enjoy the word play.

Ivan slammed his locker shut and stomped toward his boss's office. If he got blood all over Martelli's visitor chairs, so the fuck what?

Outside in the hall, there was no sign of Martelli. Ivan's steps slowed as lethargy battled his momentary anger. Surely Martelli's voice, deep and booming though it was, hadn't carried all the way from his office.

A couple officers gave him a wide berth as they walked past. Ivan didn't blame them; he must look like an escapee from a horror movie. Hell, with his dark blond hair and the Slavic features he'd inherited from his mother, he looked a lot like the Russian gangster he'd shot to death earlier. And whose blood covered him now. Dead wasn't a win, and even as bullets scudded into the walls around him, Ivan had dashed in to try and save the guy. He'd failed. Many of the drug dealers and gangsters were going to prison—some would be deported—but Ivan's foe was headed for the morgue. When the paramedics arrived, they'd found out the young man's name was Dmitri. They said you never forgot your first kill, and now he knew why.

Without knocking or otherwise announcing his presence, Ivan stalked into Martelli's office and threw himself into the blue chair on the right side. Serve him right if Martelli had to get the damn thing reupholstered.

Nose buried in a report, Martelli didn't appear to notice his arrival.

Ivan shifted in his chair a couple of times. He could have showered already.

Irritation and impatience got the better of him. "What the fuck is so important I couldn't even change clothes first, Sarge?"

"Shut the door, Bekker."

Anger heated his cheeks and neck. Was it possible to literally steam? Because Ivan was on the brink. He got up and slammed the door so hard he was sitting again before the reverberations ceased.

Lifting one grizzled, gray brow, Martelli stared at him. "Was that necessary?"

Ivan blinked at him. When in doubt, don't say a damned thing that might be incriminating.

"What happened out there?"

Squinting, he tried to determine Martelli's exact mood. Definitely pissed off, but Ivan can't have been the only one to kill their target. With the amount of bullets flying around, it had been nothing short of a localized war zone. No way was he the only one up for investigation by the Special Investigations Unit.

He'd not intended to kill anyone, but he'd done nothing wrong. He shrugged and recounted events of the day, from his perspective. Martelli and the SIU were going to need information from many, many officers before anyone could fully piece together the picture of what happened today.

"Right. Good job. I'm going to need a written statement before you leave."

"Before I leave?" What the fuck? He had no intention of writing any reports today. Not with Kurt in the hospital, condition unknown.

"Yes, I'm afraid I must insist."

"Why, Sarge?" Ivan slammed his fists down on the armrests, but that wasn't enough. He launched out of the chair with enough force to tilt it precariously before it wobbled back onto all four legs. Ivan didn't even spare it a glance as he prowled about the room. He wasn't as tall as some of the other officers, but he used his hard-won muscles to intimidate when needed. Unfortunately, Martelli was completely unaffected. Damn him. Then again, Ivan wasn't like some of the ill-tempered idiots on the squad. Made a lot of people underestimate him.

His boss knew his capabilities, though, and even though Ivan paced like a restless lion, Martelli stared indulgently like he was nothing more than a fretful kitten.

He couldn't let it go without a whimper. Whirling, he yanked the chair over and watched it skid to a stop at the wall. He stared at it, hands fisted at his side. Punching something would make him feel better—for a split second. There wasn't a damn thing in the office that wouldn't bust his knuckles if he tried, and since he normally punched with his gun hand, well... drawing or firing a gun with busted knuckles was no joy.

"Better?" Martelli asked.

Ivan unclenched his fists and slumped into the other chair. He took a bit of vicious satisfaction in getting blood and grime all over both chairs, but that wasn't enough compensation for making Ivan do paperwork today.

"Interested in knowing why I need you to do this now?" The reproach in Martelli's tone was unmistakable.

Ivan scraped at a streak of dried blood on the back of his hand that had escaped his initial hand wash.

"Fine." His mother would have slapped him upside the head if he'd spoken to her with that tone, but Martelli wasn't his mom, thank Christ.

"You, Kessel, and Gillespie are on admin leave, pending the SIU investigations. I don't know who else from the other divisions are out, but there weren't supposed to be any casualties. And there were ten, at last count. This is going to come back and bite me on the ass."

"Fuck, Sarge, how will making me do paperwork help any?"

Taking a furtive look around the office, Martelli lowered his voice enough that Ivan had to lean in to hear him.

"I've got a job for you, completely off the books."

Shock made him sit back. Martelli had grand plans to get into politics once he'd finished his twenty-five years on the force, backed by his wealthy society wife. As a result, Ivan had never known his boss to bend the rules, and now he was proposing... what, exactly?

"What kind of job?"

"You're one of my best detectives, Bekker."

He was? Ivan was damned good at his job, but finding out Martelli thought he was one of the best surprised him. Then again, maybe it made Martelli uncomfortable to show him any sort of favoritism since he was gay. Martelli was an effective leader, but he was usually deaf to the slurs and insults Ivan heard on a regular basis from some of the other officers and detectives—in that, he'd envied Kurt. Inspector Nadar in Homicide seemed a lot more politically correct than Martelli, reprimanding those who acted or spoke offensively. Most of the guys were fine; there were only a few rotten apples in the bunch.

Nevertheless... how did he respond? "Okay."

Martelli nodded, as though he'd been waiting for some sort of acknowledgment from Ivan. Also weird. "We both know we got lucky today. Only one cop with life-threatening injuries. Considering...." Martelli's voice dropped yet again.

"Considering?"

A scowl deepened the creases on Martelli's spray-tanned forehead. "Considering we've got a leak. Maybe worse."

Ivan's nostrils flared. Shit. He'd tried hard not to think it, but he'd been on more than one of these stings during his career, and this was the first time they'd been met with this degree of organized resistance.

"Worse?"

"I don't want to speculate yet. What I do want you to do is go undercover while you're on your administrative leave. I hate to ask this of you, but we've got a tip that needs looking into, and I need you on it."

Slumping back in his chair, Ivan stared at Martelli. This was so completely against regulations it wasn't even funny. If this went south, Ivan could lose his job. But police work wasn't always clean and proper, no matter how much they might wish it so. And if he lost his job over this, well, this wasn't the first time he'd considered moving into another line of work. He'd wanted to be a cop to fix things, make things better, but he'd never realized he'd have to give up his personal life.

"What's the job?"

"We got word that one of the suspected up-and-comers in Razhin's organization has advertised for a roommate. I want you to get in there and see: one, if the connection is real; and two, if you can find some inside information on Razhin. If we can't take him down, we're going to have more incidents like today."

As head of the Russian mafia in Toronto, Viktor Razhin was ultimately responsible for any drug or human trafficking the Russians had a hand in.

Martelli tapped a finger on his desk. "The information I have is that this new kid owns two properties and has spent the past few months delving into the marijuana market."

"Marijuana? That's a little small-time for Razhin, isn't it?"

"From what I can tell, the kid's an independent operator, and pot's less dangerous and requires less capital to get started than major coke, crack, or meth operations."

"And now he's grown big enough for Razhin to take an interest? Savvy little entrepreneur. But why would a guy like that need or *want* a roommate?"

Rolling his eyes, Martelli handed over a sheet of paper. "No idea. Look into that if you get a chance, but the Razhin connection is your primary concern. Here's the vitals. Make sure you shred it before you leave the office."

"Not even a file?" Ivan frowned.

"Can't afford one. I'm afraid even entering this into the system will alert the mole."

Ivan scanned the sheet, but aside from a couple names, addresses, and contact numbers there was little for him to form an opinion. Parker Wakefield. Not a picture, not a driver's license, not a school transcript, not even a credit report. Not a damned thing except for a notation that he attended the University of Toronto, was twenty-two, and had a boyfriend named Neil Travers. Ivan tried to keep the grimace off his face. Presumably Martelli trusted him, but the bullshit about being the best detective was no more than that. Martelli had chosen him for this operation because he was the only one on the team who was openly gay. Ivan knew of one other, and suspected a couple more, but no way was Martelli putting one of the homophobic asswipes on this.

"I'm a little old to be a college kid, or to need a roommate. How did you want me to play this?"

"Divorced man whose wife took him to the cleaners. I'm hoping he'll have some sympathy for you, but either way, the housing coordinator at the university owes me a favor. You'll be presented as the most viable candidate."

"Wife?" Great. Back in the closet for yet another fucking undercover mission. "Does that mean I've got Trish as backup?" His partner would make the ultimate scorned wife. Most of the department thought Trish was a right royal bitch, but Ivan enjoyed her outspokenness, her willingness to call bullshit, and her quick wit. They got along great.

Martelli shook his head, and a tight band squeezed at his heart. If Trish was dirty, Ivan would know, dammit.

"If I don't have Trish as backup, why can't I go in as a gay man who just broke up with someone?" Nothing like the damned truth to sell an undercover story.

Martelli snorted. "Don't be ridiculous. That doesn't have the same devastation as a divorce. We want him to be sympathetic and off guard."

If Ivan hadn't been sitting down, he would have fallen. His breath fled as though he'd been kicked in the gut. He'd lived with Colin longer than most departmental marriages lasted. Yet somehow, his relationship was less valid? Sure, he and Colin had never gotten married. Ivan wasn't sure how that would work for a gay cop, but Colin had never pushed, and Ivan had been content with the state of their relationship. Until he came home early one day last fall and caught Colin fucking someone else in their bed. How was his pain, his sense of betrayal, not as valid?

Why was being gay always an uphill battle? This whole job wore him down, today more than most. Especially since Martelli's urgency meant it was unlikely he'd be able to stop by the hospital and find out how Kurt was… if he was even going to live.

"So, I guess you don't need me to seduce him?" Ivan tried to suppress the sour twist to his sarcasm but didn't entirely succeed, given the puzzled look Martelli directed at him.

"No! I mean, no. Even if that pillow talk thing worked between two guys, he's way too young for you."

Martelli's emphatic words and fierce blush had Ivan raising his brows. He'd been half joking, but he wasn't sure why his boss was against a honey trap. If it weren't for the fact thirty-four was practically dead by most gay men's standards, he might be offended Martelli thought he didn't have what it took to pull a twenty-two-year-old. Hell, the way he felt right now, he wasn't sure he could pull a half-blind *ninety*-two year old.

He'd gone a little hog wild the past couple of months, but his recent practice with one-night stands didn't provide the same skills required for a successful honey trap. To be fair, most operations didn't require any of them to sleep with someone for the job. Too easy to lose perspective.

"Whatever. What about the SIU investigation? How am I going to participate? What about my gun?"

Martelli pulled out a cheap, generic cell phone and slid it across the desk. "Use this. I'll call you from another burner phone and keep you apprised of your appointments. It's not like anyone's expecting you to hang around the house all day."

Appointments. Had he lost his job along with his hypothetical wife? Or was he seriously going to have to hang out somewhere all day, pretending to fucking work? This op got shittier by the minute, but he wasn't exactly anxious to get back to his half-empty apartment.

"What about a car?" If he was going in undercover, he couldn't take his own car. It was one of the few indulgences he had, and not only was he not inclined to get it in the line of fire, he wouldn't put it past Razhin's people to discover his real identity through his car.

Martelli shook his head. "No car."

No, of course not. Why the fuck would he get to have a car? The whole op was unsanctioned. The dread and unease, which had begun churning in his stomach as soon as he realized his bullet had taken down that kid, kicked into high gear. What the hell was he doing this for? Risking his job—the only thing he had left—for a half-assed undercover operation and a boss who didn't think his relationships were worthy of regret or emotional trauma when they ended.

"Sir, I...."

"You have to." Martelli shot him a pleading look. "I don't have anyone else I can trust."

Holy hell. How had he forgotten about the mole? His discomfort and possible reprimand were nothing compared to protecting his fellow officers from a traitor. Kurt might be a new friend, but he deserved nothing less than Ivan's full attention to this case. Not when the departmental leak might be the reason Kurt had gotten gunned down.

"Fine." He couldn't even ask to be kept informed about Kurt's status. Too much intersection with his real life would only be dangerous for everyone involved, and he didn't want anyone to trace numbers on his burner phone. Then again, if Kurt didn't make it, all Ivan would have to do is open a newspaper. "I'll get you your report before I leave, Sarge. Anything else I need?"

A key and a piece of paper with an address and a phone number on it joined the nondescript cell phone. "Liz arranged everything; you can move in tomorrow."

"Liz? Who is Liz?"

"The housing coordinator at the university. She's how I found out about the opening." Martelli's gaze dropped to his desk, focused, apparently, on the stapler he hadn't stopped fiddling with over the past few minutes. Jesus. Was this Liz person his new girlfriend? For a man depending on his wife's money and connections to launch a political career, he was surprisingly incapable of keeping his pants zipped.

"Whatever. I've got a report to write." Ivan tossed the information sheet on the desk, scooped up his meager tools, and blew out of the office, slamming the door behind him.

The other officers and detectives suddenly looked a whole lot more sinister after his meeting. Home had ceased being a refuge after Colin betrayed him, and now he'd lost the comfort of work. He was too old and beat down for this shit.

IVAN quietly unlocked the door and stepped inside the house. This mission had come together fast and easy. Too easy. Ivan was partly suspicious and partly impressed. Maybe that's what happened when stings didn't need to have forms signed in triplicate and notarized by God himself. Just yesterday, he'd been sitting in Martelli's office, agreeing to his unorthodox undercover operation, and today, he was a divorced straight man. Despite the lack of departmental support, he was able to use a fake ID from his last undercover bust, so he didn't have to go in with his own ID with his real address on it.

Shaking his head, he closed the door behind him. Parker had, seemingly out of the blue, advertised for a roommate. Was it good luck? Or was it a sign this op was going down the shitter, with Ivan at the vortex? His years as a detective had taught Ivan that easy was a trick. A dangerous trompe l'oeil. But Martelli was less superstitious. Or just more sanguine when *Ivan's* safety was on the line. Besides, maybe this was what happened with off-the-books ops.

"Hello?" Ivan called out. He'd yet to meet Parker, the owner of the house. The housing coordinator at the university had facilitated the entire transaction. He'd called her while filling out his report, and she confirmed she'd tell Parker he was moving in immediately. Presumably, Ivan would meet Parker's boyfriend, but he didn't want to meet them together. He needed to establish a rapport with his erstwhile roommate because Martelli suspected Parker had a soft spot for the underdog that Ivan intended to play up.

"Hello?" Ivan called again, but he heard nothing. The housing coordinator had assured him moving in on short notice wasn't a problem, confirmed by the key his boss gave him yesterday, but Ivan expected a welcoming of some sort. One more indication Parker wasn't a decent human being. As if the drug dealing wasn't enough to convince him. Maybe the boyfriend could be saved from Parker's dangerous aspirations.

Ivan glanced quickly into the living room and kitchen. Everything was neat and tidy, not even a dish in the sink. Somewhat unexpected, but even drug dealers might have standards for cleanliness. Ostensibly, Parker was going to university, but this didn't look like any frat house he'd ever seen. Despite the lack of transcripts, Martelli believed Parker wasn't taking a full course load, and he had no visible means of income. The lack of income might explain the need for a roommate, but it didn't explain how Parker owned a house, nor why an up-and-comer in Razhin's organization would need or want a roommate during the summer semester. Beyond finding out who Parker's associates were, Ivan wanted to discover the answer to that question. Something wasn't right here, and Ivan wanted to know what it was before he was staring down the barrel of a gun.

The row house, around a hundred years old, was tiny. A small kitchen, dining room, and living room-turned-media room made up the first floor, along with a small bathroom, which Ivan hadn't expected. Most houses like this only had a single bathroom upstairs with the bedrooms. The first floor facilities weren't original, and there was an incredible amount of wood trim—likely original— painted over in white in some sort of decorating travesty. A door led to the basement, but Ivan would have plenty of time to explore down there.

"Hello?" Ivan walked up the narrow staircase, the carpet doing nothing to muffle the creaking treads. This would have been a shit house to live in as a teen who wanted to sneak in after curfew. No one replied.

At the top of the stairs a small landing, too square to be considered a hallway, led to three rooms and another bathroom.

One of the bedrooms on the left had a futon, a couple of bookshelves, and a desk with a computer. Next, Ivan found a plain, sterile bedroom, devoid of any character. Presumably his. He'd been assured he was the only roommate, but this could be a guest room, and he could be stuck in the basement. Nevertheless, he dumped his duffle bag beside the bed and gave the functional and surprisingly clean bathroom a cursory peek before standing in front of the only closed door. When no one responded to his light knock, Ivan opened the door and stuck his head into the master bedroom.

The bed was huge. E-fucking-normous. One of those California king-size beds. Or some sort of optical illusion heightened by the narrowness of the room? Either way, he'd never known a college kid to own a king-size bed. Two narrow bedside tables flanked the barge of a bed, and they had to have been greased to slide into the space between mattress and wall.

Then there was the mess. Without the time to make any kind of search, all he could do was observe. After a moment, the jumble sorted itself into merely... stuff. Lots and lots of stuff. Lush pillows and richly colored drapes accented the room, but cardboard boxes draped with T-shirts and jeans mingled with an extremely feminine vanity table and an exotic looking Asian folding screen. The headboard looked like wrought iron but was an IKEA catalogue standard. It didn't match the wardrobe and dresser, both with a distinct Asian flair that matched the folding screen. The room didn't scream drug-dealing university student, that was for fucking sure. Ivan didn't have a clue what it all meant, aside from the fact that it was going to be a bitch to search Parker's haven. God only knew what resided in the closet, but Ivan would have to find out eventually.

Ivan retreated and silently shut the door. He'd have to make time to thoroughly inspect Parker's bedroom, but later. He had no idea when his roommate might return, and getting caught snooping his first hour in the house would not spell mission success.

Back on the first floor, he was still alone, so Ivan wandered downstairs.

The basement was damp and unfinished. An old beast of a furnace hulked in a shadowed corner. A few bare bulbs extending from ceiling beams illuminated the depressive gray of the cinderblock walls. Aside from the furnace, which Ivan could hardly believe functioned, the basement held nothing more than a few more cardboard boxes darkened with damp, a washer and dryer, and shelving units.

He pounded back up to the second floor and was unpacking his clothes when the front door opened.

"Hello?"

Who the fuck was that? The smoky voice tightened Ivan's belly like someone had just stroked his balls. Ivan closed the drawer, wondering if he should respond.

"Ivan, are you here?"

Oh, shit. Parker? Why hadn't anyone warned him Parker's voice was like dark amber honey distilled with sex?

"I'll be down in a minute." Ivan wasn't sure how well his cover would work, but this wasn't the best time for second thoughts. College had been a long fucking time past. Ivan looked younger than his thirty-four years, but Parker was more than ten years younger. How were they going to connect enough for Parker to trust him? And trust him maybe more than his boyfriend, Neil?

Drawing in a deep breath, Ivan wiped his palms on his jeans and mentally ran through his cover story. He was beginning to hate the undercover work. Or was it just the Drug Squad he hated? Each role became more grueling.

Ivan walked into the kitchen, where Parker was putting groceries into the fridge. He wore a soft, well-worn green T-shirt and a pair of loose jeans. Parker was slim and tall, probably a couple of inches taller than Ivan's own five-eleven.

"Hi," Ivan said softly.

Parker didn't turn but continued with his task while Ivan took in what he could see of Parker from behind. His hair was dark brown, spiked with golden tips that looked like a blond dye job growing out, a look Ivan had a sneaking fondness for.

"Hi." Parker placed the last container of yogurt on a shelf and shut the door. "There. All done. I was hoping to finish before you got here."

Parker turned around.

Ivan clutched at the counter.

Oh holy hell. Ivan had expected a complication, but not like this. Parker was fucking gorgeous. Almost androgynous, with sharply chiseled features and soft-looking full lips. And his eyes. Eyes that looked like the smooth stones at the bottom of a creek bed. Gray, green, flecks of gold, surrounded by the thickest, longest lashes Ivan had ever seen on a man. Ivan could stare at those eyes for hours. The hair was perfect for him. It suited this damned amazing-looking man. Who could be a fucking model if he wanted to be.

Oh God. Ivan had to live with him. Try to be friends with him. Keep his hands off him and pretend to be fucking straight.

"Sorry, I'm Parker." Parker held out his hand, his sweet smile softening the planes of his face like the old silver-screen stars seen through Vaseline-smeared lenses.

Ivan stepped closer to the counter and shook Parker's hand, thankful the counter was high enough to hide the bulge growing in his pants.

"I'm Ivan." His voice was gruff, probably sounded curt. At least, he hoped it did. If Parker knew how appealing he was to Ivan, it would be impossible to find out what he needed to know. Hitting on someone's boyfriend wasn't cool, especially when it wasn't one of the stated parameters of the op. Even if Martelli believed gay men fucked instead of shaking hands, it would be difficult for Ivan to entice this hot young thing into his bed. Ivan was good-looking, but nothing like this Adonis. And he wasn't old enough to satisfy any daddy kink Parker might have.

"Nice to meet you." Parker's voice rumbled through his narrow chest. He didn't look skinny or bony, but that deep voice definitely didn't match his physique.

"Do you drink?" Parker asked.

"Yeah, sure, just about anything." True, but that made him sound like a lush.

"Oh, good. I hoped you might. I brought some beer home. Thought we could order a pizza, have a few beers, and get to know each other."

Ivan stared at Parker. This was more considerate than he'd expected from his organized crime-connected, drug-dealing roomie.

"Uh. If you want, that is." Parker's smile slipped away at Ivan's lengthy pause, replaced by a hesitant look. Ivan felt like he'd singlehandedly pulled the clouds across the sun. How could one smile make such a fucking difference?

"Sure. That sounds great. My treat." Ivan tried to regain his lost ground. An unhappy Parker would not be a forthcoming Parker.

Parker tilted his head to the side, like a bird. "Oh. But I thought…." His cheeks pinked up, and he dropped his gaze.

Christ. His fucking cover. He had to get into the mindset of Ivan Baker, loser. "Hey, it's okay. My wife took just about everything in the divorce, but I can spring for a pizza without raiding the sofa cushions for change. I promise."

Parker chuckled, and that thousand-calorie smile returned. It was a treat on which Ivan wanted to gorge himself. Why, oh why, couldn't Parker look like the fucking lowlifes he arrested all the time? Not one criminal had ever filled him with the urge to slide his fingers into their hair, desperate to pull lips down atop his own.

Fuck.

FUCK. Parker's new roommate was pissed about something. Nerves twisted his stomach. Maybe he should have asked for a woman. Parker didn't know how to make friends with guys, especially not sexy, straight, older guys who probably had boatloads of life experience and… what would they talk about? He didn't know a lot about sports or cars or sex with women. Hell, he hadn't had sex with many people at all, despite having given up his virginity six years ago.

Neil thought he was an idiot for wanting a roommate. The sweet lady at the university housing office told him mid-semester was the worst time to search for one. When she'd called telling him she had a candidate, although not a student, Parker had been ecstatic. A newly divorced man might be as lonely as he was, because the emptiness of his place was crushing him, and Neil refused to move in. He certainly hadn't expected to find the guy attractive.

"So, beer?" Parker proffered the chilled bottle, hoping the booze would ease the way. He didn't want Neil to be right. The desperation to prove Neil wrong intensified as Ivan's lips thinned and he reached out for the bottle.

"Thanks. Have you got a local pizza place you like, or should I just call Pizza Pizza?"

"Pizza Pizza's good." It was Parker's favorite, anyway. Being able to call a single phone number, no matter where you were in the city, and get a decent pizza delivered was a boon to both students and stoners alike.

"I saw you had a sweet TV out there. Want to put something on while I call?"

"Uh, sure." What the hell was he supposed to put on? Clearly they weren't going to talk. Probably that was too much to expect. They weren't on a date. Parker grimaced. He assumed straight guys used TV as an avoidance mechanism, just like the gay guys he knew.

With a sigh, he sank down on the couch. Neil had talked him into getting the entertainment system, but it hadn't taken long for Parker to realize it wasn't for Parker's benefit. He fiddled with the remote, postponing turning it on.

"What do you want on your pizza?" Ivan called from the kitchen.

Parker rubbed his belly and frowned. "Pepperoni's fine."

He couldn't tell what Ivan's grunt meant, but the subsequent low rumble was obviously the man ordering pizza, even though Parker couldn't distinguish any specific words.

A few minutes later, while Parker stared at the remote in his hands, Ivan strode out of the kitchen and flung himself down in the armchair. The room seemed smaller, somehow, even though Ivan was a couple inches shorter than Parker. Those shoulders, though, were wide enough to steal Parker's breath, and under the boring blue golf shirt was a super fit body. Not that he would have tried anything if Ivan had sat beside him on the couch. The proximity of good-looking men made him squirmy and stupid.

Ivan stretched out a hand, and Parker stared at it for a moment before he let out an embarrassed chuff of laughter and handed over the remote.

"Let's see what you've got to make this TV worthwhile."

Ivan flipped on the TV with the practiced hand of a veteran. The huge expanse of flesh on the enormous screen clued Parker in to what Neil had been watching last as the room filled with moans and the slick sound of adequately lubed fucking. The camera pulled back to bring into focus a giant cock pumping into someone's ass. Parker's entire body chilled as all available blood rushed to his face—probably not the moviemaker's intended result. He leapt over the coffee table, slamming his shin against it as he went, and scrabbled at the DVD player. Goddamn Neil.

Doing his best to block the screen with his body, Parker waited an eternity for the disc to slide out. After what seemed like several hellish minutes, the blessed blue menu screen replaced the oversized cock, set of balls, and full moon. He snatched the disc out of the player and tossed it behind the TV. Serve Neil right if it broke. Probably pirated anyway.

With dread—and a face on fire—Parker turned back to Ivan. Had he noticed it was two guys fucking? When Parker first advertised for a roommate, it never occurred to him to mention he was gay, but suddenly that seemed a huge mistake. The hard, curved biceps peeking out of his short sleeves were testament to the power Ivan could put behind a punch. Parker's shin throbbed, reminding him of how vulnerable a body could be.

"Um."

Stunned wasn't disgusted—or homicidal—was it? Or in this case, homo-cidal?

Ivan's lips worked, but he didn't say anything.

"It's not mine." Parker wanted to call back the words as soon as they escaped. Seriously, could he have sounded any more guilty?

Ivan cut a glance at the couch, and Parker's face burned hotter than before. Was he imagining Parker sitting there, jerking off? Would it be any less embarrassing—or icky—to explain it was Neil? Because Parker didn't want to think about that either. Undoubtedly, Ivan was pleased he hadn't sat on the couch. It was going to take a supreme effort of will for Parker to sit back on the couch before he'd had it scotch-guarded.

"Okay." Ivan sounded almost like he believed Parker. "You want to…?" Ivan waved the remote, and a fresh flood of mortification swamped Parker as he moved from his protective and obstructive stance in front of the TV.

Trying not to be too obvious, Parker inspected the couch. He couldn't see any new stains, and he limped around the coffee table to sit down gingerly.

Ivan flipped on the retro video station before turning to him. Parker hadn't really taken the time to look at his new roommate in the kitchen, but now he did. Ivan had the wide-set eyes and sharply defined cheekbones Parker associated with Eastern European men, similar to the guys Neil had brought around on occasion, but so rugged and gorgeous it hurt. Golden blond hair and dark blue eyes and a body without an ounce of fat, although Parker wouldn't mind making a thorough, naked inspection to be sure. Just as some of the blood left his face—finally—for a point farther south, Ivan raised a brow questioningly.

Parker coughed and glanced at the video playing on the TV. He didn't recognize it, but there was a lot of spiky, bleached hair. He shouldn't have been staring at his new roommate, assuming he hadn't scared Ivan off already. Even if Ivan wasn't straight, he was way out of Parker's league. Probably thought he was nothing more than some dumb university kid who spent all his free time whacking off on the sofa.

The silence stretched out endlessly, punctuated by the distinctive wail of eighties electronica. Ivan must not have realized the DVD had shown two guys fucking, or he would have said something, wouldn't he? Although Ivan's intent stare was very much like one of his professors trying to catch someone in a lie, which was a little weird.

"Did you, uh, find your room? Is it okay? We can move some of the furniture around. The laundry's downstairs, and we can make a schedule for cleaning and shopping and stuff and—" Parker broke off. His words had accelerated, but he hadn't been able to put on the brakes until his breath ran out, even though Ivan's eyes had widened partway through his speech. Embarrassment flared in his face—again—and he bit his lip to stop himself from saying another word. This was why he didn't have many friends aside from Neil. Neil was the only one who'd hung out with the fat kid and stuck around after Parker had shed the weight but retained his social idiocy.

Ivan frowned, and Parker frowned back, unsure where to go from here. He shifted his legs and caught his shin on the edge of the coffee table again.

"Ow. Fuck." Throbbing pain exploded where he'd hit his leg during his ungainly leap over the table, and he wrapped a hand around it, rocking and biting his lip to keep in any whimpers.

"Let me look." Ivan left his seat to drop to his knees by Parker, making him freeze.

With gentle fingers, Ivan moved Parker's hand and slid the leg of Parker's jeans up. He pressed his fingers around the contusion, the pain making Parker hiss.

"You're going to have a nasty bruise, and you broke the skin, but not badly. No fracture, I don't think. Have you got a first aid kit?" Ivan stared up into his face, and Parker had a little trouble catching his breath.

"Yes, um, in the bathroom. Under the sink." Parker waved toward the front of the house.

Ivan patted his knee and rose, heading for the bathroom.

"Most houses this old don't have bathrooms on this floor." The tile inside the bathroom made Ivan's voice warble slightly.

"True. But after my mom got sick, we had a bathroom put in so she could stay at home and not worry about stairs."

White plastic box in hand, Ivan stepped out of the bathroom and stared at Parker. Again.

"Your mom lived here?" Ivan glanced around the room, and Parker nodded.

"Yeah. Near the end, she had difficulty getting around, so we had the bathroom put in and set this room up as a bedroom."

"Where does she live now?"

Parker dropped his gaze to the purplish, bloodied lump on his shin and shrugged. His mom had been his best friend, and although he'd had a couple years to prepare for her death, it had still rocked him. Even now, almost six months later, he'd sometimes call out to her when he got home. At least Neil had never heard him do that.

"Oh, when did... I mean... I didn't...."

The sound of Ivan stumbling over his words like Parker usually did had him looking up. The sympathy on Ivan's face had his eyes burning.

"I didn't realize, Parker," Ivan said as he walked closer.

"Why would you?"

Getting himself under control was easier when Ivan transferred his attention to cleaning Parker's leg. He bit back an offer to do it himself. Would be the more manly, self-sufficient route, but it had been so long since someone had touched him tenderly, selflessly, and with true caring.

The swipe of an alcohol swab over the scrape made Parker flinch, but the unexpected waft of coolness as Ivan blew on it brought goose bumps up on his nape. Did Ivan have kids? Was that how he learned to take care of minor injuries like this?

Ivan continued on with his first aid. "How long has it been?"

"Six months. Cancer." Parker didn't need any clarification for Ivan's question.

"I'm sorry for your loss." Ivan placed a couple of bandages over the cut, his fingers warm against Parker's skin.

"Thanks." He cleared his throat.

As he pulled Parker's pant leg back down, Ivan lifted his head. Parker had never seen such beautiful blue eyes before, and the compassion filling them warmed his belly.

The doorbell rang, and Ivan sprang back, nearly toppling over onto his ass.

"Guess that's the pizza." Ivan headed for the door, pulling out his wallet.

Suddenly chilled, Parker wrapped his arms around himself. He couldn't decide if living with Ivan was going to be heaven or hell.

CHAPTER
Two

AFTER paying for the pizzas, Ivan took the boxes into the kitchen, carefully not looking into the media room. This job was already so fucked up, and no wonder this kid had flown under everyone's radar. He seemed so innocent, grieving for his mother. No one who met him would ever think he was dealing drugs. Ivan was going to need to be careful, or he'd give himself away before he figured out how much of this guy was an act, and how much was the real Parker.

Nevertheless, he needed to get ahold of himself and start ingratiating himself with Parker, not figuring out how to get him into bed. He had sex on the brain as soon as he saw Parker, and the life-sized porn appearing on the TV hadn't helped. He'd never seen anyone blush like that before, and as tempting as it had been to make some sort of comment to keep Parker flustered and embarrassed, he might have stroked out if any more blood rushed to his head.

Between tending to Parker's injury and imagining him sitting naked on the couch pleasuring himself as he watched porn, Ivan had been distracted like he'd never been on the job. Just one more reason for him to reevaluate his life and career once his administrative leave was over.

As Ivan searched for plates, he made a mental list of all the reasons he couldn't even begin to think about sex with Parker. He was a criminal, he thought Ivan was straight, he was too damned young, and, most important, he had a boyfriend. There weren't many criminals Ivan had seen who'd been adamant about the notion of fidelity, but after experiencing the lack firsthand with Colin, Ivan had no interest in being party to that. Thankfully, his cover precluded him having to do anything of the sort. Fucking weird situation. The last time he'd roomed with a complete stranger was in university, but it felt like eons since he'd had that carefree mindset, and he wasn't sure how he was going to get it back well enough to relate to a guy twelve years younger.

Once he'd gathered everything he needed, including his composure, he placed everything atop the pizza boxes and carried the food out to the living room.

Staring relentlessly at the TV, Parker hadn't relaxed a bit. Which would never do. They had to find some common ground, some way to be friends, or this job was not only going to be a complete waste of time, it might even get Ivan killed.

"I brought us out a couple more beers." They could both use the alcohol.

"Oh, thanks." Parker stared at the boxes. "I wasn't expecting my own pizza."

Ivan shrugged and slid the box of pepperoni over. Parker flipped up the box and frowned.

"Did they screw up the order?"

"Uh, no." Parker rubbed his belly. "What kind did you get?"

"Chicken and broccoli." It was never a popular choice with the other detectives but it was one of the healthiest pizza options, and he'd never been able to give up pizza entirely. When he'd hit on the combination, he'd found it quite enjoyable, and it had become his regular order. Besides, now that he was getting older, too much grease weighed him down and frequently upset his stomach. The coffee at headquarters was enough of an assault on his innards.

"Chicken and broccoli? I didn't even know you could get broccoli on pizza."

"Better for you than pepperoni." Ivan stifled a groan. Nothing like sounding like a preacher or a parent to get a kid's back up. But Parker looked intrigued more than stubborn.

"Yeah?"

"Want to try some?" He flipped the box around so the opening faced Parker.

With a shy smile, Parker reached in and grabbed a slice. This guy was a great fucking actor. He'd even be able to fool Ivan's mom, and she had a lower tolerance for bullshitters than any cop Ivan had ever come across. Of course, being a high school teacher probably explained that.

The reminder of his mom made him groan. He forgot to call her before he came here. Missing family dinners happened, but missing them without notice was completely out of the question. He'd have to find time to sneak away and let her know before Sunday.

"What's wrong?"

"Oh, nothing, just remembered a phone call I have to make."

"You can use the phone here." Parker pointed at the small table beside the couch.

"No, thanks, it's got to do with… uh… my divorce, and I don't want to think about it right now."

Parker didn't answer, just took a bite and chewed. The sympathetic smile he gave Ivan, complete with a tiny streak of tomato sauce at the corner of his lips, made Ivan want to confess everything. When the hell had undercover become so damned hard? Was it Parker? The guy could easily be a fucking model, but he had the temperament of an eager puppy. This kid had to be a sociopath putting on an act for him, otherwise he was not only the stupidest criminal going, but Razhin was going to grind him into dust before taking over whatever operation he'd managed to build for himself.

He had to remind himself he was an impoverished divorced man, and Parker was a naïve university student. Those were the parts they'd both chosen to play, and they'd do this dance for as long as it took. Ivan at least had the advantage of knowing Parker had to be putting on an act, while Parker had no reason to suspect Ivan was acting right back.

Ivan grabbed his own slice of pizza. "Like it?"

"Can I share yours? I'll put the other in the fridge. For… uh, for later."

"Sure thing."

They munched in silence for a few moments. It was like the most uncomfortable date ever, with absolutely no prospect of getting laid at the end of it. Too bad all his opening conversational gambits could easily spook someone with something to hide. In fact, anything that resembled an interrogation wouldn't be roommate-like. This was by far the most unusual undercover operation he'd been on.

"Did you have any furniture to move in? We can make room."

Ivan resisted the urge to take his thumb to Parker's face to swipe off the tomato sauce that lingered. "No, nothing really. I've got a few things in a friend's garage, which I'll grab in the next day or so, but what the wife didn't take, I didn't much want."

"Oh. I'm sorry. Are you okay? Do you have kids? Or would you rather not talk about it? Aside from a few people's parents, I don't know anyone who's been divorced."

"No kids." Thank Christ he didn't have to fake that. "I'd rather not talk about it, if you don't mind." Less talking about his cover meant fewer opportunities for the lies to bite him on the ass.

How did this kid fake that wounded look? Forget the reefer, this kid could con grandmas out of their life savings with a few blinks of his thickly lashed eyelids. "Just the divorce. And my wife. We can talk about other things."

With those few words, the wattage returned to Parker's smile. Damn him and damn Martelli and damn the fucking mole responsible for this all.

Parker pointed at the TV with a half-eaten slice. "This is the type of music you listen to? I didn't think you were that old." His eyes widened as he realized what he'd said, and another blush lit him up to the hairline.

Ivan's own skin flushed a little in response. Most of his friends were still into the grunge music and nineties rock that had so intensely influenced their high school years, but Ivan had two older sisters who loved new-wave electronica, and watching videos with them, filled with beautiful men wearing guyliner and tight clothes… Ivan figured out very early on he was gay. His first crush had been every member of Duran Duran. But he couldn't admit that here, not when he was pretending to be straight.

"I've got two older sisters who I can blame for this." He chewed on the inside of his lip to keep from grinning. Maybe he'd do exactly that the next time he managed to make it to a family dinner. He wouldn't be living up to his job as baby brother if he wasn't pissing off his sisters.

"I see. I haven't really heard a lot of this. I don't even know who a lot of these bands are."

Parker blinked again, and Ivan was able to forgive, for a moment, the additional reminder of Ivan's advanced age.

"What classes are you taking?" God. He sounded like someone's father. Again. No wonder Parker had asked if he had kids.

Parker's gaze skittered away. "Oh, just a few things. Nothing interesting."

The courses may not be interesting, but Parker's reaction certainly was both fascinating and suspicious. But pursuing it now would be a mistake.

"What about your dad? Where does he live?"

The wounded look returned tenfold and gutted Ivan. What the hell was up with this guy and his soul-sucking eyes? Ivan wanted to leap onto the couch and cuddle him and tell him everything would be okay. Totally out of character for him too. Even though he was out—in his real life—Colin had often complained about his lack of affection and had flung that in his face in the wake of Ivan's discovery of his cheating.

"I don't know. I don't know who he is."

"Oh. Sorry." This wasn't going well. What had he been thinking, diving into a situation like this, mere hours after he'd shot and killed Dmitri, a young man who could have very easily been Parker? Killing someone, even in self-defense, took its toll. There was a reason for administrative leave, aside from the whole investigation aspect, and somehow that had been overlooked by both him and Martelli. But he was here now, and moping around his own empty home wasn't going to help his state of mind.

A tremor shook his hand. "Look, Parker, I'm beat. You okay if I hit the sack? I'll clean this up in the morning."

"No, go ahead. I can clean this up before I start on my homework."

A good night's sleep would do wonders and hopefully get him back on target. Hell, he hadn't even decided on a fake profession. What if Parker had asked what he did for a living, for God's sake? What he needed was something that gave him flexible hours, but not as flexible as being unemployed. Wouldn't that make him roommate of the year? Unemployed, divorced, straight older man. Like Parker's fucking dream come true.

Ivan clenched a fist as he dragged himself up the creaky stairs. He had to stop wondering if Parker saw him as anything more than a friend or an acquaintance. Nothing else mattered.

THE unfamiliar slam of a heavy door woke Ivan, and he sat up in bed, breath coming short, as he took in the strange room. He'd awoken in a number of strange beds, but in this one he'd definitely slept alone, if for no other reason than the narrow bed didn't have much room for anyone besides himself.

Right. He was undercover. The room he was renting at Parker's.

Sunlight streamed unfettered through the windows, making the room both hotter and brighter than Ivan liked. A glance at the alarm clock confirmed he'd slept well into the afternoon. He'd slept heavily and long, but he wasn't sure he'd slept well. Fragments of dreams hung vivid in his mind, most of them centered around Parker. Early on they'd been sensual—a safe outlet for the strong attraction he'd experienced for the younger man—but they'd morphed into something darker and more painful. The last thing he remembered was Parker in Dmitri's place, blood bubbling from his lips and welling up between Ivan's hands as he tried to save him from the gunshot.

Ivan scrubbed a hand over his face. He wanted nothing more than to run into Parker's room to see if he was okay, but that was stupid. This was a job, and Parker was a criminal. When Ivan got some evidence, Parker was going to jail, and Ivan could go back to his normal life. The sooner the better, if his dreams were any indication.

He checked his phone, but there were no missed calls and no messages from Martelli. Gaining Parker's trust was the first step. Until he learned Parker's schedule and knew he could start snooping without getting caught, he couldn't even start his investigation. But there were a few other things he could do in the meantime, including grab a few boxes of clothes and books from his place so it at least looked like he was moving in for real. He hadn't even brought pajamas. Normally he slept naked, but it was different living with someone you weren't fucking. He readjusted his briefs and swung out of bed.

What he really needed was a shower, but he hadn't even had the foresight to pack a towel. Who moved into a new place without even bringing a towel? God. If Ivan got killed on this op, it was going to be his own damned fault.

Surely Parker had a towel he could borrow for a couple of days until he got himself sorted out. Ivan opened the door to the linen closet. The closet was just like something his mother would have—neat, tidy, everything folded. His own linen closet wasn't nearly as neat. Nothing about this place was what he expected for either a drug dealer or a university student. Parker wasn't what he expected, and he had to assimilate this information soon. Soft, fluffy white towel in hand, he shut the door, another original wooden door painted over in white. What he wouldn't give to strip and refinish the wood in this place. Repaint the walls to a color more in keeping with the wooden trim. Then it would look even less like student housing.

AFTER a cab, subway, streetcar, bus, and two and a half hours, Ivan arrived at his apartment with no tail. Having no car sucked, big time. How was he going to follow someone if needed? He had a sweet vehicular indulgence in the parking structure, but the new car was too distinctive, too memorable, and, most importantly, too registered to Ivan Bekker, not Ivan Baker.

He unlocked the door to his apartment and stepped inside. Making the mental shift from Baker to Bekker was a bitch. Especially because this was no normal undercover operation. He was playing two different roles—not even his real life was the truth right now. Keeping track of the lies on both sides was going to be a challenge. A challenge he didn't feel up to, unfortunately.

After dialing headquarters, he got Simon's cell phone number. If anyone could give him the scoop on Kurt's condition, it would be Kurt's partner on the force.

Phone pressed to his ear, he sank down on the showroom sofa Colin had chosen and inexplicably hadn't wanted when he'd moved out.

Simon picked up after a couple of rings. "Trent speaking."

"Hey, Simon. It's Ivan." He paused for a moment. "Bekker. From the Drug Squad."

Simon chuckled, and his tone warmed up considerably. "I know which Ivan you are. Kurt came out of surgery just fine, and he's awake. Well, he was awake. He's sleeping right now."

Relief swamped him. "That's great."

"I'm glad you called. I know Kurt enjoys hanging out with you."

Huh. Ivan hadn't spoken much to Simon, but Kurt's previous partner, Ben, had been on the Drug Squad before he'd transferred to Homicide. In one phone conversation, Simon made it crystal clear that he was a very different sort of man. Ben had always been very aloof. Good cop, but not at all social.

In a way, Ivan hadn't been surprised to learn Ben had a secret male lover. Before his death on the job just over a year ago, Ben had been a textbook case of a closeted gay man. He'd been far more surprised when he'd found out Kurt had fallen for Ben's lover, Davy. He'd also been pleased when Kurt had reached out to him as a friend after things had gone wrong with his and Davy's burgeoning relationship.

"Me too. I'm glad he's doing better. Look, I'm going to be out of touch for a bit, but let Kurt know I'll stop by and visit when I can."

"No problem. I'm not sure when he's going to be released, but he'll be moving in with Davy when he is."

"Davy? Really?" Kurt had been pining for the man for months. Ivan didn't know the specifics, but he did know that Kurt had fallen hard.

"Yep. They patched things up."

"Good. I'm glad." And he was. He was happy someone's relationship had worked out. No one deserved it more than Kurt.

"How are you doing, Ivan? A couple guys stopped by to visit, and they told us you were on leave."

"I'm doing okay. Or I will be." As soon as he finished this investigation, he'd be fine.

"Excellent. I know it was worrying Kurt."

"I gotta go, Simon. But I'll talk to Kurt as soon as I can."

"Later, Ivan."

After clicking off, Ivan breathed a sigh of relief. Simon wouldn't have sounded so relaxed if Kurt wasn't on the mend. Ivan tossed his phone on the table and stood.

What did he need to pack? Ivan wandered through his apartment, assessing his possessions. Had it really been eight months since Colin moved out? There were still empty spots where he'd taken his furniture and knickknacks. Hell, the bookshelf was half empty, and there was a clear demarcation in his closet where Colin's clothes had once lived. Pathetic. It was like he was waiting for Colin to return and slide himself back into Ivan's life like he'd never left. Not that he wanted the cheating bastard back, but the fact that he hadn't filled up the spaces left by Colin's stuff made the apartment seem less like a home. Had it been a home even when Colin was there? Ivan couldn't quite remember. The months before their catastrophic break up had been... tense and uncomfortable, as they slowly realized that perhaps the relationship wasn't developing into what either of them expected. Ivan would have had a lot more respect for Colin if he'd just ended it before sleeping around.

He was strangely eager to return to Parker's place, despite how tired he was of undercover work. The stress and strain of constantly watching words and actions, remembering what lies he'd told... well, it was a lot easier when the guy you were lying to didn't seem so sweet and innocent.

Ivan grabbed a few boxes and packed up some essentials. He hesitated at his bedside table. Lube. That was all he should bring, but he tossed a box of condoms in. Better safe than sorry, even if they tempted him to indulge where he shouldn't. No toys, though. That was a given. They'd be a dead giveaway should Parker or his associates decide to snoop around the new guy. Straight men didn't keep dildos or butt plugs in their bedside table, he was certain of that. Not unless they wanted someone to question their orientation, and Ivan wanted no questions to arise.

With his packing done, he took a few minutes to call his mother, let her know he'd be unavailable for an indeterminate amount of time.

"Yeah, Mom, I know. No, I haven't met anyone new."

He sighed and pushed at one of the boxes with the toe of his shoe, listening only partly to his mother.

"No, not lying. I promise, if I meet someone and it's serious, I'll bring him to dinner." Parker didn't count as meeting someone new, and no way was he letting an up-and-comer in Razhin's organization within spitting distance of his family.

He frowned at the four boxes he'd packed. "What? No, Mom, I gotta go." He clicked off his cell phone, cutting off his mother mid-sentence. He'd hear about it later, for sure.

How the fuck was he getting these boxes back to Parker's? All of his friends were cops, but he couldn't let any of them know about what he was doing. He didn't know who he could trust. If they weren't dirty, one of them might report to the wrong person what he and Martelli were trying to accomplish, and that could be equally detrimental. Colin's friends had left with Colin, and renting a car could be dangerous. His family was right out; he didn't want them anywhere near his work.

He tapped his phone, but just as he'd gotten to the point of scrolling through his entire contact list, his "new" phone rang, startling him.

"Hello?"

"Ivan, are you settling in?"

It took him a moment to recognize his boss's voice.

"Yep, so far."

"Good, good. You've got an appointment you need to keep. Tomorrow at 31 Bloor, Suite 1912, 3 p.m."

Ivan rolled his eyes. The SIU would take place at headquarters, so this appointment had to be the department mandated shrink-wrapping. Who the hell wanted to spill their guts on a Friday afternoon? He scratched down the address and time on the pad of paper beside his bed.

"Fine. I'll be there. What about the SIU?"

"Next week sometime. Be careful."

"Sure thing, Sarge." Ivan disconnected the call, still unsure how he was getting his boxes to Parker's without creating any undue interest in his movements.

"YOUR chariot is here," the slender blond exclaimed as he popped out of the driver's side.

"Thanks, Rick, I really appreciate it."

"Oh, no worries. It's the least I can do." Rick thrust out a hip and winked suggestively at him. Ivan laughed. He'd met Rick shortly after he'd broken up with Colin. They'd spent a very enjoyable night, and had slept together a couple of times while Ivan gorged himself on being single, during which Ivan discovered that he rather liked the guy. He'd met a couple of Rick's other friends, but only briefly. Mostly they went to clubs or bars together and left with other people. He hadn't seen Rick in several weeks, due to overtime on the task force, but they were slowly taking their friendship out of the bars. Not dating. Rick was great in the sack, but they weren't compatible, and Rick wasn't interested in a relationship anyway. Ivan had called him because he was a friend who could not easily be associated with Ivan Bekker or the police.

Ivan loaded his boxes into Rick's car, then stood back and assessed the vehicle. Rick was one of the most flamboyant gay men Ivan knew, which made the incongruity of his ridiculously inconspicuous car all the more pronounced. Definitely a bonus for what Ivan needed.

"So, you want to tell me what this is about, big boy? I thought your main squeeze moved out."

"Um, I really can't talk about it. But will you please do me a favor and take a roundabout way back home after?"

He grabbed Rick's phone and programmed his new cell number into it, under the name Baker. "Call me at this number if you notice anything unusual, but please, please only contact me if it's an emergency."

Rick raised his brow. "I guess you're not talking about an 'I might die if I can't fuck that guy' emergency." He glanced at his phone. "Baker?"

"Don't ask. Please."

With a shrug, Rick wedged his phone back into his tight jeans. "You're the boss. Ready to go?"

"Just a minute." Ivan grabbed a handful of mud from the recently watered rosebushes at the side of the garden and smeared it over both license plates. Not enough to get Rick pulled over, but enough to obscure the plate number from casual inspection, especially while in motion.

"Incognito. Cool. But you better wipe your hands good before you get in." Rick got in the driver's side and started the car.

Ivan wiped his hands off in the grass and stared at the entrance to his condo. "Wait a sec," he called to Rick and ran back inside. Might be a huge mistake, and he hoped it wouldn't be dangerous for Rick, but Ivan was desperate.

When he returned to the car, he dumped his cell phone and charger on the seat between them.

"Rick, please keep this charged for me, and if I call to meet up with you, bring it with you."

"Sure thing, big guy."

"And don't answer it."

Rick rolled his eyes and nodded. "Can we get going now?"

"One last thing. Don't tell anyone about this, okay?"

"Oh, honey, don't be ridiculous. They'd never believe me anyway."

HE WAS taking a chance, having Rick help him, but having no friends would be more suspicious, especially if he somehow managed to arrive back at Parker's with four boxes and still no sign of a car. He'd made Rick park the car far enough from the house to garner complaints about how far Rick was expected to carry boxes, but the car couldn't be seen from the house, and therefore couldn't be readily identified. So far, Ivan hadn't seen any evidence that Razhin had any eyes on Parker's house, but that could change at any moment, especially if the mole got wind of what he was doing.

"Well, this place isn't too bad. Where do you want these?"

Ivan dumped his boxes on the landing by the stairs. "Right here is fine. I'll take them upstairs later."

Rick let his boxes fall where Ivan indicated, and he brushed dust off his clothes.

A loud breathy snort caught his attention. Caught Rick's attention too.

"Hello?" Rick pushed past Ivan into the living room, and Ivan followed.

Parker sprawled across the couch, deeply asleep and snoring. Without the blushing and the clumsiness, he still looked adorable but less like someone's kid's brother. In fact, the casual pose resembled nothing more than a model ready for a shoot. The man was stunning. Stunning. And he was poised to ruin his whole fucking life by getting into bed—metaphorically—with Razhin.

Rick drew in a breath, and he spoke in hushed, reverent tones. "Is this your new squeeze, honey? No wonder you're moving in so soon. I wouldn't want to let that sweet thing out of my sight either."

"It's not what you think," Ivan whispered. He didn't want to wake Parker, but he also didn't want to stop looking at him either.

"Oh, then are you going to introduce me?" Rick's playfulness became feral and predatory. Or perhaps Ivan was imagining things.

All of Ivan's muscles tensed. Over his dead body was he introducing Parker to Rick. There were so many reasons not to, but Rick's protection suddenly plummeted in importance. And he had to get that shit out of his head as soon as possible, because jealousy over a guy he'd met a day ago was ridiculous, never mind that he was a criminal he was supposed to investigate.

"C'mon. It'll be better if you go before he wakes up."

"Whatever you say." Rick waggled his brows.

Ivan herded Rick to the door. "Remember. Call me if anything strange happens."

"Stranger than what's happened so far?"

"And try to forget this address, okay?" Ivan gave Rick's last question all the attention it deserved, which was none at all.

Rick gave him one little salacious wink. "I'm outta here. Go get him, tiger."

"Stop. It's not what you think. But thanks for your help."

Rick hugged him, and Ivan allowed himself to enjoy the contact. It had been too long since he'd held a warm male body next to him. "Good luck."

THE scent of tomato sauce woke Parker. He blinked, trying to catch his bearings. Had he left something on the stove? All he could remember was a long day and sitting down in front of the TV he hadn't even bothered turning on.

"Neil, is that you?" Parker levered himself off the couch and walked into the kitchen.

"Oh, hey, you're awake." Ivan smiled at him.

"Um, yeah." Ivan had come home and started cooking without waking him? He must have been solidly out. He'd slept poorly the night before and woken up with a headache, which had only gotten worse after his unintended nap.

"Dinner's almost ready. Did you want to get plates out?"

Parker frowned. He wasn't sure if he shouldn't just go back to bed for the night, but he couldn't recall the last time someone had cooked for him. Well, Ivan hadn't cooked *for* him, but he'd cooked and was going to share it. The dull throb in his head kept him from making a decision, and he rubbed at his temple.

"Are you okay?" Ivan set down the saucy spoon and turned toward him.

"Yeah, just a headache."

"When was the last time you ate?"

When was that? He'd been running late when he woke up. "Pizza last night, I guess."

Ivan's eyes widened. "Last night? No wonder you have a headache. Get some water and sit down."

He did as he was told, but he couldn't shake his confusion.

Slumped at the table, head in hand, he didn't hear Ivan approach until a plate of spaghetti slid in front of him. He glanced up to see Ivan settling into the seat across from him with a smile.

"Hope you like pasta."

Parker smiled back. His mom used to make spaghetti for him when he was a kid. He shoveled a mouthful in and savored the taste. Pasta fit the bill of easy to make and cheap, but he worried about its effect on his weight. One day wouldn't hurt, though.

"Yes, thanks."

"So, who's Neil?"

The warmth that had swept through him curdled slightly at the mention of Neil. They'd been friends since middle school, and Neil was still an important part of his life, even if lately they'd not really seen eye to eye.

"He's... uh... a friend." Neil had also been his first boyfriend, but he wasn't sure how Ivan would react to that information. Parker had never been in a position of having to come out to a man like Ivan, and when that man was his roommate, it made it even more awkward. He wanted Ivan to like him, and he didn't want it to be uncomfortable for either of them.

A pause hung in the air before Ivan spoke. "How was your day?"

"Uh, mine?"

Ivan chuckled. "Yes, yours. Who else is here?"

Parker's face heated. He really had to control the stammering. He'd never had a roommate before. One who was sexy and cooked him dinner and asked about his day was completely unexpected.

"Fine. I had two classes today, and I went to the library." He stuffed another forkful of pasta in his mouth and tried not to moan. How was it meals cooked by someone else always tasted better?

Ivan chewed and swallowed before licking his lips, and Parker found his gaze riveted to Ivan's mouth.

"What are you studying?"

"Right now, sociology, mostly." He wanted to be a physiotherapist, but he needed his bachelor's first.

"Mostly? Haven't you chosen a major yet?"

Parker stirred his fork around on the plate, making swirls in his sauce. He probably shouldn't eat too much more. "I'm a little behind. I took some time off to help with my mom, and when I came back, I wasn't sure I could deal with a full course load, so I'm only back part time."

Which had been a mistake. If he'd taken more classes, maybe he wouldn't notice how empty the house was, or he wouldn't be around as much to hear Neil ask why he was even bothering with school at all. Of course, if Neil knew where Parker had started spending a lot of his time, he'd probably pitch a fit.

"That's understandable. Are your classes going well?"

Parker grinned. "Yes, actually. Straight As so far."

Ivan grinned back. "Good for you. Oh, I forgot to ask. Did you want a glass of wine?"

"We don't have any wine."

"Eh, I brought a few bottles in my stuff." Ivan cocked his head to the side. "You are old enough, aren't you?"

"Yes, way old enough. I'm twenty-two."

"Oh, twenty-two," Ivan mocked gently as he left the table to grab a bottle from the cupboard. "An old man."

"Why, how old are you?" Older than Parker, for sure, but not old. Not by a stretch.

"Thirty-four." The practiced way Ivan extracted the cork made Parker feel like an uneducated kid.

Crimson liquid sloshed into a pair of wine glasses Parker didn't recall having. He didn't understand the faint grimace Ivan had on his face. Thirty-four wasn't old, especially not if you looked like Ivan, but twenty-two seemed inexperienced in comparison.

"By the way, I never asked, what do you do for a living?" If Liz at the housing office had mentioned it, he hadn't paid attention.

"Insurance salesman."

Huh. Ivan was way too good-looking to be an insurance salesman, but somehow it made him seem more like a normal guy.

Ivan sat and proffered a glass with a flourish. Parker took it and sniffed. He'd never really drunk wine before, but it smelled good. "What is this?"

"It's a light merlot. I don't know shit about wine, but there are a few that I like. This is one of them."

The unconcerned comment relaxed Parker, and he took a sip. He couldn't taste any of the things he'd heard used to describe wine, but he liked the explosion of taste and the warmth as it burned down his throat.

"It's good."

Ivan lifted his glass. "To a new roommate."

The fresh warmth in his stomach had little to do with the wine and everything to do with Ivan's attention. He knew this wasn't a date, he knew Ivan was straight, but he could pretend for a bit, couldn't he?

"To a new roommate," Parker whispered and raised his own glass to clink against Ivan's before taking another sip. Contrary to Neil's opinion, advertising for a roommate was the best idea he'd had in a long time.

"So, what kind of movies do you like? Maybe we could watch something after dinner."

Parker grinned. Wasn't a date, but all dates *should* be like this.

CHAPTER
Three

IVAN managed to find a seat at the back of the bus in the corner. Having his back and side protected suited him very well this afternoon. Four hours of roundabout public transit for a one hour appointment with a psychiatrist hardly seemed worth the effort. Especially since he had to expend more mental effort than he'd expected to hide what he was doing on Martelli's and the department's behalf. Undoubtedly the shrink would take a dim view of the truth, but Dr. Sanchez also hadn't been impressed with his half-assed, evasive answers. At this rate, he'd be on admin leave for months.

Wasn't it enough he'd relived the shooting in his dreams? He had to rehash the whole thing in the appointment too? That's, of course, where the evasion began. Because he didn't see Dmitri in his dreams, he saw Parker. He'd met him mere days ago and yet he dreamt of shooting Parker, of desperately trying to stem the bleeding, trying to coax his heart into beating again. How could he tell Sanchez that? He wasn't supposed to know Parker and couldn't even explain to himself why Parker had invaded his dreams like this. Parker was a job like any other.

Then, Sanchez had stuck his nose in Ivan's personal life. The man hadn't expressed any hint that he disapproved of Ivan's sexual orientation—and after the shit Ivan had been through since the shooting, that would have gotten him a swift punch in the face, doctor or no. The lack of a significant other shouldn't impede his progress any, although he couldn't deny the thought of going home and sacking out on the couch, maybe watching another movie with

Parker, held a great deal of appeal. Anything that didn't involve talking about his fucking feelings, for God's sake.

The appointment had left him flayed and vulnerable, and he wanted someone to get in his face—beyond normal public transit rudeness—so he could throw his weight around a bit. Land a punch or two. Indulge the hot flares of anger that flooded him at unexpected moments. But he was too close to Parker's place. Drawing any attention from the police would be foolish and dangerous.

Ivan reached up and pulled the bell. The bus lurched to a stop, and Ivan swung out of his seat, pushing his way through the Friday evening crowd.

A heavy-set man with acne-scarred cheeks glared at him, and Ivan glared back.

"Watch where you're going," the man growled out, thick Russian accent almost obscuring his words.

Ivan frowned and kept going, unsure if the bulge that hit him was a concealed gun or not. He exited the bus but turned to stare back. The Russian man stared out the window at him, gaze never leaving him as the bus moved on.

Shit. Coincidence? Or had he been followed?

Ivan clenched fingers that were suddenly bloodless and cold. Surveying the street, he spied a coffee shop and hightailed it inside, ordered the largest coffee on the menu, and commandeered one of the seats by the window. While he sipped, he stared outside, assessing each passerby for threats. He couldn't afford to bring any suspicious characters back to Parker's place. If Parker's criminal associates connected him with the cops, or decided Parker was a threat, one or both of them would die.

"Would you like another coffee, sir?"

Ivan looked up. One of the baristas was standing by his table, a concerned look on her face.

"No, I'm fine, I just got...." He frowned. The cup he'd wrapped his hand around was cold. Liquid sloshed when he lifted it; he'd barely drunk any. "What time is it?"

"Seven thirty."

He'd been here two hours. How the fuck had that happened?

"Thanks." He threw a few dollars on the table and darted out the door. No one seemed to pay him any attention, and he walked the last couple blocks to Parker's house, flicking occasional glances over his shoulder.

ONCE inside, he shut the door firmly and leaned back against it, eyes closed. Losing his focus like that, or, more to the point, focusing so intently he'd lost track of the world around him, wasn't like him. Not at all. Was this how it ended? Not anything nefarious but his own mind rebelling against the fiction and making him his own worst liability?

"You're home late. Busy day at the office?"

Ivan jumped at the unexpected voice, but when he opened his eyes to see Parker's sweet face and warm smile, his tension dissolved. He might be making himself crazy, but he was at least making headway with one part of his assignment. Parker already treated him like a friend.

"Uh, yes. Busy. Takes more time on public transit." Ivan concentrated on breathing steady and even. No sense in broadcasting his heightened awareness to Parker—just the sort of thing to make criminals suspicious.

"I suppose so. I don't mind it much, but I guess if you're used to driving, it would suck." Parker shrugged. "There's some leftover mac and cheese if you're hungry. It's nothing like your pasta, but there's only so much I can cook. You're welcome to it."

Mac and cheese. He wasn't interested in doing any grocery shopping, not without a car, but pasta two nights in a row was a bit much. Surely there was something else in the pantry. Still, something about Parker's words struck a chord.

"Have you lived here your whole life?" Ivan pulled in another deep breath, straightened, and headed for the kitchen, Parker on his heels.

"Yes, me and mom lived here. It was my grandmother's house." Huh. That explained Parker's ownership of the house. One minor mystery solved.

"And you don't drive?" Because that would make it quite difficult for him to distribute any merchandise anywhere, unless his sole distribution was taking a messenger bag onto the university campus. If so, the roommate-undercover thing would be huge overkill. Parker wasn't even big enough to be small potatoes.

Parker leaned back against the counter, giving the casual appearance of a magazine model at ease for a photo shoot, pelvis thrust out enough to draw the eye to his crotch but not enough to be crude. The young man seemed unaware of his posture, but the graceful pose couldn't be an accident. He had to be deliberately enticing Ivan, which meant Ivan hadn't been nearly as successful in his straight-man persona as he'd thought. As much as he'd like to take Parker up on the unspoken offer, he disliked the notion Parker would just casually offer himself up to his new, older roommate.

"I don't really like to drive in downtown traffic, but I still have my mother's car."

So Parker did have a car. Ivan would have to find out where he was keeping it, because he'd need to take a look there, as well.

Ivan rummaged in the fridge for the makings of a simple omelet, then began chopping vegetables.

"You don't want the mac and cheese?" Parker's voice was wounded, and when Ivan looked up, a faint shadow of hurt darkened his eyes.

"I'll have it with my omelet." Gross, but he didn't like feeling as though he'd kicked Parker's puppy. "I'm pretty hungry tonight. There's not enough there for dinner."

Just like that, Parker's sunshine returned, and Ivan smiled in automatic response.

"Oh, okay then. So, how was your day, besides busy and late?"

Ivan's jaw slackened a bit. He remembered this—sharing his day—with Colin. It had been a pleasant way to unwind—prepping dinner, talking about their day—although Ivan couldn't talk much about open cases. He'd been missing it a lot longer than the eight months he and Colin had been broken up, though. If he could recall when they'd stopped being interested in each other, he'd probably be able to pinpoint when their relationship had broken, file the information away for his next foray onto the relationship roller coaster. But he'd never expected to recreate that interaction with a suspect.

"Oh, just lots of talking, the boss bitching about quotas. In this economy, it's hard to convince people to spend money on something that doesn't have an immediate, tangible result." There. That sounded completely believable. Should he buy a briefcase? Or would Parker think it weird he didn't already have one? If asked, he could surely say he'd left his stuff at the office. If only he'd had some time to think about what he needed to bring to this job. He should—

"Shouldn't you stir that?"

Ivan blinked and stared down at the onion just beginning to smoke in the pan. "Oh, yeah, sure. Sorry, got a little distracted." Which was dangerous, and not just because of the possibility of a kitchen fire. He needed to get a fucking grip on himself.

"How was your day?" Ivan glanced at Parker again, unable to keep his gaze off the gorgeous young man for long.

"Nothing special. Just learning and studying."

Ivan quickly assembled the omelet with his nearly charred onions, and Parker followed him to the table.

"Any plans for the weekend?" Parker's gaze locked on Ivan's dinner.

"Nope. Nothing planned. Did you want some of this?" The kid didn't eat enough. Maybe he was having some trouble getting capital, which might explain him wanting a roommate and getting in bed with Razhin. Banks wouldn't approve home equity loans to pay for drug purchases, even if the resale value was higher than for most other commodities.

A brief flash of longing appeared on Parker's face before he shook his head. "No, I'm good."

"What about you? Any plans?"

Parker's full lips opened on a reply, but the sound of the front door opening and closing interrupted, making Ivan jump. He tensed, preparing to tackle the intruder.

"Hello?"

"In here," Parker called.

Ivan grimaced. Didn't he just tell himself he had to get a fucking grip? He was jumpy, but he didn't know why. He forced himself to relax, since Parker obviously knew this stranger well enough not to be concerned by him just walking into the house.

A short, muscular guy swaggered into the kitchen, and Ivan instantly recognized both the swagger and the muscles as compensation for his height. There had been times when Ivan was younger when he'd have given just about anything to grow one more inch, to hit that six foot mark. He could only imagine the frustration of being four inches away, but he'd met so many guys who'd let it affect their personality. This guy was yet another one. Despite his height, the newcomer was good-looking and probably got plenty of attention in clubs, but next to Parker, he merely appeared rough and unfinished. Like a celebrity caught unawares at the beach, while Parker was the celebrity poised for a publicity shot.

"Isn't this cute? Who is this, Parker?" Arrogance weighted his tone, and Ivan resisted the urge to draw himself up to his full height. With his own comparable muscles, he would be as imposing to this guy as Parker was with his extra height.

He did, however, set his fork down.

"This is my roommate, Ivan." The pride in Parker's voice made Ivan flick a glance over. Parker smiled brightly at him, and Ivan couldn't help but smile back. "Ivan, this is my... friend, Neil."

So this was the boyfriend? Ivan looked closer as he extended a hand out to shake. As expected, Neil grasped his hand tighter than customary, trying to prove a point he probably spent far too much of his life trying to prove.

"Nice to meet you, Neil."

Neil grunted in reply. Parker didn't exactly roll his eyes, but somehow, Ivan knew it was a near thing. Obviously, this wasn't unexpected or unusual behavior.

"So, Ivan, you're a little old to be going back to school."

Neil's antagonistic words didn't alter Parker's relaxed state, so Ivan chose not to be concerned either.

"I'm not." But it wasn't a terrible idea. At some point, he'd have to tail Parker, and pretending to take a class or two would give him a plausible reason to be on campus.

Neil frowned in exaggerated and blatantly false puzzlement. "Then why do you need a roommate?"

"Because it's cheap. The wife got everything in the divorce."

Brows raised, Neil spoke again in that sarcastic tone. "Oh? And why was that? You cheat on her? Rough her up?"

Parker gasped and put a hand on Neil's shoulder. "You shouldn't ask those things."

"Why not? I know you didn't ask, and you should have before you let some stranger move in. I just want to know how, in this day and age, a man like Ivan got cleaned out by the little woman."

Ivan took a moment to tamp down the sudden spike of anger that flared up at the venom in Neil's tone and had to resist the urge to stand and flex, just to make Neil feel inferior. Pissing off the boyfriend would not win him any brownie points with Parker.

"My wife got everything because she had excellent lawyers." Ivan wasn't going to get in a pissing match with Neil over this.

"Ivan, I'm sorry. You don't have to answer."

"Don't apologize for me, for fuck's sake." An angry flush bloomed on Neil's cheeks. "Parker, let's leave your new roommate to eat his dinner."

"But—"

"I need to talk to you."

Parker threw him an apologetic look before he left the room, and Ivan couldn't help but stare at what had to be the world's sexiest butt. God help him, but Parker and this op were going to drive him bug-fuck nuts.

As though Neil sensed Ivan's cock revving up, he wrapped a protective arm around Parker's waist. The now familiar squeak announced their progress upstairs, and as soon as the door to Parker's bedroom slammed shut, Ivan stared back down at his dinner. His appetite had completely disappeared, but he forced himself to shovel in another couple of bites before he gave up and pitched it in the garbage.

NEIL flopped down on his bed, and Parker took one of the chairs he kept in his room.

"Was that necessary? You could have been nicer."

"What for? I still don't know why you bothered with a roommate. It's not like you need one."

Parker shrugged. He'd tried to tell Neil months ago how empty the house was, how much he hated coming home to the soullessness of a place he shared with no one. He'd been hoping for another body, a person he could get along with, but he hadn't expected to get a roommate he liked this much, never mind one that was sexy enough to prompt a few—several—erotic thoughts.

"Just for some company, you know."

Neil huffed. "Nice going. You got some stuffy old dude. He's probably a perv."

"He's not a perv, for God's sake. And he's not old." Older than they were, sure, but not old.

"How do you know he's not a perv? He sure stared at your ass plenty."

Shock kept him from getting any words out, even as his face heated. "He was married."

"Doesn't mean he's not gay. And he's got a thing for your fat ass. Probably the closest he's gotten to chicken in a decade."

Neil pulled out a joint and fussed with lighting it up, completely unconcerned by Parker's reaction. Parker dug his fingers into the worn cloth arms of the chair, trying to catch his breath from the myriad of emotions Neil had ruthlessly slapped him with in a few short sentences.

The casual contempt with which Neil called him chicken was precisely the reason he didn't like the whole gay scene. He wanted to talk, get to know someone before climbing into bed with them. He wanted a boyfriend, not a fuck, but whenever Neil took him somewhere it seemed as though the labels were the most important aspect of the sexual maneuvering.

The worst, though, was the hope. Hope that Ivan might actually be gay. Might actually be into him. He already loved coming home to Ivan and hoped he'd never leave. He swung his foot in a nervous habit he'd never been able to break, making the springs of the old chair creak almost as loud as the old stairs. Both were comfortable, familiar sounds.

After a few drags on the joint, Neil glanced up at him. "Oh, for fuck's sake. You like him, don't you?"

With the curtains closed and evening drawing in, the only light was the soft, yellowish bedside lamp. Surely Neil couldn't see him flushing. "He's my roommate. And so far, he's been a good roommate. I think we could be friends."

"Friends." Neil twisted the word into something ugly and even more contemptuous than chicken. "Don't be stupid. Even if he is as boring as he seems, and isn't some weird serial killer, how could you ever be friends? You haven't traveled or had a real job. You're still in school. What could you possibly have in common?"

Parker's leg swung a little faster, the squeaking an audible indication of his agitation. "But…."

Rolling his eyes while taking another drag took some skill, but Neil managed. He held the smoke in his lungs for a moment and let it out; all the while Parker searched for words to refute Neil's arguments.

"But nothing."

Too late.

"I bet he's one of those closeted creeps who's hoping you'll shine his pole while he goes out and finds himself a new wife. Where did you even find that guy?"

Parker couldn't stop his foot swinging. "The housing coordinator at the university. She interviewed him."

"She interviewed him? And you just took her word? You're an idiot, Parker."

Humiliation churned his stomach. Had he made a mistake trusting Liz? She seemed competent and nice. Ivan had been so sweet, and he hadn't once gotten too close or touched him inappropriately like half of Neil's friends. Of course, he knew they were all doing it to fuck with him, making it easy to say no, but still.

"I like him." Parker glared at Neil. How could the guy who'd protected him all through school, stuck with him through his mom's illness and death, helped him with all the rules, regulations, and paperwork, manage to make him feel like an unattractive, incompetent idiot? Not that he'd ever tell Neil that. Neil's favorite expression was "sac up" and Parker had heard it too many times over the years.

Neil shook his head. "You're going to regret letting him live here."

"Well, you didn't want to move in."

"No way, man. I need my own space. You know that."

Parker shrugged. "I know. But I like to share my space." He hadn't realized until he was alone how empty the house really was.

"I couldn't fucking wait to live on my own. And this place could be party central, but with the oldster moved in, you won't be able to have any fun. Don't come crying to me when it all goes to shit."

It wasn't going to go to shit. No matter what Neil thought, Ivan wasn't gay. Or if he was, he wasn't attracted to Parker. No one was, really. He and Neil had been each other's firsts, many years ago when they both realized they were gay, but they made better friends than boyfriends. Since then, Neil had probably fucked ten guys for every one that liked Parker, and Parker couldn't even bring himself to fuck every one of those. Sex was too intimate for him to indulge casually, even if that made him seem girly, as Neil often called him. Fat and girly. No way a hot, sexy guy like Ivan would be interested, even though he was apparently the nicest guy in the world.

"Fine, Neil, I won't." Parker's leg hadn't stopped its swinging, though.

"Only a couple puffs left. Come get 'em. You clearly need to relax." Neil waved the glowing end of his smoke at Parker's leg.

"No, I can't."

More eye rolling greeted his denial. The secondhand smoke would be enough to mellow him eventually, but with his condition, getting too fucked up could kill him. Neil seemed to think he was exaggerating, but he'd scared the shit out of his mom once or twice back in high school, and it hadn't taken long to sink in that if he'd been alone in the house, he'd probably be dead.

Neil took his final drag and stubbed out the joint in the ashtray Parker left in his bedroom for him. "Change your mind about coming with me tonight?"

"You know I don't like those clubs." Everyone looking for hookups made Parker uncomfortable. Could never quite believe any of the guys who approached were serious. He wouldn't put it past Neil to pay them off to "help" him out. And the stares. Everyone stared at him, and each of his flaws seemed magnified under those strobing colored lights.

"My God, you're such a wuss."

"Why don't you stay home with me? We could watch a movie or something." Before his mom died, and right after, they'd done that a lot. He'd been grateful for the company, but Neil had made a lot of new friends in the intervening months, and Parker didn't fit in. Just like always.

"No way. I got business to take care of tonight. If I'm going to open my own club, I need to talk to people when the clubs are open."

That logic always seemed weird to Parker. How could anyone have a proper business meeting with the decibel level of the music? Great for dancing, terrible for talking. But Neil would know better than Parker. As soon as they'd hit their first honest to God club, Neil had wanted to own one.

"But if you're going to stay home, do something about these boxes." Neil thumped the nearest box with his fist. "And don't spend your time wishing your new roomie would get in your pants." Neil lobbed a pillow at him, smacking him in the face.

He gasped, and Neil just laughed. "Oh, Parker... I want your cock...." Neil spoke in a weird, breathy falsetto that Parker interrupted by throwing the pillow right back before he launched out of the chair and tackled Neil on the bed.

Neil just laughed his funny, doped up laugh.

"I can't believe you've got a thing for your roommate. Such a cliché."

"Cliché. That's a big word for you. Do you even know what it means?"

Neil giggled and rubbed his knuckles over the top of Parker's head. They fell back on the bed, staring up at the ceiling.

"Turn on some music, would you? I've got some time before I've got to go." Neil pulled out another joint as Parker grabbed the remote for his docking station, setting his MP3 player on shuffle and not too loud. He hadn't had a chance to discuss ground rules with Ivan, like music level and having people over.

"You can come here after, if you want." Parker hated himself for asking. Ivan had possibilities, but Neil was a fixture in his life. Neil represented stability at times when it seemed as though Parker had none.

"No way. I'm getting laid tonight. Besides, you know I can't get any sleep here."

Parker crossed an arm over his head, letting the sweetish scent of Neil's smoke relax him as he imagined the warm body beside him was someone other than his best friend. Someone he could share his life with. Someone who wanted to sleep with him. But if he couldn't even get his best friend to stay the night, how could he possibly expect a potential boyfriend to?

IVAN turned on the TV and slumped on the couch. He flipped through several stations, but couldn't find anything to distract him from the image of Neil wrapping an arm around Parker and guiding him upstairs. It was early in the evening still. Surely they weren't having sex up there? Not already. Neil had been dressed for clubbing. Then again, he could have dressed to impress his super-sexy boyfriend. Probably took a lot of work, even for a guy as good-looking as Neil, to be within striking distance of Parker's league.

A faint squeak overhead had him muting the TV. Shit. Parker's bedroom was right above his head. What he should do was start searching for evidence down here while Parker was occupied, but the unbearable rudeness of leaving him to go and have sex had his ears turning red in his anger. Sure, he wasn't a guest or anything, but he hadn't even lived here a week. Some consideration was in order, wasn't it?

He rifled through a drawer in the end table, but found he couldn't concentrate. He needed to get the fuck out of here. Maybe go for a run. He hadn't exercised since... since the day he'd shot that kid. Been the longest he'd gone without working out since he'd joined the police services. No wonder he was antsy.

Too bad all his workout clothes were upstairs.

Ivan stood at the bottom of the stairs. Would the pair hear him if he walked up the stairs? Would it matter if they did?

A faint squeak, then another and another put images in Ivan's mind. Images he didn't want. Desperation drove him up the stairs, trying to be as silent as possible.

Changing clothes in record time, he left his room, but the distinctive scent of marijuana hit his nose. He edged close to the bedroom door, not sure what his purpose was. He didn't want to hear what Neil and Parker were up to. It was none of his business. Even though he wanted to break down the door and tell them not to be idiots. Tell them drugs would ruin their lives. But that wasn't his job. He couldn't even claim to be doing it out of friendship. As comfortable as he'd become with Parker, he could hardly call them friends.

The squeaking, rhythmic and regular, made him angry and horny and embarrassed all at once.

Other undercover operations had never triggered any feelings other than an abstract anger on behalf of those hurt by the drug trade. Never this personal, spiky hurt that filled him with the desire to break down the door and toss Neil out the window. Only a few minutes in Neil's company convinced him that whatever Parker's plans with Razhin were, Neil had to have been the one to introduce him to drugs.

A thump and a giggle startled Ivan and spurred him down the stairs and out of the door before he had a chance to hear what sounds Parker made when he came. That was the kind of thing you couldn't unhear. And if they were almost done, the last thing he wanted was to encounter one or both of them right after they'd had sex. Embarrassing for all parties.

On the lawn in front of the house, Ivan sped through some stretching. With some effort, he managed to get mostly warmed up without glancing up at the windows of Parker's bedroom. It couldn't hurt to get some up close and personal reconnaissance of the area, check out unobtrusively if anyone suspicious was keeping an eye on the house.

With a deep breath, he took off into the warm evening.

CHAPTER
Four

NEIL looked at his watch and swore. "Shit, I gotta go. You sure you don't want to come to the club tonight? I've got some friends who'd like to meet you."

Neil's sudden frantic energy dispersed Parker's pleasant lethargy brought on by the third joint Neil had smoked, along with the two tokes Neil had convinced him to take.

"No, you go on. Have fun." He and Neil really did not have the same taste in men, and almost all the men Neil tried to set him up with weren't right for him, for one reason or another. Maybe Ivan would watch a movie with him.

Parker trailed after Neil and waited by the door as he grabbed his jacket and slipped it on.

"I know why you don't want to come. You're hoping your new roomie might want a piece of your fat ass, right?" Neil grabbed a handful of Parker's butt to punctuate his words, making Parker jump.

"What the hell, Neil? That's not why."

"Sure, sure. You can't lie to me, Park. We've been friends too long. Good thing he's not here. He's bad news, remember that."

"Where would he go?" Ivan's door to his bedroom hadn't been closed, he couldn't hear the washing machine in the basement, and, unless he was sitting in the dark in the living room, Neil was right: Ivan wasn't here.

Neil patted his cheek. "It's Friday night. Most people have plans, go out. Maybe he had a hot date."

Parker swallowed heavily. Ivan didn't have to answer to him about his comings and goings, but suddenly his nice evening at home had become another lonely night in an empty house. But he knew from experience this was exactly the wrong mood to accompany Neil to a club. He'd only get more depressed.

"Yeah, yeah, whatever. See you tomorrow?"

"Eh, maybe. Depends on how business goes today."

Neil wasn't always the greatest company, and Parker was mellow enough that he almost didn't care he was alone again. He flipped on the TV, but the selections made it damned clear that the cable company thought everyone was out having fun or on hot dates and therefore only needed to broadcast complete drivel.

During yet another stupid commercial, he poked around in the kitchen cupboards and the fridge, but nothing piqued his interest.

Every little sound had him glancing toward the door, wondering if Ivan was home. Which was just too pathetic. If he wasn't going to have fun, he might as well get some homework done. After grabbing his laptop, he flicked off the TV, intending to head for his room. The last thing he wanted was for Ivan to come home and see what a loser his roommate was. Too humiliating. As an afterthought, he bent down and grabbed the disc of porn he'd tossed behind the TV the day Ivan had moved in. No way was he going to watch it in the communal area, but his homework could wait until tomorrow.

Poised in the doorway of his room, Parker glanced over his shoulder at Ivan's room, the entrance dark and shadowed. Deep in the thrall of intense curiosity—possibly due to the pot—he tossed his laptop and the DVD on the bed and strode into Ivan's room.

After only a few days, the room already smelled like Ivan. Not bad, not at all. Different from the dry and disused scent of nothingness the room had had before. He sniffed again. It was actually good. He flipped on the overhead switch. Ivan wasn't lying. He didn't have a lot of stuff. His wife must be a real bitch.

Sitting on the edge of the bed, he picked up the thriller lying on the bedside table and glanced at the back cover copy. Didn't sound too bad; maybe he'd ask to borrow it later. A few other books and knickknacks sat on the squat bookshelf beside the closet. A briefcase sat on the desk with nothing else on it. Biting his lip, he traced a fingertip over the brass drawer handle of the bedside table. He couldn't open that, could he? Did he really want proof of Ivan's straightness in the form of naked boob pictures?

Instead, he stood and flung open the closet. Two boxes were stacked on the floor, and despite the small size of the closet, the few shirts and suits Ivan had didn't take up the whole space.

After taking a quick look at sizes—why, he didn't know—Parker moved on to the dresser. He sniffed at the aftershave. Nothing special, nothing fancy, but it was definitely the source of Ivan's compelling scent. Must be hard to start again at thirty-four, with nothing. If Ivan ended up being a good roommate, Parker might reconsider the rent, maybe drop it to give him a chance to get back on his feet. As Neil was so fond of saying, it wasn't like Parker needed a roommate. His mother's trust had been more than enough to pay for his expenses, as well as utilities and property taxes. He didn't have any mortgage, as both the house and cottage had been in the family for a long time. At twenty-two, thanks to his mother's savvy financial sense, he was in much better shape than Ivan.

Back by the desk, he listened carefully for the sound of footsteps on the stairs. Nothing out of the ordinary reached his ears, although this close to both downtown and the university campus, there was plenty of background noise.

The insatiable curiosity about his roommate battled and won over any hint of shame, and Parker opened the briefcase. Unexpectedly, there was no laptop, merely a haphazard mess of files, blank contracts, and actuarial tables. Boring. What did he expect, though? The most interesting stuff had to be in the bedside table, and it sang a siren song through Parker's brain. He wanted to look but knew he'd be disappointed if he did.

He stuffed the papers back in the briefcase and took another glance at the nightstand, but the next-door neighbor's dog barking convinced him to get out of Ivan's room. Irritating his new roommate was not his intention, assuming Ivan didn't get freaked by Parker being gay. Probably he should have that conversation sooner rather than later.

Scooting across to his room, he quickly shut the door behind him and waited. After several minutes, during which the front door failed to open, a sudden yawn caught him by surprise. Pathetic to be so tired at ten in the evening, but weed usually made him lethargic, even the few tokes he'd taken. Ivan might be out on a date or something and could be gone for hours. Or he could have taken a walk to the nearest convenience store and be back in minutes.

With a sigh, he stripped down and sat on the bed beside his own bedside table. The second drawer down held lube and condoms. He'd never bought a magazine—seemed a little silly when much better stuff could be had on the Internet, so the only potential indicator of his orientation was the plug and dildo. His Internet history told a much more detailed story. Some days, it was worth the effort to make use of his toys, but most times it was just depressing. He pulled out the box of condoms. Sealed, and in no danger of expiring, but also in no danger of being used either. Also depressing.

Probably he should take Neil up on his offer to introduce him to some guys, but the men Parker was interested in—his mind shied away from an image of Ivan—weren't at Neil's clubs and he didn't know how to pick one up. Parker ran a finger over the simple and minimalist contents of his sex drawer. Inside, he was still the boring, socially awkward fat kid, and sex toys weren't going to change that.

With a frown, he slammed the drawer shut and pulled open the top drawer. Lots to be said about who he was in here, but none of it good or interesting. Its contents were the reason he'd always be alone, why he'd never have a proper boyfriend, and why his best friend couldn't stand to spend the night with him.

Somehow, he'd always imagined being thinner would magically improve his life. Not eating much during the last year of his mom's life had melted most of the extra pounds away, but he wasn't skinny by any stretch. He tried not to eat too much, tried to eat healthy, but he still had love handles, and with them— ironically—he wasn't going to find anyone to love him. Even Neil joked about his fat bum and spare tire.

Even with the weight loss, he still had sleep apnea. He still needed the dreaded CPAP machine when he slept to ensure he didn't stop breathing in the middle of the night. How could he expect any man to put up with the noise, never mind Parker looking like a fighter pilot all night? Wasn't exactly conducive to cuddling or middle-of-the-night blow jobs or even just sharing a bed. All of the things he wanted and hoped to have one day.

His mom had always seemed happy just the two of them, but Parker wanted a relationship. He wanted to share his life with someone, but with the mechanical baggage and his social ineptness, there wasn't a chance in hell he was going to get it. Maybe he needed to revise his stance on one-night stands; he might have misremembered how bad they were.

Parker fitted the mask over his nose and started the machine before turning off the lamp. Even with it, he knew his snoring was sometimes intolerable, but he usually only woke up with a headache if he forgot to wear it while sleeping or napping. And after he'd scared the crap out of his mom a couple of times, he tried not to forget, even without her around to remind him. It was especially important that he wear it after smoking up, although his doctor had strongly recommended against getting high.

Flat on his back, he stared at the flickering shadows cast on his ceiling from the streetlights outside and let the consistent white noise of his CPAP machine lull him to sleep as it had done every night for years and years.

IVAN stumbled into the dark house, shivering as the chilly air hit his sweat-slick body. He'd run a fucking long way, much longer than he'd intended, but he hadn't seen a hint of surveillance. Not entirely a surprise. Drug kingpins had more resources than cops did, but even they didn't have the manpower to stake out a low-level dealer's 24/7, unless Ivan gave them a reason to be suspicious. Whether the incident on the bus was a coincidence or not, he must have played it cool enough.

He kicked off his runners before grabbing a bottle of water out of the fridge. Half the bottle disappeared in one gulp, and he leaned over the counter, panting. His legs wobbled like wet noodles, but he had run far and fast enough that he was sure to sleep through the night. He needed a decent night's sleep.

With the rapid thump of his pulse still beating in his ears, he couldn't hear a sound from the bedroom upstairs. There was no indication if the pair had fallen asleep or if they'd gone out. He'd gotten past the point of going out after ten at night unless he was looking to get laid, but Neil and Parker were plenty young enough to see ten as going out time rather than coming home time.

That alone was enough to make his shoulders slump. It shouldn't matter that a low-level criminal had more energy and a better social life than he did, and maybe after he got a decent night's sleep, he'd stop caring.

Ivan's bed and a shower were the only things convincing him to climb the creaky stairs. Otherwise, he'd be happy to collapse naked on the couch. On the landing, he froze. He didn't recall hearing the faint mechanical sound before. Edging closer to Parker's closed bedroom door, the sound got a trifle louder. It sounded like... no. It couldn't be. A vibrator? They couldn't be still having sex, could they? Ivan dashed into his bedroom and shut the door. A wipe-down with a towel would have to do for tonight. He wasn't leaving his room until morning.

The moonlight streaming into his room provided more than enough illumination such that he didn't need to turn on the light. Within seconds, he'd pitched his sweaty clothes in the hamper and grabbed a towel to wipe away the worst effects of his run. He lay back on the bed, one arm behind his head, able to relax now that he couldn't hear any of Parker's sexscapade. The sweat drying on his scalp itched, but he ignored it. He could shower in the morning, once his muscles recovered from his run.

What kind of sex did Parker like? He didn't get much of a sense from the short glimpse of the porn Parker had been so quick to turn off, but then, porn preferences didn't always translate to bedroom preferences. Parker's skin was smooth and made for licking. The shy smiles, so at odds with what Ivan expected from a drug dealer, said he'd probably react well to a few gentle sucks and nips around the ear and neck. Slowly he'd work his lips down, over the prominent collarbone that peeked out of Parker's shirts. Would the flat discs of his nipples be the same rich peach as his lips, or would they require a bit of tonguing to bring out their color?

As his cock began to fill, he wrapped his fingers around it and tugged. Would Parker grip him firmly or tentatively? Would those long fingers be cool on his overheated skin or hot, like brands? Neil didn't seem like a considerate lover—was there anything Parker had missed out on? Rimming, perhaps? What would those innocent eyes look like as he gazed up Parker's lean body, bent almost in half, while he buried his tongue in Parker's ass? Would Parker cream just from that? Would Ivan?

Ivan spat on his hand and pumped his now fully hard cock, twisting the tip a bit on each upward stroke. He had lube in his drawer, but even that took more energy than he had.

Would he ride out Parker's orgasm with a tongue up his ass or would he suck down Parker's dick, just to feel it flex against his tongue while he came? No. He wanted to see Parker shoot all over himself, helpless against the tide of orgasm; he wanted to watch every second.

Ivan gasped, and his back arched as his own orgasm exploded without warning, and he sprayed himself almost exactly as he'd imagined Parker spraying, although he pictured Parker without any chest hair. Panting, he used the towel he'd dropped beside the bed to wipe away his sticky cum. He'd be pissed at himself the next morning, but between the orgasm and the exercise, he was too blissed out to care.

As his eyelids drooped, he scanned his room one last time and sat up, sleep swept away in a flood of adrenaline. He flicked on the bedside lamp and got out of bed. His briefcase had been moved. Hadn't it? Had Parker snuck into his room and searched it while he was out running? Peering at the desk, he tried to remember how he'd left it. Not one thing of Ivan's would incriminate him, so a search would only confirm he was nothing more than the loser his undercover identity proclaimed, but it was a harsh reminder of the reality of his situation. He couldn't let his guard down for a moment. Including while fantasizing about the man he was investigating. How unprofessional and idiotic could he get?

He turned off the light and lay back down on the bed, stiff, but not in a good way. Every time he closed his eyes, he thought he heard something move, or he'd glance at another part of the room, trying to compare it with his fuzzy recall of precisely how he'd left his things. The search should ultimately make him seem harmless, but he couldn't help but wonder if he'd missed something that identified him as either cop or Ivan Bekker. Without any time to plan, he'd packed his own clothes, used his own duffel. Hell, he'd grabbed a bunch of his own books, because if he had time to read, it should be stuff he was interested in reading. Could he have missed a receipt with his name on it?

His pulse pounded, more rapid and fierce than at the peak of his run. Sleep was impossible, but this time he wasn't disappointed. Sleeping led to nightmares, and it had been a miracle he'd not woken Parker with his shouts the past couple of nights. He swung himself out of bed, flicked on the light again, and pulled on a pair of sweatpants. Since he was up, he might as well see if there was anything damaging to his cover identity. He'd start by shaking out each and every book to make sure he hadn't slipped a receipt or note between the pages. Tomorrow, he'd delve fully into his cover identity and get to know his new roommate.

PARKER plunked down on the couch, apple in hand. Why had he let Neil chase him upstairs so early last night? He hadn't had a chance to ask Ivan about groceries, and so he'd gone to the farmers market this morning, hoping to buy stuff Ivan liked too. Stupidly, he'd thought having a roommate might mean company running errands, or even just a split of errands, but they hadn't discussed it yet. Parker didn't know what was normal, but he likely shouldn't expect company for errands. That was more in the boyfriend realm than roommate. Wasn't it?

And the tiny bit of resentment that had flared at going alone? It was nothing against the thought of Ivan getting laid late last night, requiring him to sleep in. Probably everyone else in existence got laid on Friday nights while he'd gone to bed early with his contraption of doom. Pathetic.

In celebration of his patheticness, he was going to watch *Serenity*. Again. Neil wouldn't be back until much later, assuming Parker saw him again this weekend, and he'd be long finished before Neil showed up to make fun of him. Neil said sci-fi didn't get anyone laid, and to be fair, Neil certainly had more sex than Parker the geek, but how could you not love Mal? It was one of his favorite movies, and one his mother had even liked, despite her preference for murder mysteries.

He didn't need to leave the house again until school on Monday, and maybe he just wouldn't. He had plenty of movies he could watch. Maybe a *Firefly* marathon.

Five minutes into the movie and three bites into his apple, the stairs creaked. Parker tensed and stared fixedly at the screen, although his entire awareness was on the person coming down the stairs. What if Ivan had brought someone home last night? That was even worse than imagining him out on an overnight date. Should he introduce himself to her? Should he ignore her? Could he get away with pretending he was so engrossed in the movie that he didn't notice? What was normal roommate protocol in this situation?

"Good movie?"

Parker jumped. "What? Oh, yes." He forced his head to turn from the television. Ivan was alone—thank God—but he was also shirtless. His chest was stunning. Muscular and covered with a mat of hair a shade darker than the gold atop his head. Gray threadbare sweatpants draped Ivan's package in such a way as to hint at shape and size without allowing Parker to discern any details.

Ivan cleared his throat, and Parker raised his eyes, cheeks beginning to burn. How long had he been staring at Ivan's junk? No way could he have the "I'm gay, hope you don't mind" discussion. Not after he'd just ogled the man like he wanted to eat him up. Well, Parker did want to eat him up, but admitting it was a surefire way to make the straight guy uncomfortable. Which wasn't fair at all when he was in a new home.

"How are you?" Now that Parker was looking at Ivan's face, the deep circles under his eyes attested to a lack of sleep, and likely not for the reason Parker had assumed. "Late night?"

Ivan shrugged. "In a manner of speaking."

"Was it at least good?"

"I'm sure your night was much better."

Parker barely held back a sardonic laugh. His night had been shit, but he at least had sense enough not to admit that.

"Couldn't sleep after I got home from my run," Ivan continued. "Don't think I actually dropped off until well after dawn."

Parker blinked. "You went running last night?"

"Yeah, I needed something to do and you were... uh... occupied with Neil."

Ivan put a funny emphasis on the word "occupied." Maybe he'd smelled Neil's joint. "Running. I thought you were on a date."

Ivan rolled his eyes. "Yeah, because I'm such a catch."

"You want something to eat? I went to the market this morning."

"Like the St. Lawrence Market? You should have woken me. I would have gone with you. I love that place." Ivan smiled and scratched his belly.

"Oh, I just went to the local farmers market, but we could go to the St. Lawrence Market next week."

"It's a date."

The surge of pleasure those words caused was tempered by the knowledge Ivan had only used them as an expression, not because they were actually going on a date.

Ivan stepped far enough into the room to view the movie over Parker's shoulder. "Watching movies all day?"

"Probably." Parker shrugged. "I've got a paper to work on, but other than that, I'm all caught up."

"Oh, good for you. Let me take a shower, and I'll hang here, if that's okay."

What a stupid question. "Of course. We're roommates." Parker suppressed the happy little giggle that wanted to escape. Ivan didn't need to know how much he wanted to hang out. His friends at school would have killed for Parker's relaxed class schedule, but until Ivan had moved in, Parker had regretted not coming back in with a full course load. It had given him more time to think about how empty the house was. Now, though, it gave him plenty of time to make sure he was at home when Ivan was.

Ivan yawned, and Parker frowned. "Are you sure you don't want to go back to bed?"

"What? No, I'm fine. It's been a while since I could relax on the couch and watch movies. I'll be done in a few minutes." Ivan pounded upstairs. After a couple of doors slammed, the pipes in the walls rattled when Ivan turned the water on.

Slumping back into his seat, Parker tried to focus on Mal, but listening to Ivan shower, and picturing him there, superseded the sexy captain's banter, a feat Parker hadn't thought possible.

Should he grab snacks? Make Ivan breakfast? No, that was stupid. No way could he pass that off as "oh, I was making myself some…" because it was almost one, and Ivan already knew he'd been running errands this morning. Making breakfast for a man was different than sharing lunch or dinner, he was sure of it. More intimate. A boyfriend thing.

Parker was still debating with himself when Ivan pounded down the stairs, into the kitchen, and began rummaging around in the fridge.

"Hey, you got some great stuff. Probably not enough to last the week, but I can make a mean omelet with this. You want some?"

"Oh, I've got my apple."

Ivan stuck his head into the doorway. "An apple? You need more for lunch than that. An omelet works for my breakfast and your lunch."

Parker's stomach growled. The apple was supposed to be breakfast and lunch, but he still wanted more. Ivan was a great cook, and he was hungry. Too bad this truly was a case of "oh, I was making myself some…" but Parker could live with that. The most he got from Neil was an offer to add in an extra dish and an egg roll when they ordered Chinese, but Parker always ended up paying for both of them. And usually Neil couldn't sit still long enough to watch an entire movie together, much less consider spending the day doing so.

"Um, okay, sure, thanks."

Ivan worked his magic in the kitchen and less than twenty minutes later was seated in the chair beside the couch after placing a plate of eggy goodness in front of each of them.

He wanted Ivan to sit beside him, but then he'd be tempted to snuggle, and that would never do.

ALICIA waved at him across the sparsely populated lecture hall. Parker smiled and made his way over to her. He wasn't sure what sadist scheduled a statistics course three times a week at nine in the morning, but it made Mondays difficult to wake up to. On the other hand, he and Alicia had bonded the first day over the hideousness of stats and the summer semester.

"So, tell me." Alicia grabbed the sleeve of his shirt and pulled, barely giving him enough time to slide into his seat.

"Tell you what?" A tiny smirk twitched the corner of Parker's mouth.

"Come on. You didn't even text me about how it went with the new roommate."

"Hey, I wasn't the one who played hooky for a week to go to Mexico with my boyfriend. And you certainly didn't text me with any details from that."

Alicia rolled her eyes, but blushed. "Hey, if someone had opened their cottage this year, maybe we wouldn't have had to go all the way to Mexico."

"Oh, yeah, like my cottage has anything on Mexico." Although the truth was, he wasn't able to face the cottage yet, which was the reason he'd decided not to open it up this year.

"I wouldn't know, would I?"

Parker opened his mouth to continue their banter, but the professor strode into the class, brows drawn together in a frown, ready to start. If it weren't for the perpetual scowl, the man might be good-looking, but his temperament wasn't any improvement either. His students learned the first day to shut up and pay attention or they'd regret it. Of course, it was statistics, so regret was inevitable.

Too bad it was a required course. Even the humanities version for psychology and sociology majors like himself was difficult.

Two hours later, they escaped. Alicia hooked her arm in his. "Up for an early lunch? I want to hear all about the new roomie."

"Sure thing."

An early lunch wasn't unusual. Their brains were so fried after stats, they needed the break. He had no regrets about choosing to take stats as part of his lighter course load. He'd have been hard-pressed to keep up in that class with a full complement of courses.

They grabbed food and easily found a table at this early hour. Alicia's boyfriend, Chris, showed up moments later, tray laden with food.

"Hey, Chris."

"Hey, Parker." Chris gave Alicia a deep kiss, which had flustered Parker when he'd first met them, but he was used to their casual displays of affection and, by now, a tiny bit envious.

"So, tell me all about him," Alicia prompted.

Chris smiled at him. "You met a guy? You know my girl's going to want to check him out."

"Oh, uh, no, not exactly." He'd met a guy, all right. It hadn't even been a week, but if Ivan was gay, he might be the perfect man for Parker.

"Oh my God, don't you ever listen to me?" Alicia flicked Chris on the shoulder, and he pretended to be mortally wounded. They'd been dating long enough that Alicia did no more than roll her eyes. "Parker's new roommate moved in this week."

"It sucks you need a roommate. Most of them are complete shits, and the rest of them are even worse," Chris said loudly, making sure he got the attention of his own roommate who walked past. Thom merely flipped Chris off before smiling and nodding at Parker and Alicia.

Parker smiled back. He'd only met Thom a few times, but he was nice enough. Thom and Chris actually got along very well, but they both seemed to enjoy a contentious relationship.

Chris flipped Thom off in return and looked back at Parker. "Seriously, though, most of them do suck." He got a funny look on his face, and Alicia flicked his shoulder again.

"Don't say it."

"Say what?" Chris played up being both innocent and offended.

"You were going to say how Parker would be happy if his roommate did suck. Literally."

Parker did laugh this time, and no one had to know there was a grain of truth in the statement.

"What, am I wrong?" Chris turned his palms up and looked to Parker for support.

"No, not really."

Alicia gasped, but then she laughed too. "Eh, getting laid once in a while wouldn't kill you."

Kill him? No. Embarrass the crap out of him? Maybe. It had been so long since another guy had touched him, he'd probably go off in seconds like a volcano. It didn't help that almost every sight of Ivan made him hard.

"Seriously, though," Chris said again, but this time he sounded serious. "If someone's looking for a new roommate mid-semester? They probably got booted for being an asswipe. You should have waited until the beginning of a semester at least."

Parker shrugged. He'd let them think he needed a roommate for financial reasons, because he hadn't wanted to admit how lonely he was. If either of them had known, he was sure they'd invite him out more often, although he hated being the third wheel. Spending the weekend hanging out with Ivan had been unbelievably awesome.

"He's not a student, although he did say he might audit a few classes." As a matter of fact, on Sunday, Ivan had requested his class schedule. He'd love it if Ivan meant to audit his classes. Neil thought school was boring and hated listening to Parker talk about his classes. Which was one reason he'd never bothered introducing him to Alicia and Chris.

"Oh, yeah? Tell us all." Alicia waved a french fry at him to emphasize her command. Parker grabbed it from her hand and ate it. Tasted better than the small salad he'd ordered and finished already.

Parker quickly outlined his interactions with Ivan since he'd moved in.

"Holy shit, can we trade roommates?" Chris asked. "The cooking alone makes him better than Thom."

Uh, no. Thom was a nice guy, but Parker wasn't giving Ivan up.

"You like him, don't you?" Alicia asked. "Maybe you should ask him out."

Parker choked on his water. "Ask him out? No way." If he'd been talking to Neil, he would have said he didn't like Ivan that way. But Alicia was never judgmental, and he accepted that she sensed how attracted he was to Ivan.

"Why not? He's single."

"He's divorced, yes. But he had a wife. He's straight."

Alicia snorted. "Yeah, because marriages have never broken up because the guy *came out*. Might even explain why he got hosed in the divorce."

Huh. He'd never got that sense from Ivan. He'd be able to tell, wouldn't he? "I don't think he's gay. And I don't think he knows I'm gay. I haven't found the right time to tell him." Parker didn't do a great job of hiding it, but coming out and saying it to a guy like Ivan was a lot more terrifying than assuming Ivan had already guessed.

"You're not worried about his reaction, are you? Because if he was a total 'phobe, he'd have asked before he moved in, wouldn't he?" Chris grabbed one of Alicia's fries.

Was that normal behavior? Parker was pretty sure he couldn't ask a potential roommate about that—discrimination and all that—but was that the type of thing Ivan would have asked about, if he cared? "Would you ask that?"

"No way, man. I don't give a shit. But I tell you, I've heard all kinds of stories about asshole roommates. If you're nervous, we could come over, hang out while you spill."

Parker had to smile. Unspoken were the words "protect you." Chris's willingness to stand up for him meant more than he could say, and Chris was an imposing, intimidating specimen. Regardless of Ivan's orientation, he couldn't believe the man who'd so tenderly bandaged his damaged shin could become dangerous just from finding out Parker was gay. And he was pretty sure he'd hidden his attraction.

"Well, asking him out would accomplish the same thing as some grand confession. And you'd find out if he was gay and if he was into you."

"He's not into me. I'd be able to tell, so asking him out would only make things weird at home. He's only been living there less than a week!"

"Right. *You* could tell if they're into you. Parker, you could get laid right now, if you'd just open your eyes."

Parker peered around the cafeteria. All he saw was Thom sitting with a few friends. Thom gave him a little wave, and Parker waved back.

"What are you talking about?"

"So freaking blind." Chris shook his head sadly. Parker frowned at him, but neither of them explained.

Although not as bad as when Neil teased him, the topic had him a little defensive, which meant it was time to change the subject. "Tell me about Mexico."

Alicia reached over and patted his hand, giving him a sympathetic look he didn't really understand.

THE elevator doors opened, and Ivan allowed the crowd to propel him out. A bright shaft of sunlight from the glass lobby doors lit up a geometric wedge of polished granite floor. Sweat slicked his forehead like the building's AC had been set to hellfire, but the true temperature was immaterial.

Out in the sunshine was better, but not any cooler. The breeze helped, regardless of the underlying urban scents—diesel fumes, garbage, urine. He rounded a corner, unwilling to endure the claustrophobic confines of the subway just yet. Especially considering the circuitous route he needed to take to separate his two lives.

The first door he came to was a tiny falafel shop. The scent of grease, seasoned meat, and fried chickpea patties was almost too much to bear, but they had a fridge with soft drinks, and he bought two ice-cold cans, one to drink and the other to press against his forehead.

Were you supposed to lie to your therapist? Even one that had been assigned by the department? Having to lie about everything, including the worsening nightmares, had to negate any benefits. Assuming there were any. But the last thing he needed was for the guy to prescribe him sleeping pills. No way could he allow drugs to incapacitate him, not when he was sleeping in a criminal's house. A sweet, adorable, gorgeous criminal, but that only made him more dangerous. If sin wasn't alluring, crime wouldn't be rampant.

Then again, he'd never had nightmares while undercover before. He'd never had to lie on multiple fronts before. His family thought he was on legitimate undercover work. His coworkers and the SIU investigators thought he was on administrative leave, getting his head on right. Parker thought he was a straight, divorced insurance salesman. His shrink thought he was resisting therapy, setting up roadblocks, but Doc Sanchez was just one more person he couldn't trust with the truth.

When Doc Sanchez decided he needed to see him twice a week instead of once a week, Ivan hadn't realized that meant getting two different types of interrogation in one day. Stacking a meeting with the SIU investigator and a shrink on the same day seemed efficient. He'd not make that mistake again, if he could avoid it.

Fuck, was he ever tired.

Letting his head hang, he tried to stretch out the knots in his neck. They'd arrived, hard like marbles, while he'd attempted to save that bleeding kid, and nothing, not even last night's orgasm, was enough to smooth them out. The dull ache behind his eyes had to be a combination of lack of sleep and muscle tension.

Ivan checked his watch. He should get going if he didn't want to spend two hours taking some random route back to Parker's in the midst of rush hour traffic. He might really lose his fucking shit if he had to endure that.

IVAN made it home without any other incident, and he stood outside on the sidewalk. His stomach growled, and he glanced down the street. Which would require the least amount of energy: walking down a couple of blocks for takeout or making dinner?

Breathing deeply, he stared at the front door, rubbing the back of his neck. Maybe he'd just go to sleep. The absolute least effort.

Inside the house, he sniffed. It smelled like… food?

"Parker?"

Parker popped out of the kitchen with a broad smile. "Ivan. You're home. I thought you'd be later."

Ivan smiled back, letting himself slip into the strange comfort of his undercover persona. Nightmares or not, coming home to Parker was a hell of a lot better than going back to his empty apartment or trolling bars for a hookup.

"Some days are better than others."

"I made dinner. Or, I tried to. It's just soup, but I didn't think I could screw it up too badly, and it wouldn't matter much what time you got home."

Dinner was made. Amazing. When was the last time he'd come home to dinner? Months. Long before Colin moved out.

"I'm sure it's fine." He took a couple of steps toward Parker, but stopped when he realized he'd been on autopilot for a hug and kiss. Parker might be gay, but Ivan *Baker* wasn't.

"Anything on that enormous TV of yours tonight?" Ivan lacked affinity for any specific shows. With his hours, getting wrapped up in a show was pointless effort, but he was happy to watch just about anything.

Parker shrugged. He walked back into the kitchen to stir the soup. Ivan followed him and poured a glass of wine. "Want one?"

That got him another shy smile, one that seemed to say Parker was unaccustomed to simple courtesy.

"Sure, thanks."

When Parker's attention returned to the stove, Ivan grabbed the open bottle of wine.

"Are you wanting to go for another run tonight?" Parker asked.

After their slothful day on the couch Saturday, he'd spent part of Sunday showing Parker the basics of running. They hadn't gone far, but Parker didn't have any regular exercise regime that Ivan could see, and it sure as hell didn't hurt for him to counteract some of the worst college excesses.

"Liked it, did you?"

Parker made a sound Ivan took for assent. "I'm a little sore, but yeah."

"That'll go away after a few times." Ivan bobbed up and down on the balls of his feet, testing his own muscles. After the day he'd had, though, believing he'd be able to rouse himself enough for an evening run was… optimistic at best.

"Don't think I'm up for one tonight. I'm beat."

Parker twisted his head around and frowned. "You do look tired. I thought you said work was better today."

A sardonic laugh escaped his lips as he grabbed another wine glass from the top shelf. "No, I think I said some days were better than others. Just because I got home at a decent hour, more or less, doesn't mean work was any better."

He sure as shit didn't want to think about his day. These different facets of his life were a little too big to keep in his brain.

The soup bubbled and spat. With Parker's attention back on the stove, Ivan let himself study Parker. The contentment he'd felt after walking in to Parker's happy smile was something he didn't want to examine, nor did he want to consider what made Parker decide to take a criminal detour when he appeared so firmly to be on the right path.

Later. He'd let himself think about it later. Until he had a chance to search the place, until he had a chance to follow Parker and assess his associates, he'd let himself be Ivan Baker, insurance salesman. That guy was a lot less complicated. He kinda liked Ivan Baker's life.

He stepped up behind Parker, glass in hand, and slid Parker's glass of wine onto the counter beside the stove.

"There's your wine."

"Oh thanks. Can you grab bowls?"

"Sure." Ivan pulled away, unsure if the request was intended to make him back off or not. He took a small mouthful and placed his glass down before turning away to grab bowls.

"Oh shit!"

The crash of glass had Ivan whirling into a crouch, reaching for a gun he no longer carried. Parker stared down at the broken glass, red wine spattered like blood across the floor. It took a moment for Ivan to convince himself there was no danger, no reason for his pulse to shoot through the roof.

Parker bent over and grabbed at one of the larger shards. Ivan was wrong, there was a bit of danger. "Stop."

Parker froze, hand outstretched.

"Let me clean that up." Ivan took a deep breath, trying to calm his racing heart.

"I can do it."

Ivan let himself smile. "I think it's best if I only have to give you first aid once a month, don't you?"

The puzzled frown on Parker's face was quickly replaced by an embarrassed flush. For a second, Ivan thought he'd gone too far with the gentle teasing, but Parker started to laugh.

"Okay, you're right." Parker stood, and made to step away, and Ivan shook his head. Ivan grabbed him around the waist and carried him out of the kitchen to save his bare feet.

CHAPTER
Five

THIRTY minutes later, the kitchen was clean, Ivan was stuffed with a halfway decent soup and a full-way decent wine while a mindless but entertaining action movie played on Parker's enormous television. If there was a chance he could get laid, this was his idea of a perfect night.

A twinge in his neck reminded him that everything wasn't quite perfect. He rubbed at his neck, twisting his head around to try and alleviate some of the discomfort.

"You okay?"

"Yeah, yeah. Just a bit of stress, or maybe I slept on it wrong." Which wouldn't be entirely untrue. Everything about his recent sleeping habits was wrong.

"Um... I could massage it for you."

His nostrils flared. That had to be a come on. Lust pulsed lazily in his groin, but an enormous roadblock stood in the way. He might not like Neil, but that didn't excuse cheating on someone. He didn't want to do that to Neil. Not after his own experience. The conflicts of his morals, the requirements of his job, and his overwhelming desire for Parker became tangled in his mind.

Following an appropriate course of action became harder each minute. What Ivan Bekker wanted to do didn't matter; what would Ivan *Baker* do in this situation?

If Ivan Baker wasn't so straight, and that's why he got divorced... he might allow Parker to give him a massage.

"Yeah, sure, that would be okay." Good. He didn't sound too eager to feel Parker's fingers on him.

Parker smiled like Ivan had somehow granted his most fervent wish. "Want to sit here in front of me? We can move the table."

Sit on the floor? Well, his muscles weren't that stiff, and if he sat on the floor he could easily convince himself it was completely innocent.

He settled between Parker's knees, the heat of Parker's body warming the air around him. The second Parker's fingers touched him, Ivan lost track of the movie's plot. With effort, he held back a moan as those strong fingers dug into the knots threatening to turn his neck into stone.

Minutes passed, and Parker didn't seem to tire. As the majority of the tight spots eased, his dull headache receded. How long had it been since he'd been this relaxed? Parker's touch morphed into gentle stroking interspersed with firm pressure. Another groan threatened to escape as new sexual tension built. He hung his head lower, giving Parker more access to his back. *Ivan's* most fervent wish right now was to pull off his shirt and let Parker touch the bare skin of his back, but he didn't fucking dare. There were so many reasons not to swing around and push Parker back on the couch under him, but the only one he could focus on right now was that Parker had a boyfriend. Whatever tenderness Ivan imagined was nothing more than Parker being a considerate roommate. Also highly unexpected from a drug dealer, but he wasn't supposed to know that. Ivan Baker didn't know that, and pretending he knew nothing eased his mind.

"Um, hey," Parker whispered. Ivan raised his head and turned to look. Parker's mouth was much closer to his than he expected, close enough that his warm breath tickled Ivan's upper lip. He licked his lips, drawing Parker's darkened gaze, and Ivan wondered if he could stop the inevitable head tilt as he angled for a kiss.

THE sudden pounding on the door broke the mood as effectively as a gunshot. Parker pulled away, and Ivan sprang to his feet, reaching instinctively for his gun. Which was nowhere in the vicinity, much less on his body. Damn. Parker remained on the couch, stunned, his glance bouncing from Ivan to the door.

Although it was muffled enough that Ivan couldn't tell whether it was a man or a woman, the "open this fucking door," was quite clear. And the shouter was furious.

"Are you expecting someone?"

Parker shook his head before he stepped around Ivan and made for the door. Ivan grabbed his arm. "Wait up. They sound angry."

"I can't. I shouldn't ignore them, should I?"

What planet had this kid been living on? When you started dipping your toes in the drug dealing pool, angry people were often accompanied by guns or knives. Parker was ready to open the door like there was a pair of Jehovah's Witnesses on the other side, wanting to talk about the state of his soul. Yet neither he nor Parker had a weapon of any sort.

"They'll probably give up and go away." Unless they decided to come back and shoot out the windows.

The door rattled again. "Ivan Bekker, you shithead. Get your ass out here."

Parker raised a brow. "Seems to be for you."

Yeah, but using his real name. He'd give anything for the reassuring weight of his Glock right about now. "Stay here." It was the only protection he could provide, but Parker ignored the instruction as he moved in behind.

Ivan tugged on the doorknob, but as usual, it didn't budge. He had to yank on it to open the humidity-swollen door, and it swung wide, leaving him completely unprotected and vulnerable to... "Trish?"

He should have recognized her voice right away, but he hadn't been expecting her. Not here.

"What the fuck are you doing here, Ivan? Where the hell have you been? And who the hell is that?" Trish stabbed a finger over Ivan's shoulder.

"Calm down." His partner was pissed, and a sick feeling grabbed hold of his gut. How had she found him? Had he been wrong to believe she didn't have anything to do with the mole in the department?

"Don't you tell me to calm down. You can't disappear like that, without—"

Ivan pushed her back with his body and shut the door behind him. She was going to blow his cover—if her presence meant it hadn't been already. But he couldn't see a trace of guile or murderous intent in her eyes. His gut said to trust her, and his head said he didn't have any other choice.

"I'm not discussing this with you here. Not until you calm down." Ivan pitched his voice loud and angry, but when Trish looked about ready to explode, he put a finger to her lips, hoping to silence her before she bit his finger or said anything more damaging.

"Play along. I'm Ivan Baker. You're my ex-wife," he whispered.

Trish's eyes widened, her gaze flickering to the door behind him and back again.

"Amicable divorce?" she whispered back.

Ivan grunted. "Didn't sound like it a minute ago. And no, you took me to the cleaners."

An evil grin lit up her face. "Damned right."

"Come on." Ivan grabbed her by the arm and dragged her down to the sidewalk. "Pretend you're pissed, and wave your arms and shit, but talk quietly, okay?"

Trish got up in his face, slipping into her role perfectly. "I am pissed at you. What the fuck are you doing, going AWOL while you're under investigation? Surely you're not shacking up with that guy already, are you?"

Shaking his finger in her face, Ivan replied, "I'm not AWOL. Sarge knows where I am. And I'm not shacking up. I'm his roommate. But seriously, you can't tell anyone."

"Your phone is off, and you're living somewhere else." Trish's voice rose, and Ivan shushed her.

"Just pretending. I'm undercover."

"What the fuck? Bekker—"

Ivan cleared his throat and looked around.

"Sorry, sorry. But you're on leave. Why are you resurrecting Ivan Baker?" Her hands moved to her hips, looking for all the world like a scolding mother.

Ivan shrugged. "Didn't have any choice. It's a long story, and I can't tell it to you now."

"Meet me for coffee? Or dinner? I'm worried about you. This could get you suspended or fired."

At the moment, he wasn't sure either would be a bad thing. He just didn't want to get himself or Parker killed in the meantime.

"Just go. I'll call when I can."

"You better. Or Trish *Baker* will be back, making more ruckus."

She pushed her body aggressively into his and grabbed at his crotch. Yelping, he leapt back. "What the fuck was that for?"

Another evil grin twisted her lips. "No matter who left or why, you gotta remind them of what they're missing. Besides, it looked good for your boy in there."

Ivan followed her slight head tilt to see the curtain at the front windows twitch. If nothing else, this would cement his cover story. Hopefully.

"How did you even find me?"

"Guess you'll have to make a date with me to find out."

Ivan stared at her. Was her levity real? Or a way to put him off his guard?

"Oh, for God's sake. I followed you from your shrink. And it wasn't easy, you sneaky bastard."

If anyone could follow him, it would be Trish. She was the sneaky one of the pair of them, and he hadn't sensed her at all. He'd have to be on his guard, although his instincts told him she wasn't anything more than worried about him.

"Get going before anyone else sees you, runs your plates."

"I'm going, but seriously. Be careful."

"I'll be fine. How's Kurt?" He worried letting anyone know he cared might drag Kurt into this mess if they thought Kurt was a way to influence him. Kurt had to concentrate on healing up, not getting sucked into this mess.

"Stable. Doing okay."

He heaved in a relieved breath. Even if Trish was involved, surely she couldn't be suspicious of him asking after a fellow detective.

Trish gave his forearm a tiny squeeze before she got in her little Mazda and drove off. This whole op could have come crashing down around his ears if she'd driven a squad car to berate him. Still could if Razhin's guys had eyes on the place and decided to run her plates, but he hadn't seen any evidence of surveillance. Yet.

Letting his shoulders slump, he trudged back into the house. Parker was conspicuously absent from the main floor, which was a shame. Dealing with Trish had undone all the good the massage had done, and Ivan would be more than glad for Parker to pick up where he left off. The interruption had been timely, though, because ten seconds later, Ivan would have known how well Parker's lips fit against his own, and he suspected they might fit better than anyone else he'd met.

THE unfamiliar sound of a phone chirping had Ivan throwing his covers off, heart racing, as he stared around the room, trying to get his bearings. As soon as he identified his surroundings as his room in Parker's house, he took a breath and tried to locate the source of the chirping. He dug the phone out of his pants pocket but didn't catch the call before it dropped. Stabbing a few buttons, he changed the ring to something he'd not only recognize but that didn't sound like a diseased alarm clock. He hadn't recognized the phone number, but only one person should be calling him on this cell.

He rubbed his eyes, then looked at the time again. How had he slept in until eleven? For a change, nightmares hadn't disturbed his sleep. Standing, he tossed the phone onto the bed and stretched. The phone call was an unwelcome reminder that he was here to do a job, not to hang out watching movies with Parker and getting massages, even though he'd been more content doing that than he had in a long time.

A quick mental check of the schedule Parker had laid out for him and he remembered he should be alone until three or so. Plenty of time for breakfast and a decent search of Parker's room, maybe a few other places in the house. Once he knew more, got more familiar with Parker's schedule, he might have to tail him. He didn't know when Parker met with his suppliers, but he had to sometime. Being a student was actually a great cover, although he would have expected a little more activity in the form of "friends" dropping by. For long enough to exchange money for product, perhaps some of them staying for a slightly lengthier chat, thinking they really were friends with their dealer, or in a misguided attempt to pick up Parker. In fact, for such an attractive guy, Ivan was amazed he'd been able to commandeer as much of his time as he had.

He yanked on a pair of jeans but didn't bother with a shirt and padded downstairs. The creaking steps had already gained a homey familiarity. Grabbing an apple to munch on, he stared into the fridge. Was it worth making an elaborate breakfast? He could make an early dinner for the two of them; there were plenty of groceries for a simple stir fry.

Coughing as he almost choked on a bite of apple, Ivan straightened and slammed the fridge door shut. He kept letting himself get lulled into the mindset that this was some sort of super-long date, or even a relationship. They weren't really living together; Parker had a boyfriend, and possibly an extended engagement with prison.

A strange light-headedness came over him, and he sat heavily at the kitchen table. Fuck. He'd seen some of the aftermath of a young kid—a long-time gang member, only a couple years younger than Parker—who'd gotten involved in some stupid turf war and ended up in prison. The guy had been like candy for convicts starved for years. Parker would have the same appeal, and unless he had some street-fighting skills he'd thus far hidden from Ivan, he'd be even less suited to surviving in prison.

First things first. He had to know what he was up against. And that meant finding out whatever he could about Parker's operation while avoiding a full report out to Martelli as long as possible. Ivan was out here on his own, and by God, he was going to make full use of that autonomy. After all, just because Martelli had a tip and Parker had smoked up with Neil didn't mean he was about to get into bed with Razhin. Tips had been wrong before.

Even if Parker intended to work with Razhin, surely Parker, with his soft heart and considerate ways and still missing his late mother, could be steered in a direction that wouldn't lead straight to jail.

He chucked the apple core in the trash and washed his hands before heading back up the creaky stairs. Silence was the only response to his knocking on Parker's door. Taking a deep breath, he opened the door.

The double windows were both open a couple of inches, making the curtains flutter in the hot summer breeze. The fresh air was nice, but Ivan couldn't stop himself from crossing the room to look out the window, assessing the possibility for a burglar to access the house via these completely unprotected windows. Not that the locks would be any sort of deterrent for a determined housebreaker, but open windows were a temptation when the house might be otherwise resisted.

The slanted porch roof sat benignly under his gaze. It wouldn't be difficult to swing up on the roof and enter the window, but for two factors: the roof clearly needed repairs—was the rest of the roof in such disrepair? If so, Parker should probably be made aware of it—and, while there was a tree that provided some partial shade, there were few branches to obscure the sightline of both windows from the street. The likelihood of being observed would be the most effective deterrent. Besides, it would be difficult to broach the subject with Parker. *Oh, by the way, I was in your room, and it's not safe to keep your windows open....*

Yeah, that wouldn't go over well at all. Might even get him an award for worst roommate ever, if it didn't get his ass kicked out.

Another breeze wafted into the room, carrying with it a preview of noon's heat. Perhaps Parker only left the window open occasionally, on days when it wasn't supposed to get too wildly hot. Otherwise this room must get stifling, especially without much shade and no cross breeze with the door closed. His own room had the advantage of several full, mature trees in the tiny backyard to keep it from getting too warm in the sunlight. Then again, Parker's room only got direct sunlight in the early morning.

He turned back to the room and headed straight for the bed with its twisted sheets. Skimming a hand over the rumpled pillow, he believed for a moment he could still smell Parker on the sheets. If not for Trish's timely and yet untimely interruption, he might have woken up on these same sheets. The mattress was firm, with a pillow top. Much like the one he and Colin had been considering purchasing before they'd split. Now Ivan was glad they hadn't spent the money, but it was an unusual purchase for a university student.

Stroking Parker's damned sheets wasn't what he was here to do, and he forced himself to snatch his hand away as he knelt. He dug a hand between the mattress and box spring. Not the most inventive hiding space, but convenient for a surprising number of criminals with a lack of forethought.

Ivan made his way around the bed but found nothing besides mattress tags. A couple pairs of shoes and a hoodie resided under the bed, with enough dust bunnies to relieve him of the suspicion that Parker had some sort of obsessive compulsive cleaning disorder. Probably keeping things clean and tidy, especially in the kitchen and bathroom, had been a necessary habit while caring for his mother, a habit he hadn't eschewed after her death. For which Ivan was grateful. His own dorm when he'd been at school had been a sty, and he'd endured enough squalor while undercover to appreciate that Parker's place was even nicer than being at home. Aside from the whole maybe-having-to-arrest-him thing.

Ivan shook his head. Too soon to worry about that. He hadn't found anything worthy of an investigation or a warrant or anything. If there was a part of him that hoped he wouldn't? So what?

Sitting on the bed, he considered where he should look next. He didn't want to waste time slogging through the cardboard boxes if he didn't have to. People didn't hide important shit in cardboard boxes unless they had to, and Parker didn't have to.

Nightstand, closet, or dresser. He'd have to search all of them eventually. He bypassed the intimacy of the nightstand in favor of the dresser and rifled carefully through each drawer, looking for anything that might be a connection to the drug trade. Hell, a joint or two wasn't even illegal anymore. As much as he'd wanted to bust in to keep Parker from getting high the other night, he didn't have a legal leg to stand on. A bit of weed for personal use wasn't a problem, but Martelli believed there was much more passing through Parker's hands. After checking the contents of each drawer, he pulled each drawer out and checked for anything taped to the undersides of the drawers or on the interior of the dresser.

Aside from dust and a couple of skimpy thongs—stuck way in the back with the tags still attached—Ivan found sweet fuck all. The thongs captured his imagination for more moments than he'd care to admit. He'd never been much of a thong admirer, but he was strangely pleased Parker hadn't seen fit to model them for Neil.

He straightened and stretched, letting his vertebrae pop and crackle. Having already decided to leave the boxes for another time—assuming it became necessary to search them—he glanced at his watch. Another two hours at least. He could get the nightstand out of the way, and he'd still have time to get started on the closet.

Starting with the second drawer was a mistake, and Ivan slammed it shut almost as soon as he opened it. Sex toys. Not many, considering Parker could clearly afford more if he wanted.

Then again, what if those two toys were Parker's favorites? For all Ivan knew, one of the cardboard boxes contained a plethora of toys inferior at pleasuring Parker than the two in the drawer. Ivan shook himself. No matter the toy situation, the most important one was the living, breathing boyfriend, and thinking about Parker with toys was infinitely easier and more arousing than imagining him with Neil.

Steeling himself for another, maybe kinkier, surprise, Ivan pulled open the top drawer. He blinked. What the hell was that? Anyone who needed a toy involving vacuum hoses and an electrical outlet was way kinkier than he was. Gingerly, he pulled up one of the coils to make sure there wasn't anything hiding at the bottom of the drawer. A mask, like a fighter pilot, came attached to it. Which didn't make its purpose any clearer, but at least it was more obvious which end of the body it was devised for.

The explosive creak of the humidity-swollen front door propelled Ivan from his seat on the bed. He stuffed the coils back in the drawer and shut it as fast as he could without slamming it. He hadn't lost two hours doing this, not a chance. Parker must be home early for some reason. Ivan slipped out of the room and shut the door just as the first squeaky tread announced Parker's ascent. Hiding out in his room would be the best option, but what if Parker had come home early due to illness? He'd need to know because that would alter dinner plans.

Instead, he slipped into the bathroom and quickly turned on the tap to wet his hands. He dried them off on the hand towel then emerged. Nothing more innocuous than using the can.

"Neil?"

Ivan almost stumbled back from the shock. Neil was the last person he expected to see at the top of the stairs, and yet, maybe it shouldn't be that much of surprise. "Where's Parker?"

Neil stared at him like he'd lost his mind, but was it such a crazy question? He hadn't gotten the impression Neil lived here, nor was he aware Neil had a key. Even so, were the two truly at a point in their relationship where Neil would come by while Parker wasn't home? If so, they were likely on the verge of making that official. Ivan frowned. He shouldn't fucking care about Parker's social life.

"I don't know. School or something."

He brushed past Ivan and reached for Parker's doorknob.

"Does Parker know you're here?"

Neil drew back, a scowl on his face. "Dunno. Does he know you're here? Aren't you supposed to be at work? You've got rent to pay, remember."

The venom in Neil's voice surprised him, and he had to search a moment or two for an appropriate response. Because yes, what the fuck was he doing home at this hour? Stupid fake insurance job. Should have chosen a work-at-home profession.... Wait. "I was able to work from home today."

The responding snort was disbelieving. "Whatever. If I find out you lied about your job and you're stiffing Parker on the rent, you'll be out on your ear faster than your wife tossed you out. He doesn't need a tenant, and I told him so at the beginning."

"I'm not lying." He couldn't afford to have either one of them look any closer into his falsified background. Not if he hoped to avoid attention from Razhin's people.

"Whatever. I have just as much right to be here as you do." Neil reached for the door, but Ivan's hand grabbed Neil's forearm without any conscious thought.

"Really? So I get no consideration as a rent-paying tenant? You can just waltz in whenever you want, with no warning?"

"Why? What do you have to hide? Besides the fact you want Parker's ass." Neil's derisive laugh cut deeply, and Ivan's face heated. He'd met Neil only once before. How had he known?

"No. Of course not."

Neil continued as though Ivan hadn't spoken. "Afraid I'll walk in while you're trying to put the moves on my boy? Good fucking luck. You're way too old for him."

Ivan's flush intensified. He knew that, but it hadn't stopped him from wanting Parker. Nor had the existence of Parker's boyfriend, who had every reason to be pissed off.

"I don't know if you thought moving in here would get you some younger tail, or if you thought Parker would be naïve enough to give it up to your closeted ass, but believe me, it won't work. You'll have to troll elsewhere."

Neil opened Parker's door and slammed it in Ivan's face before he could completely register that Neil thought Ivan moving in was some sort of twisted ploy to get sex from an unsuspecting younger guy. The lock clicked, and all further sounds were obscured by music blasting from the docking station Ivan had noticed earlier.

Ivan slipped back into his own room. Shutting the door didn't shut out the underlying bass beat seeping under both doors. It also didn't do anything for his disquiet. Neil's entitled attitude had been unexpected, but even more so was his own unsettled reaction. He had no idea what to think or what to do. Busting open Parker's door and tossing Neil out—his first instinct whenever Neil was around—would irreparably harm the budding connection he was building with Parker.

In many ways, he couldn't even fault Neil's antagonism. Ivan did want to fuck Parker, and Parker was Neil's boyfriend. Ivan tried to imagine how he'd feel if a boyfriend of his had a roommate who wanted to jump his bones. Not happy was the answer, and he sure wouldn't want to be friends with the guy drooling over his man.

Problem was, each day it got harder and harder to keep from touching Parker, to keep from letting himself settle into an imagined relationship. He'd never felt this comfortable and safe with anyone else. No matter what happened outside Parker's house, inside felt like a time-out from his crazy life. He had a job to do, and Parker was going to jail at the end of it, but the longer he could ignore that, the better. No matter how sweet Parker was at home, Ivan didn't have it in him to let a drug dealer get away with it. It wasn't the first time he'd gotten along with a criminal while undercover, but it was the first one he wanted in his life... Ivan Bekker's life, not the fake Ivan Baker's life.

He'd already imagined introducing Parker to his parents, to his sisters. Rick had seen him; so had Trish. Parker, despite the age difference, would fit with his friends and family.

Fuck it. He had to get out of here. Go for a run, get groceries, something. Something to keep his mind off the knowledge that Neil was hanging out on Parker's plush mattress because he belonged there, because Parker wanted him there.

Parker had twisted his mind, and it was scary as fuck. For a moment he wished he had someone he could talk to, but there was no one. Even his new therapist was off limits, and he was already pushing his luck by walking such a fine line between his real life and his undercover role.

Parker bounded up the stairs and burst into his room.

"Oh, Neil, hey." His friend was stretched out on his bed like he owned the thing. Funny thing was, Neil had never spent the night on it, although they had fucked on it a time or two. His mom, a few months before her death, had insisted Parker have a new bed, one of the best money could buy, because she wanted to make sure he did everything in his power to get enough sleep. She knew how stressful her dying days had been, and the bed had made the sleepless nights more comfortable at least.

"Hey. I thought you finished early today. Thought we could hang."

"No. Today was one of my long days. What about tonight?" It wasn't, not exactly, but telling Neil he sometimes spent twenty hours a week volunteering at the trauma rehab center would only gain him an eye roll and some gentle or not-so-gentle mocking. Neil didn't get his desire to finish school and have a career. Neil thought he should invest all the money his mother had left him in Neil's nightclub scheme. Not that he didn't believe in Neil's dream, but the trust his mother had set up didn't work that way, and he didn't have any way to repay a loan against the property. Maybe if he rented out the cottage in Muskoka he'd have an income that the banks would consider acceptable, but he didn't want to. As he'd told Ivan during one of their conversations over the weekend, he had so many good memories of his mother and grandparents at the cottage, he couldn't bear to sell or rent it, but neither was he ready to go back and visit it. Not yet.

"Nope, can't do it. People to meet, business to take care of."

The words might have been a passive-aggressive dig designed to provoke Parker's guilt for not handing over the funds to start the nightclub, but he chose to take it as proof that Neil was going to make his dreams happen on his own. It would be better that way. He'd take more pride in accomplishing such a huge goal on his own, and Parker admired the passion Neil demonstrated.

"Where's Ivan?" If Ivan had a good day, he should probably be home from work already.

"*Where's Ivan?* How the hell should I know?" The sneer in Neil's voice told Parker that Ivan had become a new topic on Neil's taboo list.

Parker slung his knapsack in the corner and opened the closet, looking for more comfortable clothes. "Just thought he'd be home by now."

"He was here when I got here. Which was weird because it was like… two."

"Two?" Neil had been hanging out in his room since two? "What did you do?"

Neil gestured negligently at the docking station. "Listened to some new tunes for the club. Toked up. Had a nap. You know."

That was kind of an epiphany. Neil had smoked up in his room, and he hadn't even noticed. How often did Neil come over and do that? Often enough that Parker had become immune to the scent. Kind of pathetic. Ivan must think he was some sort of druggie.

"You sure you can't hang tonight? Have you eaten?"

"I told you, I've got people to see."

But he had time to hang out all by himself at Parker's? He opened the curtains wide, letting in some bright sunlight, and searched the bed for signs of someone else. Even though Parker had made it clear last time that having sex in his bed was a hard line Neil wasn't to cross again, Neil might have had a guy over.

Neil swung out of bed, but aside from the wrinkles from sleeping in his clothes, there was nothing to indicate there'd been sex of any kind in his bed. If Parker wasn't getting any there, his best friend couldn't either. Not when Neil had an apartment of his own to pork his one-night stands.

"Gotta get going. But you watch out. I don't trust that Ivan guy."

Oh jeez. What now? "Why not?"

Neil's lip curled, just a bit. "He was home when I got here. You sure he's got a job and can pay the rent?"

"I thought I didn't need rent money." How many times had Neil told him he didn't need the money when he'd decided to advertise for a roommate? Loneliness was a stupid reason in Neil's opinion. If they'd been dating, he would have believed Neil was jealous, but Neil had never been jealous of him. Neil was his best and oldest friend and had stuck with him through some of the worst times in Parker's life. He owed him his loyalty, and if that meant working around Neil's quirks, well, that was what friends did.

Neil huffed out a breath that stopped just short of a derisive scoff. "You don't. But since the geezer is here, you might as well be getting rent money out of it."

Geezer? Had Neil *seen* Ivan? Sure, he was older, but so fucking hot it almost hurt to look at him. Ivan was the kind of guy Parker drooled over in magazines and porn but would never have the nerve to approach for a date.

"He might have been off sick or something." Ivan hadn't been sleeping well. A couple of times, Parker had heard noises in Ivan's room. He'd thought about going in to see if Ivan was okay, but that didn't seem appropriate, and Ivan always quieted down before Parker made a decision.

"He said he was working from home, but I don't know. I just don't trust that guy. I think he's here for your ass. Maybe he's a stalker and you wanting a roommate allowed him to waltz right in."

"A stalker? Neil, that's ridiculous. And he's not here for my ass." Oh, if only. Parker would offer it up without a second thought if Ivan was interested. "I told you he's straight. I've met his wife."

"I don't care if you met the man's harem. That man is gay and wants to pork you. He probably spent the day sniffing your briefs."

A flush of heat crept into Parker's face and a flicker of hope lit inside him. Kinda sick that he found the idea flattering and hot. Could Ivan be gay? Was that maybe why he'd gotten divorced?

"You sure you won't stay? I've got a horror movie we could watch." He didn't, but Neil hated horror. For some reason, having both Neil and Ivan in the house together was like navigating through a mine field. He didn't want to spend the evening navigating Neil-bombs and deflecting catty, unsubtle comments.

"God, Parker, go buy some taste with the rent money the oldster is giving you." He rolled his eyes and picked up his messenger bag. "See you later."

"Bye, Neil."

Parker stood by the window and, after a few seconds, saw Neil walk down the driveway. After Neil had gone, he continued to stand, unwilling to admit he was watching for the return of his roommate. He should probably study, but he was all caught up, and he didn't feel like hanging out in his room. Seemed a little antisocial, should Ivan come home. He quickly changed into a more comfortable pair of jeans and a well-worn, holey shirt and went down to watch TV.

The front door swung open with a loud bang just as he set foot on the landing, and he jumped back. His first thought—that Neil had forgotten something—was instantly dispelled by the red-faced, sweat-slicked blond who stood in the doorway.

"Ivan." Parker didn't have breath for any other words. The white T-shirt clung to work-hardened muscles, almost transparent. Even that didn't compare to the barely there cut-off sweatpants that had been through the wash so often they were almost as threadbare as the shirt Ivan wore. He didn't know where Ivan had been, but he looked delicious. Moisture had darkened Ivan's blond hair to amber honey, and it stuck up in random spikes. Dark circles under his eyes attested to his exhaustion.

"Oh. Parker. Hey. I was out for a run."

A run. The day's heat and humidity had taken its toll—unless the man had jogged clear across the city and back—because he hadn't looked nearly this sweaty and exhausted when Parker had gone with him. Then again, Ivan might have been taking it easy on the newbie.

"I could have gone with you, if you'd waited."

Ivan somehow managed to shrug with an eyebrow and skirted Parker to grab a bottle of water from the fridge. The brush-off may have been no more than an illustration of Ivan's exhaustion, but it gave Parker a twinge in his gut. Ivan's attitude made him reluctant to try and find out if Neil was right. He'd had his fair share of rejection in his life, and he wasn't ready to experience it from his new roommate.

Nevertheless, Parker trailed him into the kitchen. "Did you want me to put something on for dinner?"

The dark scowl he got in return sent him back a step. Maybe he'd been too needy. Did roommates normally spend this much time together? He knew Chris and Thom were friends, but Chris spent all his time with Alicia.

Parker almost apologized, but he didn't know what he'd done wrong, and Neil had given him shit in the past for being too apologetic. Besides, he wasn't hungry anymore.

When Ivan tilted his head back to drain his water, Parker took the coward's way out and sat in front of the television. He'd gotten spoiled, spending his evenings with Ivan. It had only been a few days, but perhaps this was why he didn't have a boyfriend. He expected too much time and attention from them.

He flipped on the set but couldn't make sense of the show he was watching.

"Where's Neil?" Ivan leaned against the doorframe, a little less red than before, but every bit as damp and delicious as he'd been a few moments ago.

"Gone. Why?" Parker didn't want to accentuate their age difference, because he wanted Ivan to look at him like a man… assuming he was, as Neil suspected, gay. The sullen bite to his tone probably didn't help his case any.

The pinched look on Ivan's face smoothed out, and as the rest of him relaxed, Parker became aware of how tense and rigid he'd held himself ever since he'd come home.

"No reason. Just thought I'd clear out, didn't want to intrude on your time together."

Intrude on their time together? Rather odd way to phrase that, but the sentiment was nice. Even if Parker wanted to spend time with Ivan far more than with Neil. Neil never seemed to care what Parker wanted to do.

"He had to work tonight. We could watch another movie." Parker maybe watched too many movies, but he loved them, and he didn't much like the places Neil took him, when he bothered to invite him at all. Probably he should take up Alicia on one of her many offers to go out. Actually, yes, he would. Next time she asked, he'd go, no matter what. His sudden conviction made him smile. For a moment, before Ivan smiled back, his expression was completely indecipherable.

"What about homework? I don't want to keep you from your school work."

"Nope. I'm all caught up."

"How about something different?"

Different? Parker's belly fluttered as he imagined the different things they could do, especially if they started with a massage like the other night. Touching Ivan gave him such pleasure, even if Ivan didn't want to touch him back.

"Sure. What were you thinking?" Please let it be kissing or sex or....

"Do you play cards?"

Frowning, he stared at Ivan for a moment, trying to figure out where "cards" fit into "touch him," before he processed the question.

"I used to play Cribbage with my mom, and Neil's tried to teach me poker, but I can't figure out the strategy behind it."

"I think I remember how Cribbage works, so we can play that, but you don't need to know strategy to have fun with poker." Cotton muffled the last few words as Ivan pulled up the hem of his T-shirt to wipe off his face. The wide expanse of chiseled abs, bisected by a fuzzy golden trail leading to Ivan's waistband, had Parker mesmerized.

The shirt dropped, returning Parker's logic circuits to almost normal. "But Neil said—"

Ivan snorted and rolled his eyes. "Strategy's only important when you're playing the game for money, in a casino. Fucking up serious players' strategy by making rookie moves can piss them off. I'm just talking regular guys'-night-out style poker. Mostly for fun, although sometimes you might have a twenty-buck buy in. Hell, I used to be in a regular game where one guy had to have a cheat sheet about which hand was better."

That sounded a hell of a lot better than the drill sergeant teaching style Neil had, as though he was trying to get Parker ready for a poker death match. At least Parker could remember a full house beat a flush.

"Okay, sounds like fun." Fun. The essential missing ingredient when playing cards with Neil.

"We can start with Cribbage, if you'd like."

"What about dinner?"

This time, Ivan's smile was full and lit up his whole face. "You don't have proper dinner on poker night. There's no time to make chili, and I'm too damned hot anyway, but we've got veggies and dip and cheese. That will be sufficient."

The grin was infectious and sparked excitement in Parker's belly, along with a tiny niggling disappointment that there wouldn't be any excuses for incidental touching, as there would have been if he'd given Ivan another massage or convinced Ivan to sit on the couch beside him.

"Did you want to get started on the munchies while I shower?" Ivan turned on his heel and pounded up the stairs after Parker nodded.

He'd barely started preparations when water rattled the pipes in the old house, heralding the start of Ivan's shower. Parker had to grip the edges of the counter to steady himself as a barrage of images hit him—Ivan, wet and soapy and slick, touching himself, rubbing himself. Steam curling up to the ceiling, condensation blurring the edges of the mirror and window.

Parker could slip inside and watch Ivan's movements distorted through the clear shower curtain. He'd rinse off by closing his eyes and turning his face up to the showerhead, a blissful look on his face. Then he'd lean one arm against the tile while grabbing his hard cock with the other and….

The water shut off, cutting Parker's fantasy off before the details made him hornier.

Desire lit an eager throb in his groin, and he gulped in air, hoping to cool the fire before Ivan came back downstairs. The last thing he needed was to greet Ivan while packing a full-on erection. It was unlikely Ivan would take it as a compliment.

By the time Ivan's footsteps fell in the kitchen, Parker had almost finished preparing their snacks, but a half erection lingered. He surreptitiously adjusted himself before turning to Ivan, hoping his hard-on wasn't too obvious.

"Did you want a beer?"

"Nope. Just water. I ran far enough that my legs feel like rubber, and I need to rehydrate. But you have one if you want." Ivan waved a deck of cards at him and slapped it on the table before grabbing a couple of bowls from the counter.

"We're using your cards, are we?" Parker recognized them from his mini snoop in Ivan's room. He placed the last of their munchies on the table.

"Does it matter?"

Parker made sure his face was properly solemn. "Well, they could be marked. I wouldn't know the difference."

Ivan's eyes widened before he laughed. "No, I told you, this is for fun. Marked cards are for business." He winked, and Parker laughed too.

"Just because I'm a gentleman, and you can be sure I don't cheat, I'll let you deal first."

Parker rolled his eyes before grabbing the deck and shuffling the cards. "I gotta warn you, I'm pretty good at Cribbage."

"So what? I'll whip you at poker."

Smiling wide, Parker dealt out the cards.

CHAPTER
Six

"I'M OFF to work now. I should be home in time for dinner." Ivan ignored the twinge of déjà vu those words caused. He'd often said the same thing to Colin, and he suspected such words weren't typical for roommates. In fact, he knew they weren't, but somehow, he and Parker had fallen into a much closer relationship than he'd ever had with any roommate. Having never had a roommate before, Parker probably didn't realize how unusual this was, but Ivan didn't much care. He wasn't ready to let go of the comfort Parker gave. Not yet. Not until he had concrete proof of anything. Undercover could last months, although he'd be surprised if Martelli would be able to cover for him for that long. He needed to wrap this up quickly for Martelli… but also as slowly as possible for Parker.

Unwilling to risk getting caught in the house two days in a row by a jealous and suspicious Neil, Ivan was implementing the other half of his plan. One good thing about all the running he'd been doing was that he'd scoped out a few places where he could observe the house if he needed to. He headed to one now, because Parker was due to leave shortly for classes. He'd observed enough to know that Parker always walked to the campus, and Ivan would have to follow him, possibly for several days, to ensure he was going where he said he was going, as well as to observe any people Parker interacted with.

If necessary, he'd take pictures with his phone. Next time he went in for his therapy appointment, or the next SIU interview, he'd make a stop home, or somewhere safe, to download them.

He leaned against a wooden telephone pole. While he waited, he picked out old, rusty staples used to attach millions of flyers over the years.

Parker came into view, not precisely smiling, but clearly happy with the world. Parker's joy smoothed his agitation and made him smile. He wiggled his fingers, itching to touch Parker's spiky hair.

Once Parker had moved far enough away, Ivan slipped out of his concealed hiding space and followed Parker's round butt at a safe distance. After nearly face-planting three times and bumping half a dozen pedestrians' shoulders, he had to consider that perhaps he was a little too intent on that delectable ass.

The sidewalks were clogged with students heading to classes, bottlenecking at the entrance to a subway station, but Parker didn't stop to talk to anyone. He skirted large groups, but moved like a man with a goal. Martelli was certain the student gig was merely an easy way to access buyers; Ivan wasn't so sure. Many of the common areas didn't require student IDs; all Parker would need to do is loiter and he'd probably sweep in the customers. Ivan had also witnessed Parker doing homework, so he kept up appearances with at least one class, and Ivan needed to verify how much of the schedule Parker had given him was true. Once he assimilated Parker's schedule, he'd be able to better assess potential exchange places or drop spots. To date, there was no evidence Parker used his house for any illegal activity, unless Neil was working for or with him.

A number of men and women gave Parker appreciative glances as he passed, and a few even checked out his ass as he passed, although as far as Ivan could tell, Parker remained oblivious to the attention. Whether it was because he was taken or because he was clueless about his own appeal was a mystery still to be solved. *After* the bigger mystery of who his suppliers were. Ivan would take note of buyers, but those would be small fish, especially if they were careful to buy no more than legal for "personal use."

Parker crossed the road and strode up the steps to a non-descript, squat building. The funnel effect of the doorway on the press of bodies urged Ivan to close the distance between them, as he didn't want to lose his quarry.

The sudden approximation of a crowd elevated the temperature. Sweat broke out on his upper lip. Didn't these places have air conditioning? Gasping a little at the imagined sensation of lack of air, his heart rate soared even higher. Large backpacks and briefcases buffeted him from every direction, and trying not to think about how many weapons they could conceal only made him calculate numbers more feverishly.

Parker's height and the distinctive blond tips of his hair were the only reasons Ivan was able to keep him in sight, and he plowed doggedly after the younger man. Once past the first hallway intersection, enough people veered off to allow Ivan to breathe better.

Up a flight of stairs, Parker opened a door. Ivan assessed the layout of the room as he passed the slowly closing door and continued on. Ideally, he'd be able to find a door that opened at the back of the lecture hall, and he could slip into the room without Parker seeing him. Failing that, he'd have to find a place to keep the entrance under observation and hope Parker left using the same door he entered.

Ivan stood opposite the next door and waited. Moments later, another student opened the door, revealing the same lecture hall Parker had entered. Pulling his ball cap lower over his eyes, Ivan slipped into the room, scanning for Parker. About midway, Parker's distinctive hair acted as a beacon, and Ivan slid into a chair and slouched down, just in case Parker decided to glance at the back of the room.

Problem was, just about everyone in this class, aside from Parker, looked shifty and suspicious. Especially the ones whose gazes glanced over him. For those, he tried to assess whether they sat near Parker or spoke to him. Exchanged eye contact with Parker. Four girls and two guys had ranged themselves within close proximity of Parker, but the stadium style seating and the distance made it difficult to tell if they had any ulterior motives or whether they were simply drawn by his gorgeous face.

The constant staring had Ivan gritting his teeth, so he concentrated on Parker and his reactions.

Parker wasn't as oblivious to the attention as he had been out on the street, but his scrunched-in shoulders and bent head told Ivan he wasn't comfortable. Not the reaction of a guy trying to drum up drug business.

The professor strode in, closely followed by a girl, clearly searching for someone. Parker's whole body language changed, and he waved at her. She smiled and scooted up to the seat beside Parker and kissed him on the cheek. The fact that Parker was gay was the only thing that kept Ivan from springing up and ripping her away. He wasn't sure why he was so zealously invested in protecting Neil's claim on Parker. Even if Neil were out of the picture, there was no way Ivan would be able to step into position as a viable boyfriend. Just thinking that way about a guy he was investigating, a guy who was likely destined for prison, was... ludicrous. Pathetic. And a career-killer, although his career was the least of his worries right now.

Who was that girl? A friend? Customer? Another dealer? The light pink T-shirt looked innocent enough.

Ivan let his gaze wander over the assembled students once more. Almost everyone had laptops or tablets out. What a change from his university days, when he'd taken notes with pen and paper. Back then, a few ambitious souls would record the lecture. It wasn't even that long ago. Foolishly, he hadn't even brought a pen with him. Why the hell hadn't he planned this excursion better? Having nothing to take notes with possibly made him the most suspicious person in the room. Well, except for the guy by the far wall, who appeared to be recovering from a significant bender the night before.

The professor called the class to order and began to speak. Ivan ignored him completely in favor of staring at Parker's profile. Concentration was a sexy look on him, and he appeared genuinely interested in the topic. Occasionally he let his glance stray toward the pink girl, but she concentrated on the lecture as well, not Parker. Which made Ivan hate her just a little less.

TWO hours passed quickly; watching Parker was more interesting than any other surveillance gig he'd done. The rustling of laptop bags and the click of laptop lids closing warned Ivan that the class was drawing to a close, despite the fact that the professor's lecture hadn't broken stride. Ivan ducked his head and slipped out and stationed himself at the end of the hallway, hopefully far enough that even if Parker deigned to glance his way, he wouldn't notice Ivan observing him.

Parker and the pink girl emerged from the class, laughing and smiling with each other. Ivan waited until they'd almost reached the door before he began to trail them.

He almost lost them through the doors and rushed to catch up. The pink girl was too short to see through the crush, and he had to swerve around several students trying to push their way into the building. Outside, Ivan stretched up on his toes, looking for Parker's spiky dyed hair.

There. Ivan sped up, determined not to lose sight of Parker.

They stopped. Ivan came to a stop too, rocking slightly as he paused. Out in the courtyard, there was absolutely no cover and no reason for Parker to have stopped.

As one, Parker and the pink girl turned around as though they knew someone was following them and they were determined to confront him.

Ivan's breath stopped as Parker's gaze met his and recognition flooded his features. Heat streaked across his cheeks. Somehow, this young amateur drug-dealer had made him on surveillance. It had been years since he'd experienced that degree of failure.

"Ivan?"

"You know this guy?" Pink girl looked him up and down, assessing him.

"He's my roommate." Parker's cheeks bloomed with color, too, but Ivan didn't know why he'd be embarrassed.

"This is your roommate?" Pink girl looked even more interested, and she stepped close, peering under the bill of his ball cap. "Hmm."

Her pursed lips and thoughtful expression made Ivan more nervous than facing down a dozen drug dealers with automatic weapons. He was also unpleasantly reminded of his mother trying to catch him in a lie.

"I'm Alicia." She thrust her hand out at him, and Ivan had no choice but to shake it. She had a firmer grip than he'd expected considering her Barbie clothes.

"Ivan."

"Yeah, so he said." She smirked and jerked a thumb in Parker's direction.

This time, the heat in his face intensified because of embarrassment from a different cause. He glanced back at Parker, who was still staring at him quizzically.

"What are you doing here?"

God. Thinking fast on his feet was one of Ivan's particular skills, but lately, trying to put together thoughts was like trying to swim through pudding.

"I... I mentioned auditing courses, right?" Fuck. He had, hadn't he? "I thought I'd check some out. Maybe choose something for next semester."

Ivan let out a breath. That sounded perfectly reasonable.

"Auditing courses, you say?" Alicia's voice held a note of something Ivan had difficulty recognizing. It wasn't disbelief. Not precisely. And she couldn't seem to stop smiling, although Ivan was much more concerned with Parker's reaction. "What a coincidence to see you here."

"It is, isn't it?" Mild panic twisted his stomach. He couldn't fuck this up. "I've been wandering around campus for a bit and thought I recognized Parker."

Parker's smile got a bit brighter, on par with the smiles he got when Parker had whipped him at Cribbage. Poker hadn't gone much better for Ivan, but losing had been worth it because they'd had such a good time.

"We're heading to the deli for lunch. Want to come?"

Ivan stared into Parker's eyes, checking if the invitation was genuine. But there was no hesitation or wariness in Parker's expression, and since his surveillance was clearly over for today, he might as well work on solidifying his relationship with Parker. For a change, there was a part of an undercover assignment that he actually enjoyed, and every good thing he could learn about Parker was a way he could help him when it came to an arrest.

THE deli had some decent sandwiches and surprisingly tasty fries. They found a table outside under an umbrella. The humidity made their clothes stick to them, but the sky was clear and sunny, and the occasional breeze kept the temperature from being unbearable. Ivan took a seat next to Parker. Alicia gave him a little smile that said she was reading something more into his actions than he intended, but changing seats now would only draw attention to whatever had made Alicia smirk.

Two attractive guys headed for their table, the dark-haired one looking unhappy about something. Ivan tensed. They didn't look strung out or drunk, but he'd have difficulty keeping Parker and Alicia safe while taking them both down if they were here to cause trouble. His inability to call for backup freaked him out more than it had on any other undercover assignment. Was that because everything had the appearance of innocence? Parker's life, on the surface, was innocuous, nothing for anyone to take note of, yet Ivan knew it was all a lie. Or most of it was, and he was having difficulty discerning which parts were. That alone was enough to make him jumpy as hell.

"Ivan, this is my boyfriend, Chris, and his roommate, Thom. Guys, this is Parker's roommate."

"You sure you should be eating those fries? Aren't guys your age supposed to watch their cholesterol?" Thom's scowl deepened, and Ivan scowled right back. He was a decorated police officer, one of the best detectives in the Drug Squad. He was getting a little sick of Parker's friends calling him old. He wasn't that fucking old, even if there was a twelve-year age difference between him and Parker. Okay. Well, maybe that wasn't the best example.

He bit his tongue against a vicious reply, but couldn't hold back his grin when Chris kicked Thom under the table. Ivan hadn't missed the hungry expression Thom directed at Parker, but Parker remained relaxed beside him. A quick glance confirmed Parker hadn't returned interest.

Glares passed between the other two men, along with some abbreviated sentences. Oddly, Parker picked up on the tension between Chris and Thom but didn't seem to have a clue he was the cause. Ivan wasn't going to be the one to enlighten him. If Thom didn't have the balls to step up, Ivan wasn't going to help him.

"Yeah, right." Alicia snorted. "Did you see his hot bod? I think he can eat a fry or two."

Ivan waggled his eyebrows at Alicia before he bared his teeth at Thom in an approximation of a smile, the same smile that had intimidated suspects tougher than Thom. To his credit, though, Thom didn't back down. He copied the smile and tossed it right back at him. There was a better way to deal with Thom, because as much as Thom wanted Parker, Parker was oblivious, as he'd been to every person who'd ogled his ass today.

"So, Parker, tell me about your other classes." Ivan nudged Parker's thigh with his own, picking up the conversation as though the altercation hadn't happened.

Parker's eyes widened, and he stuttered a moment before he spoke. Alicia smiled indulgently, and Ivan did also, even though he didn't want to. He'd hoped to find out something about Parker's patterns and contacts, but it all seemed so innocent.

When Thom picked up on Ivan's tactic—getting Parker talking—he started interrupting to ask questions, which backfired. The intent regard from both of them flustered the shit out of Parker, to the point Ivan was ready to kick Thom under the table.

Parker pushed his half-eaten salad away and checked his phone. "Oh, I forgot. I've… I've got somewhere to be."

He shoved away from the table, grabbed his bag, and was gone before anyone could respond.

"Didn't he, uh, have another class this afternoon?" Ivan had had every intention of auditing that class as well. Had Parker got a text message from a supplier? A buyer? Whichever it was, the way he'd left guaranteed Ivan couldn't follow.

"Yes. I guess he's skipping." Alicia shook her head. "If you still want to audit, I've got an anthropology course this afternoon."

Ivan stared after Parker until he disappeared, then turned his attention back to his lunch companions.

"Uh, thanks, but I should probably go into the office for a bit." Ivan finished his sandwich, slowly enough to avoid seeming rude, but he was itching to leave. Each minute that ticked by added a new layer to his anger. First Parker had made his surveillance, then he'd ditched him with his friends. Goddamn, Parker.

"Nice to meet you all." Ivan made a mental note of their names and appearances, just in case they were involved, although the whole lunch had been almost painfully innocuous.

He nodded to Parker's friends and walked back to the house.

THERE was no one in the house. Where the hell had Parker gone? When would he be back? Ivan wiped sweat off his forehead and frowned.

Perhaps Parker was already suspicious and that's why he'd ditched Ivan. He needed to finish searching Parker's room; Parker could be home at any time.

He left Parker's door open, just in case he needed to depart quickly. He had no intention of either Neil or Parker catching him by surprise.

A file box sat on the closet shelf close to the door. Ivan pulled it down, grunting a bit from the unexpected weight. Could be guns. Bricks of marijuana. He placed the box on the ground and flipped off the lid.

Shit. Money. Lots and lots of money. Possibly worse than guns or marijuana. He'd seen people killed for a tenth of this much cash. His first instinct was to grab it and run, but money by itself wasn't evidence of a damn thing. Ivan replaced the lid. A small part of him had suspected—hoped—Parker wasn't involved in anything shady. But in his experience, this much cash was never, ever innocent.

Maybe there was an explanation. Even if the money meant exactly what Martelli thought, maybe Ivan could find a way to convince Parker he had so much more potential than becoming a petty criminal. The guy was smart and good-looking. Finishing school and embarking on a legitimate career would keep him safe and healthy, unlike becoming a criminal.

What the fuck was wrong with Parker?

Shit. Cameras. What the fuck was wrong with *him*? With this much money, it made sense Parker might have a camera as security and he should have thought of it earlier. He was better than this, normally. Had he already outed himself to Parker? Adrenaline flooded his veins.

Ivan scanned the closet but couldn't find any evidence of a camera. He hoisted the box up and replaced it on the shelf. He exited the closet and closed the door behind him. Standing in front of the closet, Ivan visually inspected each corner of the bedroom, seeking any place where a camera could be hidden or any of the standard nanny-cam containers.

Nothing. No beady black eye spied on him. He heaved in a deep breath, trying desperately to slow his racing heart, to halt the involuntary tremble in his fingers. Blood pounded in his ears, blocking out the street noises. Conducting any sort of search when he didn't know where Parker was or when he'd be back was a rookie move, anyway. He slipped out of the room, determined that Parker would have no reason to be suspicious when he finally returned home.

THE sticky front door opened and slammed shut on the floor above Ivan. He glanced toward the stairs but continued to deliberately fold his now-clean clothes. He had no interest in another run-in with Neil, and Parker ditching him today still smarted. Problem was, now that he'd had a few hours to reflect, he wasn't sure what prompted his bad mood: the fact that the much younger man had managed to easily throw off his surveillance, the huge amount of cash in his closet, or the fact that Parker had left him behind.

Either way, he was in no hurry to head upstairs. Unfortunately, Ivan didn't have a whole lot of clothes here, and folding them, however precisely, didn't take all that long. With nothing else in the unfinished basement to occupy him, remaining downstairs would be nothing short of cowardly. Besides, these crazy mood swings weren't normal for him. Not at all. This was a chance to prove that he could overcome them. His force of will was stronger than that.

Maybe he'd get lucky. Maybe Parker would have gone to his room to study or… something. He took a deep breath and tucked the laundry basket under his arm before striding up the stairs.

As he reached the top of the stairs, breathy sobs became audible. With a frown, he set the laundry basket down and padded into the living room.

Parker was curled up on the couch, arms wrapped tightly around long legs pulled up to his chest, head tilted away from Ivan. His narrow shoulders shook, and a crystalline tear quivered on his chin, sparkling in a late afternoon sunbeam before it dropped onto his shirt. He would kill whoever had hurt Parker. Unless he'd broken up with Neil. The tiny spurt of joy was completely inappropriate in the face of Parker's misery.

"What's wrong?"

Parker gasped and jumped, hands clutching the sofa cushions. "Oh. I didn't think you were home." He swiped the backs of his hands across his face and sniffed loudly before he stood up.

"Just doing some laundry. Are you hurt?" No blood or contusions were evident, but Parker had to be involved with some unpleasant people, and those people often punctuated conversations with their fists.

"No. I'm fine." Parker's gaze darted around like a man getting ready to run, a look Ivan was plenty familiar with, although usually when he saw it he was about to slap on cuffs. "I'll just go upstairs."

"Sit down." Ivan hadn't dusted off his official take-charge voice since the raid where he'd killed that kid, Dmitri, but Parker responded instantly and dropped back into a seated position. Red-rimmed eyes stared up at him, greener than he'd ever seen them.

The pain in Parker's eyes begged for surcease, and Ivan was helpless against the sweetness.

This might be a mistake, but he couldn't leave Parker like this. Ivan sat beside him and pulled Parker into his arms. If he foolishly sensed a realignment in his own personal universe as Parker settled against his chest like Ivan had been made to cradle him, well, he'd chalk that up to the weird-ass mood swings. Whatever it was couldn't be real.

"Did you want me to call Neil?" Or was Parker here crying because of something Neil had done?

Parker's breath hitched. "No. He'd think I was an idiot for... this."

So. No break up, then. "What's wrong? I don't think you're an idiot." Tempting and gorgeous and almost perfect, but never an idiot. Except when it came to his choice of boyfriend.

"I... I... volunteer. At the trauma rehab."

Ivan blinked, trying to make sense of the statement. Despite the fact Parker had kept this bit of information to himself until now, Ivan couldn't figure out how that related to the tears. Instead of prodding, though, he smoothed his hand up and down Parker's back as a fresh spurt of tears dampened his shirt.

"I told you I'm going for a degree in sociology, right?"

Ivan grunted in the affirmative after he realized Parker hadn't lifted his head to see Ivan nod.

"Well, once I've got this degree, I'd like to get my master's in physical therapy. Anyway, even though going back to school part time seemed like a good idea, I found it didn't fill up the time. I found myself alone a lot. Brooding. The house was so... empty."

And why the fuck hadn't Neil done something about that? Parker had said something about him trying to start up a nightclub, but other than that, Ivan didn't know what the hell else he did with his time. If Ivan had spare time to spend with a fun, happy, sweet boyfriend like Parker, not a damned thing would keep him away.

"What about Neil?"

Parker's shoulder lifted under Ivan's hand in a weak attempt at a shrug. "He was great keeping me together right after my mom died, but I couldn't require him to keep me company."

Ivan's muscles tensed for a moment as he valiantly refrained from shaking Parker, because it was truly Neil he wanted to shake, or worse. Keeping your boyfriend company while he got used to a new chapter in his life didn't automatically mean slipping into a codependent relationship or anything. Parker's oddly-timed desire for a roommate suddenly made a lot more sense. The house wasn't large, but it was much bigger than one man needed, especially one who didn't have hoards of friends hanging out all the time or who did have a boyfriend who clearly wouldn't move in.

"Anyway, I figured volunteering at the trauma rehab center would look good on my resume, and I've already had lots of experience taking care of a terminal patient."

Ivan's eyebrows nearly crawled off his forehead in shock. "And you thought volunteering with terminal patients would be a good thing so soon after your mother's death?"

Parker let out a watery snort. "No. I'm really not an idiot. Maybe someday I will, because it did help, knowing I made things easier for her. But no, I was assigned to assist one of the physical therapists. She works with some terminal patients, but mostly she works with accident victims, ones whose mobility had been severely impacted."

That didn't sound too bad. Probably a lot less depressing. "But… something happened today."

Parker nodded against his neck and tried to burrow closer. "Steve. He was a couple years older than me. He'd been paralyzed in a motorcycle crash. His moods were sometimes erratic—the therapy can be difficult—but mostly he was upbeat and determined. He… he killed himself."

A fresh river of warm tears wet his shirt as Parker shook again. Ivan had seen a lot of shit over his life, but Parker was far more compassionate than he was. He felt things so strongly.

"I'm sorry, Parker. That has to be hard, losing someone you know and care about like that." Was it better or worse than shooting some young kid in the line of duty, then failing to revive them? Ivan pulled Parker closer, gaining as much comfort from Parker as he gave back.

"I didn't know. I didn't know it had gotten that bad for him."

Ivan wrapped his other arm around Parker, trying to give him all the strength he could. "Sometimes we can't know. Sometimes people don't let you see everything you want to see."

Parker curled around him for several minutes until the silent tears tapered off, and he sniffed several times. Tears and sweat from their close proximity moistened both of their shirts, the damp a little uncomfortable.

As soon as Parker levered himself up, Ivan forced his arms to fall away.

"C'mon. Get up," Ivan coaxed. "Grab a water from the fridge. You're probably a little dehydrated. I'll grab us a couple of fresh shirts."

Head hanging down, Parker obeyed.

Ivan grabbed two clean T-shirts from his laundry basket while Parker took advantage of the time to blow his nose. When Ivan entered the kitchen, Parker had dried his eyes and retrieved a bottle of water from the fridge. Ivan tossed the cotton shirts on the counter and yanked his shirt over his head. He gestured for Parker's, and he quickly stripped his off as well. Ivan took both shirts and tossed them toward the basement stairs. He'd throw them in the washing machine later.

Turning back to Parker, their situation hit him right square in the groin. Parker lifted the bottle to his lips and drained it, the action drawing attention to his prominent Adam's apple and the stretch of skin between peaked nipples. Ivan, shirtless, stood eighteen inches from an equally shirtless and golden skinned Parker. Sweet Parker who cried for the loss of a man who'd chosen to leave this life behind. Who'd taken care of his sick mother. Whose boyfriend left him lonely and alone. Who was the sexiest, most gorgeous man Ivan had ever seen. Who made Ivan laugh and smile even when he shouldn't.

The temptation was too much. The warmth in his heart was too overwhelming. Ivan reached out a hand and pressed it against the soft skin of Parker's belly.

Parker didn't actually cringe, but Ivan sensed him almost fold up in response, and his cheekbones burned bright.

"Is this okay?" Ivan asked.

"I guess. But I'm not, you know... toned like you are." Parker's voice was as soft and hesitant as the fingertip he trailed along Ivan's bare six-pack. Ivan hissed, the feeling of Parker touching him wildly erotic.

"I adore this bit." Ivan stroked gently, hoping Parker was squirming from something other than self-consciousness. Parker wasn't as toned as Ivan, true, but he wasn't fat, and Ivan wasn't lying. He adored that Parker's belly wasn't like his own.

"Why?"

"It makes you less intimidating."

"Intimidating? I'm not intimidating."

The statement seemed to truly puzzle Parker. Ivan continued to hold his palm against Parker's warm stomach and stared into his eyes.

"Oh, but you are. This is the one part of you that's not perfect."

Parker gasped as the red in his cheeks dialed up.

"Anyone would be lucky to have you. You're sweet and good-hearted and so damned gorgeous you could be a model." Ivan let his gaze rove over those perfect features. The ones that resonated inside him like a gong. If there was a way to set Parker on the right path, keep him from being a full-fledged criminal, Ivan would do anything. Prison would kill Parker; he'd be ripped to shreds. As much as Ivan wanted to say it was his humanitarian nature to protect Parker, it was more visceral, more primitive than that. Parker might not be his in truth, might never be his, but heart and soul, Ivan wanted him. Wanted him enough to toss his morals and principals out the window, both professional and personal. And all the goodness in Parker? He wasn't meant for a life of crime. Whatever choices he'd made so far had to have been mistakes. Somehow, he'd convince both Parker and Martelli of that.

"But I'm... not perfect." Parker sounded breathless and strangled, those riverbed eyes wide, pupils dark. Heat from Parker's bare chest kissed Ivan's, and he wanted to touch more, like he had earlier. He wanted to be as close as they'd been on the couch, but with only skin between them. He wanted that more than he wanted his next breath.

The ravages of tears were still visible around Parker's eyes and nose, redder than his flushed cheeks, and Ivan wished he could take Parker's pain away.

Ivan bit his lip and stared into those warm eyes, wanting more than anything to convince Parker he was perfect. Perfect for him. Neil should be the one here, comforting Parker. Ivan should feel guilty; he wanted something that didn't belong to him. And if the touch of Parker's smooth skin burning like a brand was all he'd ever have, he didn't want to step back. If Parker looked, though, he could probably see in Ivan's eyes everything he didn't dare say.

As Ivan continued to stare, Parker's eyes flared. Parker stepped closer, trapping Ivan's hand between them, and cupped Ivan's cheeks in his hands. Lowering his head, Parker pressed his supple, full lips against Ivan's. It was every bit as glorious as Ivan had imagined. Ivan debated with himself for all of half a second before he deepened the kiss, allowing Parker's response to escalate, become frantic. Ivan slid both hands around Parker's slim waist, reveling in the sensation of the satiny skin of the younger man. Parker pushed his hips into Ivan's, and Ivan groaned into the kiss.

Knowing Parker was as hard as he was sealed the deal. He'd take what Parker offered. He'd try to provide the solace Parker needed. There would be plenty of time in the morning to hate himself for making Parker break faith with his boyfriend.

PARKER had never been kissed like Ivan kissed him. Voracious and sweet at the same time. Soft lips, hot tongue, eager hands, and a hard body all came into play. Warm under his palms, Ivan's skin was supple and covered with springy hair. The few guys he'd slept with had been waxed within an inch of their lives, but Ivan's hair made him shiver. This was a man wrapped around him, a man with his tongue exploring Parker's mouth. A man that said Parker was perfect, and—although Ivan must have imperfect eyesight—there was no mistaking his hunger. No mistaking the hard cock pressed against him.

Ivan guided their kiss, lightning hot and electric, and Parker did his best to meld their bodies. As much as he disbelieved Ivan's assertions of his perfection, the wariness he'd had with Neil's friends didn't exist. All he wanted was more.

"Hey." Ivan separated their lips and pulled back an inch or two. His eyes were a stunning blue this close up, and his lips were reddened and every bit as delicious as they looked.

"Yeah?" This wasn't all he was going to get, was it? Then again… Ivan was straight. Straight or not, Ivan could fucking kiss.

"You okay with this?" There was a weird look in Ivan's eyes, but it sure wasn't confusion.

"Yeah." Apparently he wasn't capable of any other words. The skin just below Ivan's lightly stubbled jaw caught his eye, and despite the fact that he'd never been the aggressor with anyone, Parker licked the spot before he scraped his teeth gently downward and sucked.

Ivan groaned and gripped Parker tighter. He didn't stop tasting Ivan, but the reaction warmed him from the inside out, and if his mouth hadn't been busy, he would have smiled.

Parker could feast for days on Ivan's salty, soft skin. He moved his lips back up to Ivan's jaw and rubbed his lips over the stubble, enjoying the rasp and tingle. Ivan slid a hand under Parker's waistband to grip his ass, and it was his turn to throw his head back, gasping.

When Parker bent his head again, intending to take up where he'd left off, Ivan grinned at him and grabbed his chin with his other hand. Didn't Ivan like—

Before he could finish the thought, Ivan had pressed their lips together again, and Parker couldn't complain. Didn't want to complain. He could kiss Ivan forever. Except kissing forever meant they'd never get on to the next, exciting bits.

Ivan's hand on his chin moved slowly down his torso and tickled at his belly, flicking the top button of his jeans open. Somehow, he held his breath, even as he returned Ivan's kisses. He'd need more practice to be able to keep two hands and tongue moving all at the same time.

With a swift movement, Ivan delved into his pants, one hand cupping the head of his cock, the other sending fingers sliding across his hole, and Parker moaned into Ivan's mouth.

Stroking on both sides made Parker squirm. Concentrating on breathing and kissing and feeling and touching overwhelmed him, and he pulled his lips from Ivan's, panting. The feral look in Ivan's dark blue eyes trapped breath in his lungs. He'd never had someone look at him like that before, not even when past lovers had been poised with cock at his hole. His balls contracted, and he frantically pushed Ivan away.

Ivan's molten expression cooled as a frown creased his forehead. "Are you okay? I'm sorry, I shouldn't have—"

Parker cut him off with a finger to his lips and a shaky grin. "I'm fine. I was about to be... uh... exceedingly fine all over your fingers."

The frown hung there for a moment before the heat returned. Between the smug smile and the sapphire blue eyes that had no business being so hot, Parker broke into a sweat. How was he supposed to demonstrate any control at all with the temptation of Ivan? He'd have to if he didn't want this over too soon.

Ivan had other ideas, though. He wrenched Parker's jeans open and shoved them down his hips. He pushed Parker against the counter and dropped to his knees, swallowing half of Parker's dick in one smooth move. Proof positive of why Ivan's marriage had failed, because there was no way he'd never done this before.

Then, there was no more room in Parker's head for thinking as Ivan sucked him all the way into his throat, burning away all regrets and coherent thoughts in a white-hot burst of pleasure.

Parker arched his back and sent volley after volley of cum spurting into Ivan's welcoming mouth, tangling his fingers in the short blond hair to anchor himself.

He rested his head against the cupboard as he tried to catch his breath. Ivan continued to lick his sensitive cock, cleaning him, but embarrassment kept Parker from watching. Seconds. He'd lasted seconds under Ivan's skill and enthusiasm. And now he'd be expected to reciprocate, and as much as he wanted to lick Ivan all over, there would be no disguising that he wasn't as good at this as Ivan was.

Still, he couldn't leave Ivan hanging. Biting his lip, he bent his head, and Ivan, sensing the weight of his gaze, looked up. Parker gasped a little. Ivan's pink lips, slightly swollen from their effort, rested a fraction of an inch from his still shiny dick, and Ivan's breath was warm on his skin. The odds of getting Ivan to do that again were miniscule, given Parker's pathetic lack of control, and a new regret blossomed in his chest, because he might never know what Ivan's lips looked like sucking him down.

Why hadn't he given in to some of Neil's friends? Most of them made his skin crawl, but practice was the key to getting better, and he was clearly terrible at sex. No wonder he'd never been able to keep a boyfriend.

"I'm sorry." Embarrassment strangled the words as they clawed their way out of Parker's throat.

"For what?" Ivan stood, trailing his fingers along Parker's belly as he did so. An impressive erection strained the fly of his jeans, while Parker's own jeans pooled at his feet.

For what? Ivan had been right there in the trenches. Parker waved his hand at his half-hard dick. "For going off so quickly."

Ivan stared uncertainly over Parker's shoulders. "I wanted to give you another out."

"Another out?" Why had having his dick in Ivan's mouth so abysmally affected his comprehension?

Idly stroking Parker's collarbone—covering his nape with goose bumps—Ivan continued to avoid his gaze. "One last chance to change your mind. About sleeping with me."

Crazy swarms of butterflies danced in his stomach, and he blurted out the first thing that came to mind. "I don't want to change my mind. I want you." But then he wanted to swallow his tongue; he'd never come out and said that to anyone.

It had been the right thing to say. Ivan finally looked him in the eye, pupils blown out with a desire that arced between them like electricity, shocking Parker's dick to life once more.

Ivan wiggled his brows. "Besides, it was so fucking hot, watching you."

Parker laughed nervously, acutely aware of his total nudity. "You watched."

"Oh, yes." The words were throaty, deeper than Ivan's normal tone, and they reached right into Parker's psyche. He'd probably do whatever Ivan wanted whenever he used that tone.

"Um."

"I also noticed this." Ivan licked along his collarbone, making him shiver. No one had touched that area, not with intent, and Parker hadn't realized how sensitive the skin there was. Or maybe it was just Ivan. Ivan, who stared at him as though he were… delicious.

Ivan moved his mouth back up to Parker's and kissed him, the lingering saltiness of Parker's release flavoring his tongue. Parker moaned deep in his throat and pressed himself up against Ivan's muscular body.

"So, you haven't changed your mind?" Ivan spoke the words against Parker's lips, almost kissing while talking.

Yeah, right. If anyone was going to change his mind, it would be the former straight guy.

"No." Parker's breath intermingled with Ivan's, and he suddenly understood why some guys didn't like to kiss. In many ways, it was more intimate than any other sex act. "Have you? Did you want me to?"

"No. God, no."

Well, then. "Are you going to fuck me here?" And where the hell had this sexually forward man come from? Neil would be so proud.

Parker did some grinning of his own when Ivan groaned and flexed his hips against him.

"Let's go." Ivan stepped back, allowing Parker to step away from the counter. He took another step toward the door and promptly tripped over the crumpled jeans.

Ivan caught him before he face-planted on the floor, but the near miss caused another rush of blood to his face.

"C'mon now. I gave you a chance to change your mind. Don't go braining yourself just to get out of it."

Parker laughed at Ivan's teasing and got a gentle smack on his ass as he continued to the stairs.

ON THE landing, Parker paused, Ivan's footfalls close behind. His bed was bigger and better, but.... An image of him wearing his stupid, noisy, weird CPAP machine pushed him toward Ivan's bedroom. Sure, the CPAP was a necessary evil, because it made sure he didn't stop breathing in the middle of the night, but after the teasing Neil had given him, he sure didn't want Ivan to see him in it. It would be a lot easier for him to get up and leave Ivan's bed than it would be to convince Ivan he needed to leave, assuming Ivan would even consider actually sleeping next to him all night.

"You sure? The bed's pretty small in there."

"You planning on much space between us?" No, really, what had happened to him?

Ivan turned into the feral beast Parker had caught a glimpse of earlier, as he practically stalked across the landing. "Not a fucking inch."

Parker barely got the door opened before Ivan crowded him from behind, his hands caressing Parker's ribcage with long vigorous strokes.

When the tips of Ivan's roughened fingertips passed over his nipples almost without intention, Parker jumped. Nothing Ivan did was wrong. Parker loved everything. Even when Ivan tipped him over on the bed, with his ass thrust up into the air, leaving him vulnerable.

He'd have preferred to have sex face to face, but he'd already had one spectacular orgasm; he wasn't going to be picky about how he had the second. Not when Ivan was the one distributing them.

But he was mistaken. Ivan rubbed his butt for a moment, squeezing the cheeks, before he urged him onto the bed. Parker lay back and only had to wait a few seconds while Ivan stripped off his jeans and briefs. Ivan crawled up over him from the bottom of the bed like a hungry lion. The complete lack of hesitation on Ivan's part, at least when it came to naked man bits touching other naked man bits, reinforced Parker's earlier revelation that Ivan was no novice at fucking guys.

Parker thanked whatever deity that looked out for shy gay boys because if they both had been hesitant, it might have been months of dancing around their attraction before anything happened. In the morning, Parker might have to consider whether sleeping with a guy he barely knew, and his roommate to boot, was good idea, but for now, he wanted Ivan inside him so bad he couldn't stop his legs from splaying open, his knees drawing up toward his chest of their own volition.

Ivan's gaze traveled up from his groin, making him both self-conscious and aroused. He didn't think he'd ever been on display like this, with his partner happy to just look at him. With slow, deliberate movements, Ivan pressed their cocks together, and they both hissed. So hot, so hard. Parker couldn't stop his hips from thrusting up. Jeez, he wasn't going to go off again so soon, was he?

However, Ivan did not seem to be in a hurry to get lube and condoms, and Parker knew damn well he had both, although he wasn't going to mention that.

With Ivan's lips and tongue moving over Parker's neck, ears, and chest—making sure to focus on the newly discovered erogenous zone along his collarbone—he managed to distract Parker from thinking about fucking, because even fucking had never felt as good, like Ivan could play with him forever.

The steady friction of Ivan's erection against his, made enticingly slick by precum, pulled him closer and closer to the edge.

Every inch of skin pressed against Ivan's tingled from the contact. Parker ran his palms up Ivan's fuzzy forearms before reaching around and digging his fingers into Ivan's smooth back, giving himself more leverage for his upward thrusts to meet Ivan's downward ones.

Next time, he'd explore Ivan top to bottom. Those hard muscles begged for closer examination, including licking and sucking.

Ivan wormed a hand underneath Parker's ass and grabbed his ass cheek, assisting Parker's thrusts. Parker followed suit and grabbed Ivan's flexing ass with both hands.

Then came the moment of no return. Parker wasn't going to last any longer. Dammit. "Ivan, I'm gonna—"

Ivan moved quickly and kissed him, tongue tangling wildly with the deep, chesty groan that accompanied Parker spurting all over his belly.

He relaxed back onto the mattress, too blissed to care that he'd had two awesome orgasms to Ivan's none. Ivan still tongue fucked his mouth and still rode his cock against Parker's now slick one.

While still enjoying the twitchy aftershocks of his orgasm and the rhythmic flex of Ivan's glutes under his palms, Ivan pulled out of the kiss and threw his head back while his entire body stiffened.

The sudden stillness of the man above him left him free to concentrate on the subtle jerking of Ivan's spewing cock and the gush of warmth over his cock and balls. Ivan slumped against him, his breath harsh and choppy in Parker's ear. Parker smiled at the ceiling. If they didn't move soon, they'd be glued together, but there was nowhere else Parker would rather be.

He'd have to be careful, though. Ivan may have proven himself to be not as straight as Parker believed, but he had just gotten out of a volatile and acrimonious marriage. The odds of him wanting to jump into a relationship would be almost nil, but as they lay together, sweaty and sated, he could dream. Dream that they'd do this every night. When Ivan came home from a hard day selling insurance—and Parker had never imagined such a job would be so stressful—Parker could soothe him, feed him, and take him to bed.

Huh. Sort of like Ivan had done for him just now. Maybe the dream wasn't too wildly improbable.

Ivan's breathing evened out, and he planted a light kiss on Parker's neck before he reached down to grab a T-shirt from the floor. He slid off to Parker's side and swiped at their groins with the T-shirt.

"Gross." Parker made sure the teasing was evident in his voice.

Ivan lifted a brow. "Well, I could have used your shirt."

"You couldn't. Mine's still downstairs."

"Whatever. How 'bout I show you gross." Ivan straddled him again, threatening to rub the damp cotton in his face. Parker struggled and flipped his face from side to side, trying to avoid the impromptu cumrag, but the laughter made everything a little halfhearted.

When they were both out of breath from the mock fight, Ivan threw the crumpled shirt across the room and tucked Parker up to his chest, lips brushing over his nape in faint approximations of kisses.

His eyelids grew heavy as he relaxed in the warmth of Ivan's arms. A deep breath, which sounded alarmingly like a snore, jerked him into full consciousness. He couldn't fall asleep here. That just wasn't possible.

He eased out from under Ivan's arms. He didn't even have any clothes to gather, because they were all still downstairs. He'd have to grab them in the morning.

"Where are you going?" Ivan's sleepy voice made Parker pause.

"To my room."

"You could stay here, you know. I don't mind."

Parker glanced at Ivan over his shoulder. He wanted to. He really did. But he shouldn't sleep without his stupid, ugly machine. If his lack of sexual prowess hadn't scared Ivan off, that surely would. He didn't think any boyfriend would be able to overlook the CPAP, never mind right after the first time they'd had sex. How could they? Parker could barely look at himself without shuddering.

"I can't. I just… can't." Parker turned and fled. Sleeping—actually sleeping—with a guy would mean more to him than simple sex, and he was pretty sure that's all Ivan thought this was. All he had to do was keep Ivan interested until he got over the negative emotions from his divorce, and living together would give him lots of opportunities to.

Inside his room, his bed looked so big, and tonight of all nights it wasn't going be nearly as comfortable as it usually was.

Sighing, he sat down and pulled the hated black tubing and mask out of his nightstand and prepared himself for sleep. He lay back on his chilly sheets, breathing apparatus on, wishing Ivan were still wrapped around him, wishing he could still smell Ivan's sweat and cum.

CHAPTER
Seven

BLOOD covered Parker's chest, and splatters speckled the ashen skin of his face. Ivan worked frantically to stem the bleeding and keep him breathing, keep his heart pumping, but he knew, as those green riverbed eyes clouded over, he was going to fail. Again. With a deep whooping breath, like the nightmare had managed to physically strangle him, Ivan sat up in bed and panted.

Nostrils flaring, he grabbed the corner of the sheet and swiped at the sweat pouring off his face and chest. Parker wasn't the only one he failed to save in his dreams, but he was definitely the most frequent visitor to his nightmares. And the most terrifying. In a matter of days, he'd managed to become a very important person in Ivan's life, and as much as he'd like to say it was because of the investigation, he didn't think that was it.

He'd been hurt, unreasonably so, by Parker returning to his room last night. No matter how many chances Ivan gave him, after all was said and done, the guilt of cheating must have gotten to him. Hell, it got to Ivan too. He thought in the cold light of morning he'd have no regrets; he'd somehow be absolved of all guilt because they hadn't had anal sex. Yeah, he was a real fucking hero. But anal sex wasn't the be-all and end-all of sex. Lips were kissed. Bare skin was stroked. Cocks were touched and sucked. People came. Penetration meant nothing in the wake of that. They'd had sex.

Ivan had knowingly conspired with Parker to cheat on Neil. Hating Neil didn't make it better. No excuses were valid, as he'd told Colin. He still felt that, but now he could add blackened, choking guilt on top of his other issues. Which didn't take into account his job. Getting involved with a suspect was not only the territory of sappy romance novels, but a big fucking professional taboo.

He knew what had prompted the dream tonight. He'd expected the presence of Parker in his arms to keep the dreams at bay, but he'd left. Completely unexpectedly. Ivan never thought his narrow, extra firm bed would ever be comfortable, especially not with a second person, but he'd been pleasantly surprised. He'd also been surprised by Parker's choice to have sex in Ivan's room. This morning, it wasn't so surprising. Probably he'd been aware all along that the bed would be a continuous reminder of his infidelity, as Ivan's bed at home had been until he'd replaced it.

Grabbing a pair of sweatpants, he stood and pulled them on, trying to ignore the dried cum he'd missed the night before. He needed to get in the shower and get the fuck out of here before Parker woke up.

A glance at the clock assured him he had plenty of time. The nightmares, which littered his dreams with the dead and kept him semiconscious most of the night, had at least ensured he'd awoken before the sun. Students Parker's age weren't usually morning people.

AFTER a quick shower, which didn't seem to disturb Parker's sleep, he dressed quickly. Ivan grabbed his sheets and the soiled T-shirt and ran downstairs to throw them in the washing machine. Sleeping on those sheets tonight would be… difficult at best.

As he poured detergent into the machine and started it, his stomach roiled, a sickly mix of hunger and regret. He'd planned for another day hanging out with Parker, "auditing" classes, but pretending nothing had happened last night, especially if they ran into Neil, would be impossible. He was already holding on to so many secrets they were straining his mind at the seams like an overfilled balloon. One extra pressure and all his careful preparations would explode in a messy, life-threatening disaster.

He'd have to follow Parker again because searching the house was just out. He couldn't stay here alone all day, remembering. Sex was sex and he'd engaged in lots of it, before Colin, with Colin, and after Colin. But not even with Colin, at the idyllic beginning of their relationship, had it ever fucked with his mind like sex with Parker had. This wasn't a normal situation, not at all, and he had to remember that.

Ivan dragged himself upstairs, intending to grab a quick breakfast before he stationed himself in his observation post to wait for Parker to head out for classes. Then he tripped over Parker's well-worn jeans and briefs on the kitchen floor. The regret overtook the hunger and boiled up into anger that burned so bright he could barely breathe. Damn Parker for making him the other man, and damn him for being everything Ivan wanted. A low growling came from his throat, and he slammed his fist into the wall.

Pain splintered across his knuckles and flew up his arm. He pulled his arm back, cradling his fist. At least he hadn't turned his hand into mulch against a concrete wall. Only a small dent and some flakes of paint to show where he'd lost control. And damn Parker for being a criminal in the first place. If Parker hadn't decided to become a criminal, Ivan would have never met him, and at the moment, that could only be a good thing.

The agony in his knuckles pulsed in time to the anger heating his ears as blood welled up from scrapes, and he wanted to shake Parker. This was all his fucking fault. He wanted to shout at Parker, beat Neil's stupid face in. When he realized he'd taken a few steps toward the stairs, he took a deep shuddery breath and held it, hoping to calm himself. The sound of Parker shutting the bathroom door stretched the already abused threads of his self-control. He had to get the fuck out.

His left hand shook so much he had difficulty closing his fingers around the door handle, but the humidity had been negligible overnight, and he didn't have to put all his weight into getting the door open. His heart rate sped up when the toilet flushed.

Get out, get out, get out.

Ivan slammed the door behind him and hit the sidewalk running. He didn't know where he was running to, but he ran like his life depended on it.

PARKER stumbled out of the bathroom. He hadn't slept nearly as well as he should have after two spec-fucking-tacular orgasms, but he only had himself and CPAP to blame. Losing all that weight while taking care of his mom should have made his sleep apnea go away. But it hadn't. Even if he'd decided to spend the night with Ivan, take the risk of sleeping without his machine, knowing he snored louder than a half-dozen chainsaws would make it impossible to face Ivan in the morning. One day, he'd like to wake up in someone's arms, someone he cared about, but the black tubing and hideous mask was an effective deterrent.

Then again, he'd never imagined someone as sexy and sweet as Ivan would ever be interested in him. *Baby steps, baby steps.*

No force on earth could have stopped him from glancing in Ivan's open door. The empty room and the stripped mattress was an unexpected slap to the face. Ivan must have awoken at the crack of dawn, foiling Parker's hope that he could stare at a sleeping Ivan, twisted up in the sheets they'd had sex in, maybe smile at the memory of Ivan's playfulness.

Ah well. It didn't much surprise him that Ivan would wash his sheets after sex. It was a habit Parker actually approved of, after one disgusting incident with a date earlier in the year. The guy's sheets had been positively crunchy, and it didn't matter whether it was from other guys or himself. Parker had fled, and he'd never been so happy in his life that dating prospects were so few and far between.

"Ivan?" There was no answer, so he walked downstairs and tried again. Nothing. Where had he gone? Yesterday he'd said he was going come with Parker again to the university. He didn't know why Ivan had decided to audit his courses, but he'd enjoyed having his friends meet Ivan. He'd enjoyed spending time with him out in public. Made them seem a little more than roommates. He laughed. After last night, roommates didn't seem like quite the right description, but he didn't know if there was a term that wouldn't freak Ivan out. Roommates with benefits? Or could they graduate to friends with benefits? Liberal application of said benefits might see another upgrade to their status in a few months, and Parker was going to work toward that goal like he'd worked toward no other.

The main floor was empty except for his jeans and underwear on the kitchen floor, bringing on sweet memories from the previous night. Would Ivan be willing to repeat their kitchen interlude? This time Parker would watch and hopefully last a little longer.

The distinctive metallic thunk of a washing machine slightly off-kilter drew his attention to the basement.

"Ivan?" he called down, but got no answer. A quick trip downstairs revealed an empty basement. With a frown, and slower steps, Parker climbed back to the main floor.

Where the hell had Ivan gone? Had he gone for an early morning run? If he didn't get back soon, he wouldn't have time to shower before Parker left for class. This close to midterms, it was dangerous to skip out on lectures. Parker threw an apple and a granola bar into his bag. While his bread was toasting, he ran his jeans and briefs back upstairs, getting back down just as the toast popped up. As he grabbed a plate out of the cupboard, a shadow on the wall beside the cabinet caught his eye. Plate in hand, he peered at the spot. Was that a dent? He ran his fingers over the wall, paint flaking to the floor in response. The wall was depressed under his fingers. This house had been his home forever, and he knew every inch like he knew his own body. That dent was new. How odd.

He swiftly slapped peanut butter on his toast, along with a tiny smear of jam, and sat at the table, staring at the rounded depression. What would cause that? And when had it happened?

After washing the dishes and generally puttering, he could stall no longer. Ivan wasn't coming back. Maybe he'd forgotten, or maybe his boss had needed him back at work, but either way, Parker's day had dimmed.

With one last brief touch of the counter, where he'd rested while Ivan had blown his mind while blowing his dick, Parker slung his bag over his shoulder and left the house.

IVAN pounded on the door to the house. He really hoped he had the right address. He paced the length of the tiny porch while he waited. No way could he expect an immediate answer. The heat in the air was becoming oppressive as it neared noon, but that didn't factor into Ivan's desperation to get in the house.

A glance at his watch confirmed he'd not been outside for several minutes, but he pounded his fist—his left one—on the door again. His right one was swollen and scabbed and had been a bitch to protect on public transit in the midst of the early morning rush hour. More than once he'd had to bite back a shout of pain as some unsuspecting passenger jostled him or knocked into it with a laptop bag or purse.

The light rumble of a car engine had him turning to face the street. He was—mostly— certain no one had followed him, but it wouldn't surprise him if beat cops were doing regular drive-bys, just in case. He flattened himself against the house and peered through the floppy branches of the evergreen growing at the corner of the porch. The white Crown Vic could be an unmarked cop car, or it could be an elderly person. Pretty much no one else drove those things.

Squinting, he stared intently at the driver, who was driving probably ten or so under the limit for a residential street. The flash of glasses and white hair registered just as the door banged open behind him. He leapt into the bushes while he whirled around to face the new threat.

Heart pounding, he crouched into a defensive posture. It took him a few seconds to recognize the man in front of him.

"Ivan? Is that you?"

Ivan stretched to his full height and stepped back on the porch, trying to tamp down the embarrassment at his overreaction. That didn't stop him from taking another nervous glance around the neighborhood before he spoke.

"Kurt, I need to talk to you."

"Sure, c'mon inside."

"Is your boy home?"

"My boy? Really?" Kurt rolled his eyes, but ushered Ivan inside and shut the door behind them. "Davy's at work."

The cool air hit Ivan's face, the chill refreshing after the heat of the sun. He didn't much care if Kurt objected to his terminology, so long as they were alone. And he'd drawn a complete blank on Davy's name, so boy did just fine.

He followed Kurt's slow progress to the living room, where he sat gingerly on the couch. No wonder it had taken him so long to answer the door; the guy was clearly hurting. He'd lost several pounds since he'd been shot, on top of the pounds he'd lost fretting about coming out. The man needed a sandwich or three.

Kurt flipped the TV off and gestured at one of the chairs. Ivan sat on the edge, unable to relax.

Ivan took a deep breath. "I'm sorry. I'm being a shitty friend. I'm glad things worked out with Davy. You'll have to tell me about it sometime."

"You got someplace to be? Simon told me what happened to you during the raid. Obviously he didn't hear about it until later, but he did tell me you were on leave until further notice." Kurt frowned. "Surely the SIU didn't find you at fault for that kid's death?"

Ivan choked down a gasp. He hadn't wanted to talk about Dmitri at all. Especially not when the image of Parker in his place was still so vivid in his mind. So, he ignored the question.

"Kurt, man, I need help. I don't know who to trust."

"Of course. What's up?"

Ivan flexed his hand and hissed as the pain clawed him.

"Shit, Ivan, who the hell did you hit? And why?"

"Long story. But it was a what, not a who."

"Looks like you've cracked your knuckles. Let me get something to wrap up that hand, then you can tell me your story."

Kurt stood, holding himself stiff and careful. Maybe he still had stitches. Ivan wasn't even sure how long he'd been out of the hospital, but Ivan was still pissed this job had kept him from visiting.

"I don't know." Jittery like he'd had a dozen espressos topped off with a couple lattes, Ivan bounced up to look out the window.

"It's not like either of us have any place we need to be." Kurt left the room, moving slowly but steadily.

He was wrong. Ivan was supposed to be someplace else. Probably he should have left a note for Parker, letting him know he wasn't going to class today, but it was far too late to have that regret, which was minor enough that it drowned in a much bigger sea of regret about having sex. Besides, he wrote for shit with his left hand; Parker wouldn't have been able to read it.

After pacing the perimeter of the room a couple of times, he flicked the curtain back again, checking for surveillance. Nothing. Yet.

"What are you looking for?" Kurt's unheard return startled him, but not to the point he was ready to attack, like he'd been in front of the house.

"Nothing." Yet.

"Come sit on the table here. It's easier if I don't have to bend or twist."

Ivan didn't want to cause Kurt any pain—he'd been the source of pain for far too many people lately—so he did as he was he told.

Kurt peered up at him, blue eyes concerned. "You look like shit. You want to tell me what's up, or do I have to beat it out of you?"

The intentional humor surprised a grunt out of him—not quite a laugh, but as close as he could possibly come today. Kurt was a tough motherfucker, but right now, a one-armed monkey could take him.

"Seriously, Ivan. You said you needed help. Tell me how I can help you." Kurt picked up his hand and began cleaning and wrapping.

Ivan spoke as Kurt finished up his first aid. The whole mess only started several days ago, but it seemed like years. He managed to outline how he'd ended up in Parker's house before Kurt paused in his first aid and looked closely at him.

"What the fuck, Ivan? Sarge had no business putting you undercover like that." Kurt ran agitated fingers through his auburn hair, making it stand up in all directions before he completed wrapping Ivan's hand. "It's completely against regulations. You could lose your job over this. And any arrests might not even stick."

Ivan shrugged and fiddled with the buttons on the TV remote that sat next to him. Those issues had worried him, too, but with a mole in the department and him not wanting anyone to arrest Parker anyway, he wondered if he was even cut out for this job anymore.

"That's... not really the issue."

Kurt frowned and hissed. "Shit, I can't do that."

"Are you okay?"

"Yes. Or I will be. Just taking time to heal, you know."

Ivan let out the breath he hadn't realized he'd been holding. His stupid shit, his hand, his issues, were nothing compared to what Kurt had been through. He stood, ready to run.

"I should go. I need to deal with this on my own."

"Sit the fuck down, Ivan." Kurt grimaced and stood as well, drawing his shoulders back. Despite the recent weight loss, Kurt was still bigger and showed no hesitation in reminding Ivan of the fact.

"Kurt, I—"

"You gonna make me make you sit?"

"Fuck, no." Kurt would try, no matter what additional injury it would cause. There was no mistaking the look in Kurt's eyes, and Ivan couldn't be responsible.

This time, he slumped into a chair facing Kurt, who sat gingerly down again.

"Talk, Ivan. Now."

"If someone's passing inside info to the Russian mafia, you're the only one I can trust. Which is why I'm here. I... don't know what to do." Ivan dropped his head into his hand.

"You need to stop this. There's no way this kid is any sort of major player. You'd have heard about it before now."

"I haven't finished yet." Ivan continued to tell his story, and Kurt listened intently.

"Okay, wait, Sarge might be on to something. Even if his mom left him an excellent inheritance, there's no reason for him to be keeping that much money in his closet."

Ivan glanced around the room, trying to postpone admitting the very worst thing. The thing that would get him fired, that made this whole investigation useless.

"Yeah. I know. But that's not all. Kurt... I'm so fucked. This kid." No. He couldn't call him kid. "Parker. He's... I'm... we...."

Kurt's back straightened, and his eyes widened. "You fucked him?"

Ivan's breath gusted out. "Yeah. And he's no kid." That had to be made clear. He had enough guilt weighing him down without adding cradle robbing.

"So... why? It wasn't necessary for the cover, right? I thought you said you went in as a divorced man?"

Oh God. No. So not necessary for the cover. But he couldn't stop himself. He stared at Kurt, not wanting to say it out loud. "It'll never happen again. I swear."

Kurt's expression softened, and Ivan stared over his shoulder. "Oh. Shit."

"Um. Yeah." At least he didn't have to come out and say he just hadn't been able to stop himself. He'd had to have one taste. Just one.

"What are you going to do?"

Ivan smiled, or at least as much as he could. Since Kurt was now living with Davy, Ivan supposed he'd gotten his happy ending, but Ivan had seen him before he and Davy had gotten together, and he'd been pretty fucked up. Kurt wasn't going to bitch him out for being stupid, and he appreciated Kurt's friendship more than he could say. Even though there was no happy ending in his own future, he was glad Kurt had found Davy. The worry and distress and emotional pain that had hung over Kurt like a cloak the last time they'd gone out was gone. Kurt's issues were all physical, lucky ass.

"I don't know."

"Go to Sarge. Tell him it's a bust. What you're doing is fucking dangerous."

"Yeah, but if I leave, will it be more dangerous for Parker?"

"For Parker? Why?"

"The leak. What if Razhin finds out we were investigating him? I don't think Parker realizes how dangerous those people are."

"Shit, man, you can't do it. You can't talk him out of it. If he finds out you're a cop, you're the one in danger, and no one is going to prison. You can't do it."

"I can. I think. You haven't met him, Kurt. He's so naïve. So sweet. I don't think he realizes how insidious the drug trade is. He and—" Ivan cut himself off. Last thing he wanted to talk about was Parker's goddamned boyfriend. "Anyway, I don't think he's so far gone yet."

"He's far gone enough that Sarge has heard of him."

"I don't care. Sarge has to be mistaken. Arresting Parker will kill him. He doesn't have a criminal mindset at all."

He hadn't realized how passionate he'd gotten about defending Parker. The drug trade saw more than its fair share of repeat offenders, enough that Ivan didn't much believe they could be rehabilitated, but Parker was different. He had to be. Ivan couldn't bear it if he died or was broken in prison.

Kurt pressed his lips together, but the weight of his too knowing stare was too much to take. Instead, he let his gaze dart around the room. A rather shockingly white room, now that he was paying attention.

"Ivan, listen to me."

"You ever hear of paint? It comes in colors. You should think about it."

"Ivan, for God's sake."

Ivan sighed and looked Kurt full in the face.

"This is wrong. I don't know why you agreed to this. I don't know why Sarge asked you to. But this stinks."

"Yeah, I know." Ivan let out a laugh bordering on hysterical. "I never even thought Sarge liked me much. Surprised me all to hell when he trusted me with this, but there are times, times when I feel eyes on me. People watching, even though I can't see them. I think he expected me to fail. That he's setting me up for… something. That's crazy, though, isn't it?"

Ivan bit his lip until it bled, because more hysterical laughter bubbled up in his chest, and he couldn't let Kurt hear it. He was losing his fucking mind.

"Ivan, man, you're one of the best detectives I know. I can't believe Sarge is setting you up. I can't see any possible reason for that. None. Maybe there is a mole, and maybe Sarge got rattled by that, enough that he fucked up your assignment. And believe me, he seriously fucked up here. I'm telling you right now, I don't want you to continue this. But if you feel you must, I'll let Simon know. I can't do much; I'm on leave too. But you can go to him, if you need anything. Got it?"

Simon. As a newcomer to the force, he'd be unlikely to be connected to the mole, and besides, this was obviously a Drug Squad issue, not Homicide.

Ivan nodded. "Thanks."

"As for the white." Kurt waved a hand at the walls. "We're having a painting party in a couple of weeks. I'd love it if you were there."

"There's nothing I'd like better. I'll try, okay?" Ivan didn't think he'd be there, and Kurt's expression said he agreed. Ivan would either be still undercover, or perhaps he'd be dead, if he was wrong about Parker's role in Razhin's organization.

He stood. Kurt needed to rest, and Ivan needed to get home— to Parker's. If he got his ass in gear, he'd have maybe an hour to go through some of those other boxes in Parker's closet, make sure he wasn't missing anything before Parker got home from the trauma center. Parker's volunteer work was yet another reason he refused to consider Parker a lost cause.

"SO WHERE'S that sexy roomie of yours?" Alicia poked Parker's shoulder, and he tried to grin.

"I don't know. He was gone when I woke up."

"Well, maybe he needed to go into work. Spending all his time staring at your fine ass isn't going to pay any alimony, you know?"

Parker looked away. Ivan had already spent a good deal of time with his very naked ass and apparently wanted nothing more to do with it. When would he learn? Sex was sex. Once it was done, he should be able to forget it. Until now, it hadn't even been that hard, but today, the cold shoulder hurt more than he'd expected. Unlike the few other guys he'd slept with, he truly thought Ivan had liked him, not just been interested in a quick fuck.

"He's not interested in my ass." Not now that he'd already had it.

Alicia's eyebrows rose before she laughed. "You can't really be that blind, can you?"

Yes, apparently he could. His eyes burned, and he blinked, trying to clear them. "What are you talking about?"

Alicia bent over to pull out her tablet. "Like you don't know. Shit, I thought Chris was going to have to break up a fight between Ivan and Thom."

"Thom? What does he have to do with it?" The confusion helped him gain some control over his emotions.

"Holy shitballs. You really are that blind, aren't you?" Alicia shook her head. "Thom is totally hot for you. Chris said last night was mighty depressing in the apartment, with Thom moping about. It wasn't hard to see the sizzle between you and Ivan, that's for sure. We could have cooked steak yesterday with the heat between you two."

Parker pressed a hand to his cheeks to ensure they weren't actually on fire. "I had no idea Thom was interested. I thought...." He hadn't actually thought much, aside from the fact that he assumed Thom didn't like him. How had he not known? Then again, even knowing he was going to get ditched today, he wasn't sure he would have picked Thom over Ivan. Maybe not the smartest thing;

Thom seemed like a very nice guy, and he was cute. But Ivan consumed Parker's thoughts.

"Oh, well, I don't know. It was probably just sex."

Alicia's mouth dropped open, and this time Parker was sure his cheeks had lit up. He hadn't meant to admit that to anyone.

"You had sex with Ivan? I'm shocked and yet, I'm not surprised at all. You need to tell me everything!"

Everything? Jeez, he was already embarrassed and hurt. He stared at Alicia. "He's not here today. He left the house without leaving me a note. What more do I need to say?"

"Oh." Alicia gave him a sad smile and squeezed his forearm. "I'm sure there's a good reason. Don't you worry. That intensity of feeling just doesn't go away, no matter what Thom hopes."

The professor walked into the class, giving him a reprieve. He tried to pay attention, but all he could think about was whether or not Alicia was right and how he was going to explain skipping lunch today. Getting an early start at the center would give him other things to think about.

SWEAT poured off Ivan as he collapsed against the door. The day was fucking hot and both of the subway cars he'd ridden on had faulty air conditioning. He also thought someone had picked up his trail, so he'd gotten out early and walked… well, it would have been twelve or so blocks if he'd been able to take a direct route, but he'd meandered with purpose, trying to identify who, if anyone, was following.

He heaved in a few gasping breaths. Running for exercise hadn't really prepared him for this level of vigilance and paranoia. He'd rather run a marathon or two than constantly feel those invisible eyes at his back.

After popping down to the basement to put his laundry in the dryer—as well as to verify no one was down there—Ivan made a quick round through the house. As he suspected, no one was there. As long as Neil didn't decide to drop by again without notice, he should have an hour or so to finish his search of Parker's closet.

He changed shirts and toweled off; no sense in alerting Parker by sweating all over his stuff.

More or less clean and dry, he walked into Parker's room and headed straight for the closet, despite the large bed lurking behind him. Regret over not getting to share that bed with Parker was ridiculous, and if Ivan didn't figure out how to turn Parker from his path, well, the guy should have as many nights on a comfortable bed as possible. Prison beds didn't come equipped with pillow-top mattresses.

Carefully, he lifted down the file box where he'd found the money. A quick look confirmed the money was still there. Finding out where the fuck it came from was a job for another day. He flipped quickly through the files. Parker didn't have much of a filing system. Deeds and invoices and utility bills for two different properties were mixed together and out of date order. Seemed at odds with the student who was always caught up on his homework, but then, he'd been responsible for all the bills for a relatively short period of time.

Ivan found documents relating to a trust fund that paid for Parker's expenses, which explained a lot, but didn't explain the large expenditures for what he presumed was the cottage in Muskoka that Parker had mentioned. He skimmed the purchases, and a pit of despair opened in his stomach. These were indicative of expenses associated with growing marijuana on a large scale. The cottage in Muskoka must be on a large parcel of land. Shit. The money must be from Razhin, bankrolling the conversion. He had less time than he thought to get Parker out of this situation. He might already be in too deep for Razhin to let him go, if the fat packet of cash was any indication.

He shoved everything back into the box and replaced it. Fuck, fuck, fuck. There was another box on the shelf at the back of the closet. Looked like a mini steamer trunk. He couldn't imagine anything more incriminating than what he'd found so far, but he might as well check while he was here.

The stiff hinges told him the box wasn't opened very often. Inside was a scattered mess of photos. As long as there weren't any photos of Parker posing beside a marijuana plant, there probably wasn't anything of interest, but that didn't stop him from rifling through. He saw a couple shots of Parker's mom, who he recognized from the few pictures Parker had propped on the mantel downstairs.

He skimmed over the others, looking for pictures of Parker, but it wasn't until he found one with Parker's mom, her arm wrapped around a young teen, did Ivan realize he'd missed... a shitload of Parker pictures.

Taking a handful out of the box, he walked out into Parker's bedroom to look at the pictures in the sunlight that streamed in through the windows. At least Parker had enough sense to keep the windows closed on days with record-high heat and humidity.

Parker's younger self was adorable. There were hints of his stunning face in those pictures, but the kid was pudgy, those sharp cheekbones hidden beneath the padding of baby fat. There were a couple of Neil as well, who looked much the same as he did now. He couldn't find any pictures that appeared to be from the last two years, which presumably was when Parker's mom had deteriorated to the point where she hadn't wanted pictures. Somewhere in those two years, Parker had shed probably fifty pounds to reveal the gorgeous guy underneath. The smile was the same, and Ivan touched a fingertip to one of the pictures. Parker's hesitancy and uncertainty, as well as his lack of arrogance, made a lot more sense now. He probably wasn't used to being the object of everyone's attention.

Movement outside the window had Ivan glancing up. Parker was on the sidewalk, almost in front of the house. Shit. He'd completely lost track of time looking at those pictures. Swiftly, he shoved the pictures back in the box and replaced them on the shelf before dashing out of the closet, carefully closing Parker's bedroom door just as the front door downstairs opened. His glance darted between bathroom and bedroom. He needed a few minutes to calm his rapid heartbeat and shallow breathing, so he opted for the bedroom and closed that door softly as well, hoping to indicate he'd been there for a while.

His ears strained, listening for Parker. The telltale squeak made him hold his breath, waiting for Parker to go into his bedroom. Then he could relax. Think about options.

CHAPTER
Eight

PARKER stood for a moment, staring at Ivan's closed door. He'd gotten home before Parker, which was unusual. Was he having difficulty at work? If insurance agents worked on commission, maybe he was having trouble selling policies. Might explain some of Ivan's slightly erratic behavior.

He reached a hand out, intending to knock, but the memory of Ivan's disappearance this morning brought up all his feelings of inadequacy. If Ivan thought they were friends, or at least, slightly more than a one-night stand, he'd confide in Parker. And then he'd know where he stood.

His own bedroom was both comfortable and comforting, but he wanted to be curled up with Ivan on his narrow twin mattress more than anything. Sex was optional. Ivan's arms around him had eased him so thoroughly, he hadn't even realized how badly he'd needed someone to touch him, hold him.

With a sigh worthy of the angsty, emo teen he'd been, he pushed open his door and slammed it behind him and threw himself on the bed. He stared at the open door of his closet, the two club shirts crumpled on the closet floor along with their hangers, and frowned.

He usually closed his closet door before he left, a weird hang up he'd not left behind in childhood. He'd hated having the closet door open when he was a kid, the clothes and shoes, so innocuous during the day, became shadows of monsters lurking, waiting for him to sleep. He'd gotten into the habit of closing his closet door and never left it open. Granted, he'd been in an unsettled frame of mind that morning after realizing Ivan had taken off, but it was hard to believe that had been enough to disrupt a habit of years.

Besides, he was also sure he hadn't touched his club clothes in weeks. Not since the last time he'd gone with Neil and almost gotten mauled. Neil seemed to think he needed to get laid and had introduced him to someone he thought would fit the bill. But the guy had gotten rough. Parker had escaped before too much had happened, a little bruised and smarting under Neil's derision for not following through. Clubs were never really his thing—if he wasn't being stared at like a freak, he was being ignored—and he'd managed to avoid all of Neil's subsequent invitations. If it weren't for Neil's business meetings, he'd have had a harder time putting Neil off.

Parker pushed himself off the bed and rehung the shirts. Which brought his attention to the file box on the shelf right above. Alicia's comment hadn't left his mind in the intervening days. Should he have opened the cottage this year? It wasn't too late. The place was strongly tied to memories of his mother—good ones, not like some of the depressing ones that lingered here. It was the reason he'd redone most of the furnishing downstairs and had completely rearranged the master bedroom so it didn't remind him of times when his mother had been healthy and happy and living in this room.

Once his mother's health had started failing, they'd stopped going to the cottage. Would going back be better or worse since his mom had passed? Maybe inviting some of his new friends to go might help. He'd told Neil he'd never sell the place, but he also might never go back. Perhaps he'd been a bit hasty, although he could be forgiven. He'd made that pronouncement just weeks after his mother's death, after Neil had asked him about the cottage.

He was certain he had the name of a company that would go in and get cottages ready for the summer season somewhere in that file box. Couldn't hurt to give them a call, find out what would be involved and how much it would cost.

He tugged out the file box and took it over to the bed. He flipped open the top, but he didn't recognize—at first—the wrapped bundles of money. Panicked, he pulled a few out and tossed them on the bed.

With a forefinger, he reached out and touched one, gently, like it might bite. What the fuck was this? He had no frame of reference to even estimate how much money there was. The one bundle had a paper wrapper from the bank, but the other bundles were a mishmash of large bills.

Where the fuck had it come from? If Neil had known about it, he'd have asked if he could borrow it for his damned nightclub. There had to be more than enough here to bankroll the nightclub venture.

A screechy laugh from one of the neighborhood kids, loud enough to be heard through the closed window, startled him. Ivan's door opened and closed, and Parker scrambled to stuff the money back in the box. He replaced everything in the closet. The money could sit there for a few days until he figured out what to do. Calling the police to tell them he'd found money in his closet didn't sound exactly sane, but it might be his best course of action. In a few days. Once he'd had time to consider. Neil would accuse him of hiding his head in the sand, but he couldn't help it. Sometimes pretending something wasn't happening was the only way he could deal with it.

Taking a few deep breaths, he checked himself out in the mirror. Nope, he didn't look like a guy who'd just had several thousand dollars in cash materialize in his closet.

IVAN was poking through the fridge when he got downstairs. Maybe Parker could help with dinner, assuming he hadn't been completely blown off.

"Hey, Ivan, you're home early."

Ivan whirled, nearly whacking his head on the freezer door handle. "What, oh, hi, Parker. I didn't hear you."

Parker somehow managed to refrain from rolling his eyes. Way to state the obvious.

"How was work?" Probably he should just ask where Ivan had been, instead of giving him an easy out.

"Work? Oh, right, yes, work was fine. Busy."

Busy. That's why he was home before Parker. Uh-huh. And his obvious confusion over the question pained Parker. Did Ivan really think Parker completely incapable of recognizing a lie when he heard it? He didn't want to ask this, but Ivan's jumpiness made it necessary for his peace of mind.

"Um, can I ask you a question?"

The small movement Ivan gave might have been a shrug, Parker couldn't quite tell, but the attitude of exaggerated boredom hurt.

"It's... well... have you been in my room?" The second he blurted out the words, he wanted to grab them back. He sounded so accusatory, but he just had no explanation for the money and wanted to rule out Ivan.

No longer bored, Ivan straightened and glared. "That would be an invasion of your privacy. Besides, you made it quite clear I am not welcome in your room."

Was this all because he slept in his own room last night? Why would Ivan care? Still, if explaining his condition would put things right with the tentative friendship, and—dare he hope—relationship they were developing, Parker would admit it and hope it didn't put Ivan off.

"Look, about last night—"

Ivan waved a hand. "No. You don't need to say anything. It was a mistake. It shouldn't have happened, and it won't happen again. We're good."

Parker blinked, but before he could shake off his shock, Ivan had grabbed an apple and disappeared upstairs like the hounds of hell were nipping at his heels.

A mistake. He was always a fucking mistake. The best night of his life shouldn't have happened and wouldn't happen again. Parker hadn't even had a chance to ask if Ivan would be auditing more classes. Clearly that had been a ploy to get him to let his guard down. The only comfort—and it was so petty he could hardly call it comfort—was that Parker had had two orgasms to Ivan's one. Then again, maybe it was Parker's lack of experience that had turned Ivan off. Bad lay was a label he didn't much care for, especially with Ivan. At least Ivan had cut him off before he'd admitted to his sleep apnea, which would make his humiliation complete.

With shaking fingers, he drew out his cell phone and called Alicia.

"Um, hey, you interested in hanging out tonight?" The last thing Parker wanted was to spend the evening trying to avoid Ivan.

"Well, I was going to go to a movie with Chris and Thom. You're welcome to join us."

"Are you sure? What about Thom?" He didn't want to hurt the guy, but he sure wasn't going to leap into bed with him.

"He'll be fine. He's a nice guy, although he may try to get you to change your mind about Ivan."

It wouldn't work. It would take time to get over his silly infatuation with Ivan, and one night with a nice guy wasn't going to cut it. But it would keep him from thinking about Ivan and his hurtful behavior. At least, Parker hoped it would.

"What time?"

"Want to meet at Lettie's in an hour? We're grabbing a bite first."

"Sure."

Parker disconnected the call and drummed his fingers against the counter. An hour. If he left now, he could hang out at the bookstore or a coffee shop or something until it was time to meet his friends. He had no interest in waiting around here. He briefly considered leaving Ivan a note, but clearly the man didn't give a shit what Parker did, or when or who he did it with.

He tucked his phone back in his pocket, made sure he had his wallet, and left.

IVAN was a shit. He couldn't handle this. He'd regretted his outburst within minutes of having it and had gone back downstairs to apologize, but Parker was nowhere to be found. He'd tried waiting up, even if it meant seeing Parker and Neil come home together, even if it meant watching them go into Parker's room together. But his restless, nightmare-filled sleep had only left him more and more tired each day, and he fell asleep before Parker had gotten home. For a change, though, his dreams had been filled with a variety of erotic movies starring him and Parker.

He'd greeted the morning no more rested than usual, but instead of being drenched in a cold sweat, his pajamas had been sticky with cum. After cleaning up, he wandered downstairs with bleary, gritty eyes to discover Parker had already left. Or perhaps he'd never come home. And that thought had ached like a tooth with an abscess all day. He'd tried not to think about it but the ache didn't go away.

Today had been hard enough without so many flavors of Parker-induced guilt coating him. He'd had to endure another damned SIU interview, had to lie his way through yet another useless therapy session, and then, on his circuitous route home, he'd been trapped on a bus when an accident snarled traffic. Finally, when he'd been about ready to punch the guy who kept bumping into him as the heat and body odor increased with every minute, Ivan pushed his way out of the bus. He hadn't trusted his mood with commuters who couldn't keep their fucking bags to themselves, so he'd walked again. The intermittent clouds gave a bit of break in the heat.

When he realized his feet had taken him to the university campus, and he was mentally following a map to get him to Parker's Friday afternoon class, he growled and forced himself to walk past the stadium, then the Bata Shoe Museum, which his sisters loved, and went into the first pub he found.

The cool, dark interior soothed his jangled nerves, and a beer or two could only help. Once he was calm, once he'd given Parker enough time to get home, Ivan would follow and apologize. Parker had cheated, and Ivan could hardly blame him for not wanting to repeat the mistake. Being the other man was a position Ivan had never thought he'd ever fill, but when it came to Parker, he was afraid he wouldn't be able to say no if Parker crooked his finger.

PARKER sat on the couch, arms crossed, on the fourth episode of a *Doctor Who* marathon. Normally, he could lose himself for hours in his favorite sci-fi shows, but instead, he kept obsessively checking the time. He'd been hoping to come home to… a home. Since Ivan had made him dinner the first time, coming home to Ivan had felt right. Having sex had changed everything, and he still wasn't sure if the problem was him or if Ivan was nothing more than a closeted jerk. He'd stayed late after class, loitering in a coffee shop, hoping he'd find Ivan preparing dinner when he walked in the door, but the house had been empty. Completely empty. If they couldn't get past this, how could they continue to live in the same place? Parker would be willing to pretend they'd never had sex if he could get his new friend back. He missed Ivan.

Paranoid, he'd even checked Ivan's room when he got home, to make sure his stuff was still there. That he hadn't moved out without a word. Logic told him that moving out would be an extreme reaction, but then, he'd never wanted someone to stay so much.

As the shadows lengthened and time marched on, Parker had to concede that Ivan might not be coming home. Hell, he might even have a date. Would Ivan date a guy, or was he truly in the closet far enough that he'd try to get involved with another woman? Parker wrapped his arms around his stomach and rocked to stave off the sudden stab of pain the thought caused.

He should have said yes to Thom. Thom had gotten him alone at the movie last night—which had actually felt alarmingly like a double date—and asked him out for tonight. Parker had actually had to use the phrase "it's complicated" for the first time in his life. When had his sex life ever been complicated? Never. Even now, alone in this empty house, perhaps it wasn't so complicated after all. Ivan wasn't here. Ivan didn't want him, not for anything other than getting his rocks off.

Thom had been very sweet about the rejection, and if only Alicia or Chris had pointed out Thom earlier, maybe he'd have been involved in a relationship. Maybe he wouldn't have advertised for a roommate, and he'd never have met Ivan.

His heart twisted. Never knowing Ivan was… unthinkable. Somehow, his emotions had gotten over-involved with Ivan, and now he was facing his own rejection. Maybe he should reconsider. Call Thom and see if he was still available. With Thom, perhaps he could uncomplicate his sex life. Put Ivan back in roommate status where he belonged instead of considering him potential boyfriend material.

One day, he'd be able to picture living here with someone other than Ivan, even if he hadn't quite been able to picture sleeping next to Ivan while wearing his wretched fighter pilot mask.

The front door opened with a bang, and Parker sprang to his feet, mood lightening in an instant.

"Ivan?"

"Oh, fuck, no." Neil bustled into the kitchen, laden with grocery bags. "How could you possibly mistake me for that old fart?"

Parker ignored the clearly rhetorical question. "What are you doing here?"

Neil rolled his eyes. "Nice to see you too."

"What's all this?" Parker stood back while Neil unloaded bag after bag of snacks, specialty beer, and top-shelf liquor.

"We're having people over tonight. A party."

Closing his eyes, Parker counted to ten. Then twenty. "A party? Why here?"

"I want to make a good impression. They're possible investors in the business, and my place is too small."

A real friend wouldn't point out that Neil could afford a better apartment if he didn't spend so much money on clothes, shoes, and weed, so he remained silent.

"I don't want to have anyone over."

"For God's sake, Parker. You're even more of a boring old fart than your roommate."

Boring old fart? None of those words described Ivan. "That's a little excessive."

"Oh whatever, Parker. You're going to dry up into one of those 'get off my lawn' geezers before you're even twenty-five. You need to get laid, and I need investors. There are potentials for both coming in...." Neil twisted his wrist to check the time on yet another expensive toy. "Less than thirty minutes. So help me get this place ready, okay?"

Parker didn't move. He'd never really said no to Neil before. Grateful to Neil for his friendship, Parker usually let Neil have his way. As much as he didn't feel up to socializing, maybe it wouldn't hurt to meet some of the guys Neil thought he might hit it off with. After all, he wasn't doing so well in selecting his own sexual partners. And he really didn't have anything else to do but sulk in front of the television. Which was all kinds of pathetic.

"Fine. Give me the chips." He dumped them into bowls and took them out to the living room. Neil followed him with dishes of nuts.

"And turn off that geekazoid shit." Neil didn't wait for Parker to obey, but picked up the remote and changed it to one of the cable music stations. Not the same one Ivan liked, and Parker almost pinched himself for thinking about Ivan again. "Only fat fucks like that futuristic shit, and you can do better than that."

Parker bit his lip against the reply he'd been tempted to make. Not that long ago, Parker had been one of the fat fucks Neil spoke of so contemptuously, but that had nothing to do with tastes in entertainment, no matter how Neil liked to generalize. Tonight he'd see who Neil invited for him, and tomorrow he could call Thom and set up a date.

ONE beer had given way to five. Or six? Maybe seven, along with a plate of nachos to soak up the alcohol. Ivan usually ate healthy low-fat food, but the greasy, cheese-covered chips had been perfect. Maybe it was his equivalent of drowning his sorrows with ice cream. By the time night fell, he'd watched an entire baseball game. Although he couldn't remember the team or score if his life depended on it, the server knew his name, and he was pleasantly buzzed. Able to face Parker—and Neil, if he had to.

He walked back to Parker's place, music from a nearby party hitting his ears. Seemed early for that kind of ruckus. His watch, though, said otherwise. Shit, it was almost eleven. Not too late for a party, but he'd definitely spent longer in that pub than he'd realized.

When he turned up the walkway, it took him a few moments to realize the party was coming from Parker's house. What the hell? Didn't the roommate at least deserve a warning? Or an invite? Surely that was the polite thing to do. A flash of white fabric in the narrow pathway between Parker's house and the neighbor's gave him a reprieve from entering.

With some remnants of stealth, he crept around the side of the house. The sight that greeted his eyes held him in place for a moment. Neil was on his knees in the dirt, sucking a dick which did not belong to Parker. Elation flooded him, that maybe Parker could be convinced to dump Neil, but quick on its heels was anger that Neil would cheat on Parker. Then confusion, because Parker had cheated too. God, he was so fucking confused, and the alcohol swimming in his brain wasn't helping. Whipping out his phone, he snapped a picture. Just in case Parker needed proof, although just having the picture was pathetic and petty.

He backed away as silently as he could and bounded into the house. He pushed past several men accompanied by scantily clad women with full makeup and four-inch heels. None of these people bore any resemblance to what he imagined Parker's friends to look like, but what did he know? Maybe they were clients.

That thought sobered him up a little, and he pushed into the living room, searching. He finally found Parker, pressed up against the wall by a dark-haired man about the same height as Parker, but more muscular. They were kissing, and Parker was writhing. Anger flooded his mind, and he wrenched the guy away from Parker.

"What the fuck are you doing?" Ivan wasn't sure which of them he was talking to, but the big guy answered.

"I saw him first."

"So what?"

"So you can just move along before I bust your face open."

Whatever. Just because this guy had won a couple of bar brawls, he fancied himself a fighter. But his stance, intimidating to a novice, was all wrong.

"Just because you saw him first doesn't mean jack shit, asshole."

A vein ticked in the guy's forehead, and he cracked his knuckles. Which wrestling show had he picked that up from?

"What did you call me?"

"Like I'm the first person to call you that. Drama queen."

He took his eyes off the guy for a second to stare at Parker, which is when the guy chose to make his move. Ivan took advantage of his momentum, blocking his punch and slamming him into the wall. The guy dropped to the floor, moaning and clutching his head.

Ivan ignored him. The loser wasn't going to be any more trouble, and he didn't give a shit that the whole party had paused to stare at their altercation. None of them mattered. Only Parker mattered, who'd been kissing this asshole while his *boyfriend* had been blowing some other dude outside. "Who the hell is that, and what the hell is going on here?"

Parker stared down at the big guy for a moment before he stepped over him, approaching Ivan. "I think he said his name was Bran? Brad? Not sure."

Not sure. He'd been kissing some guy, and he didn't even know his name. The anger bloomed brighter, and he curled his hands into fists. With the alcohol numbing him, he barely felt the knuckles he'd cracked earlier. Punching anyone, even Brad, wasn't going to make anything better. Parker reached out to touch his arm, and Ivan stepped back. He couldn't let Parker touch him. He couldn't.

"Neil invited some people over for a party."

"Oh, really? And does he know what you were getting up to with Brad?" Ivan shook his head. He couldn't get into this at the moment, not while staring at Parker's kiss-swollen lips. "Never mind. But next time, I expect to be informed about any prospective party. I live here too."

Neil sidled up beside Parker and wrapped an arm around Parker's waist. How had Ivan missed him entering the room? "It's Parker's house, he can do whatever he wants. He sure as fuck doesn't need your permission, Ivan."

They stood beside each other, both of their lips swollen, Parker's from kissing and Neil's from his recent sojourn with another guy's dick. Ivan shook from the effort of not letting his fists fly. When Neil smirked at him and kissed Parker's cheek with those lips that had minutes ago been wrapped around a stranger's dick, Ivan's hand flew to his side.

Clarity wiped away his anger in seconds as he realized how close he'd been to throttling Neil. Parker had his emotions all twisted around, and he was out of fucking control. If he'd had his service weapon on him, Neil would have a bullet hole in him, and that scared the mad right out of him.

He stared at the two young men. As much as he wanted to leave the house, he couldn't be seen to retreat that far. He nodded sharply at them and went upstairs.

Behind him, Neil spoke. "Brad, you okay? That's just Parker's weird roommate. Old guys can be such a fucking drag."

The weird roommate. Also unstable, he'd proven that without a doubt. This investigation was full of win.

PARKER scrubbed at his lips with the sleeve of his shirt and tried not to grimace while Neil helped Brad off the floor. Brad was like every other guy Neil had introduced him to. Grabby, arrogant, and assuming he'd bend over for anyone who claimed they had a big dick. Unlike most of the others, Brad was into kissing, but unlike his recent experience with Ivan, kissing Brad was… not good. Besides the slobbery kissing, the guy stank. What was it about guys with a bit of cash to flash? Never thought they had to be considerate or even fucking clean.

Staring at the stairs where Ivan had escaped, it took Neil elbowing him in the ribs to get his attention.

"What?"

Neil glared at him. "Really? You like the closeted old fart, don't you?"

Parker shrugged. He and Neil had never had the same taste in guys, for which Parker had taken a lot of shit. Even with the way they'd left things last, and after Ivan's strangely violent outburst, he liked Ivan a hell of a lot more than Brad. He couldn't forget those nights eating dinner together, watching movies. Hanging out together or with friends. Smoking-hot sex. That was the kind of relationship Parker wanted. The relationship he'd envisioned having with Ivan.

"Try not to let anything get broken, okay? I'm going to bed."

"To bed? Not alone, I'm guessing."

The scathing, contemptuous look Ivan had directed Parker's way didn't bode well, but he wanted to clear the air between them, if he could.

Without a backward glance, Parker ascended the stairs. Aside from Neil, he hadn't known a single person at the party, and he didn't give a rat's ass if any of them thought he was rude.

On the second floor, Parker stood between the two closed doors. The house was well built—the music, loud downstairs, was sufficiently muted upstairs that neither he nor Ivan should have trouble sleeping. He should just go to bed, but he wasn't tired, and the tension between him and Ivan was so shitty, especially compared to the way they'd meshed so well together. Story of his life, but he didn't want Ivan to disappear like other prospective boyfriends had. Music or not, if he didn't clear the air with Ivan, he wouldn't be able to sleep for worrying about it. And if he was awake and worrying, he'd have to add the alarming stack of cash that had materialized amongst his papers. Which was incentive enough to take a few more steps toward Ivan's closed door.

Parker licked suddenly dry lips, sucked in a deep breath, and knocked. And waited. He let his breath out. Waited some more. Had he knocked hard enough? Had Ivan heard him? Surely he hadn't managed to fall asleep in the ten minutes it took him to come up.

He glanced around, as though someone might see him being a complete dork, then pressed his ear against the door. Silence, not even the undertone of voices on television, reached his ears.

He raised his hand to knock again, but jumped back when Ivan yelled "What?"

"Can I come in?"

The muted grumble might not have been an affirmative answer, but Parker chose to take it as such and turned the knob.

Ivan sat on the bed, a towel wrapped around his hand, first aid tape on the nightstand.

"I didn't realize you'd hurt yourself." Although now that he was paying proper attention, he remembered a flash of white on Ivan's hand during his scrap with Brad.

"I, uh, did it earlier, but I made it worse." Ivan's gaze skittered over the room, landing everywhere but on Parker.

Parker sat down beside him and lifted Ivan's hand into his lap. He peeled away the cool, damp towel, revealing the curling tape of a previous wrap job. With care, he pulled away the tape. The bruising was bad, but there were only a few scabs.

"How'd you manage this?" Punching people wasn't something insurance agents did in the course of the day. Not for the first time, he wondered just how well Ivan's job was going. Maybe they could work something out with the rent to ease the financial burden.

"I, uh, owe you a repair for the wall in the kitchen."

Parker squeezed Ivan's hand in surprise and he gasped in pain. "Oh, sorry."

Ivan had punched the wall? When? Why?

"Don't you have a party to attend?" Surly Ivan had suddenly turned into petulant Ivan.

Parker quickly finished the wrap job. "It was Neil's party. I didn't know anyone. I'd rather stay up here with you." There. He'd put himself out there for a change, his heart fluttering.

"You knew Brad. Sort of."

Parker frowned and tried to catch Ivan's eye, but failed. Clearly, Ivan didn't care about what he'd said. "Neil's forever trying to set me up with his friends. Brad was just a bit pushier than most."

Ivan sat up straight, then bounded off the bed and towered over Parker. "Neil tries to set you up? For God's sake, Parker. Why do you put up with that? And he's cheating on you too. You deserve so much better than that."

He didn't even know what to say. Ivan was angry at him and on his behalf, all at the same time? For a full minute, Parker stared at Ivan, trying to make those words make sense.

"Neil's not cheating on me. We're just friends."

Ivan froze. "He's not your boyfriend?"

A few tendrils of anger wove through his brain. Clearly Ivan thought he was a cheater too. "I know not everyone believes the same, but I wouldn't cheat." And he was a little hurt Ivan would think that of him.

Ivan reached a hand out to touch his cheek. "I'm sorry."

"For?" He'd had enough confusion and he didn't want any more crossed wires.

"I.... My...." Ivan's face blanched, and he shook his head as though trying to clear his thoughts. "Sorry. I've been burned before by someone cheating on me."

Couldn't have been his wife, or she wouldn't have been able to take him for everything. "Have you... did you cheat on someone when we...." It wasn't entirely impossible that Ivan was already seeing someone else. Or what if he'd been cheating on his wife with a man he cared about?

"No. I would never. I mean...." Ivan sighed and sat down next to him. "I wanted you ever since I met you. I started liking you. I hated myself for giving in the other night, because I thought you were taken."

The brittle edge of tension Parker had carried smashed to pieces and disappeared. "Which is why you said it was a mistake and would never happen again."

Which meant, just maybe, he could have Ivan. For his own. Roommate turned boyfriend—a bit cliché, and perhaps a little too soon, but he wouldn't object. Not with Ivan. Parker already cared, so much.

"Yeah. I didn't want that, for either of us, but I couldn't resist."

This time when Ivan cupped his cheek, Parker turned into the caress. Ivan trailed fingers along his jaw, the faint scrape a little embarrassing as he'd been in such a hurry to leave that morning he'd forgotten to shave.

"Couldn't resist?" Other guys had said that before, but he'd never believed them. Always sounded like a cheesy line, but Ivan was so damned sincere. Ivan's lips curled up in a tiny, knowing smile, and he trailed his fingers down Parker's neck to dip under the edge of his shirt. The first stroke over his collarbone had Parker gasping, quickly followed by an enthusiastic response in his groin.

Within seconds, they were naked, Ivan's comfortingly warm weight pressing him into the mattress. Ivan smiled down at him before he swooped down, lips moving over Parker's.

Ivan's arousal rubbed against his, and Parker's mouth opened on a groan. Ivan's tongue delved deep, and Parker sucked on it.

They writhed together, Parker's passion feeding off Ivan's, growing and filling the room. The last time hadn't been a fluke. This was what sex was supposed to be like; this was what he'd been missing with his past boyfriends and one-night stands. Ivan was so fucking hot, but that wasn't it. Ivan was a good guy, and he treated Parker so well. Made him sexier than anyone he'd ever met.

Ivan slid his lips down, his tongue darting out, tasting Parker's neck. He shifted, trapping Parker's erection against those firm abs. Ivan lifted his head, a wicked, devilish smile curving those skillful lips. Before he could ask what Ivan was up to, Ivan dropped his head and licked Parker's collarbone.

"Ivan, fuck." Parker ground his hips up, his cock sliding against Ivan's belly, the fuzz creating a delicate scrape along the sensitive flesh.

Those lips moved down, and without hesitation, Ivan sucked down Parker's dick. Twisting the sheets in his fists, Parker moaned and spread his legs. It had been so long since he'd been fucked by anything other than toys, but if Ivan kept up this delicious torture, he'd be done. And he wanted—needed—to prove himself worthy of Ivan's attention.

"Stop, please."

Golden brows creased as Ivan lifted his head. The air chilled Parker's wet, overheated skin.

"What's wrong?"

Parker squirmed. "Nothing. But I'm close, and…." Could he say it? Could he come out and say it? But he didn't have to. Ivan's eyes darkened, and his hips bucked against the bed. They were definitely on the same wavelength.

Light strokes along Parker's length kept his desire high while Ivan stretched for the nightstand. He dropped lube and condoms beside Parker, the plastic bottle cold against his skin.

Ivan's tongue swiped away the clear precum welling in Parker's slit while he opened the foil packet and slid the condom on himself. He grabbed the bottle of lube and flicked the top open.

"How often do you use that dildo in your drawer?"

Lust had heated Parker's skin, but he still managed an additional embarrassed flush. The toy was surprisingly close to Ivan's proportions. "Often enough."

Ivan's eyes crossed briefly, and he bucked his hips again, clearly as eager to fuck him as Parker was to get fucked.

"Hurry, please." He wanted Ivan so badly he was about ready to crawl out of his skin.

With a throaty growl, Ivan slithered up to align their bodies. One hand slicked Parker, then slathered more lube over the condom. Settling between Parker's legs, Ivan guided his cock to Parker's hole, the tip exerting only the slightest pressure against his body. This time, Ivan's smile was lustful, yes, but also so sweet, so full of tenderness.

"Just relax," Ivan whispered before he leaned down and captured Parker's lips. His cock slid inside while Ivan's tongue fucked into his mouth.

The fluid thrusts of Ivan's hips were driving Parker out of his mind. He did his best to move with Ivan, but between the sensual kisses and the perfect rhythmic pressure on his prostate he was losing control.

Ivan pulled back, breaking the kiss. The new position changed the angle of Ivan's thrusts, forcing guttural groans from deep within Parker's chest.

"So fucking hot." Ivan smiled down at him and wrapped a hand around Parker's erection.

Parker arched his back, legs stiffening for a moment before he exploded, shouting Ivan's name. His cock jerked and spit, coating Ivan's hand. Seconds later, Ivan squeezed his eyes shut and shuddered between his legs, finding his own release.

Parker lay limp and sated while Ivan dealt with the condom and gently cleaned him up. He'd never had better sex, but it was the sweet kiss and whispered words of gratitude that gave him hope for a future with Ivan.

CHAPTER
Nine

IVAN was so fucked, and not in the good way.

He tucked Parker closer to him, enjoying the heat of Parker's skin against his own, and flipped on the tiny television on his dresser. He'd had sex with a suspect, again. For several hours, he'd forgotten he wasn't Ivan Baker, insurance salesman, having drama with a potential boyfriend. He'd forgotten the main reason why having sex was a mistake, and it wasn't the cheating. When Parker told him he was single, it was like thick, scudding clouds had suddenly disappeared, leaving sunshine and rainbows everywhere. He wanted Parker to be his more than anything, but the evidence of some serious drug-related crimes was mounting, and it wouldn't be long before he'd have to go to Martelli with it.

But if he was going to save Parker, he needed to get Parker to trust him, and that meant not pushing him away. Meant spending as much time with him as he could. A little voice inside his head—far away and faint, sounding a lot like Trish—said he was rationalizing to get what he wanted, but he shushed her. This undercover op had been pure fucking hell, and maybe Parker was his compensation.

He lightly stroked Parker's bare skin as Parker's breath evened out and his body relaxed into that state just before sleep. This time, maybe Parker's presence would chase away the nightmares. If nothing else, he'd be able to wake up and see Parker was fine, alive, and breathing.

Too soon for him to try and sleep, he contented himself with half listening to the TV while he stared down at Parker, trying to memorize this moment for when he had to return to his apartment alone.

Parker's breathing quickly edged into snoring, which made Ivan smile. For such a slender, sweet guy, he had one hell of snore on him. Good thing Ivan could sleep through just about anything, although his recent sleep patterns had put a lie to that. Still, he had a good feeling about tonight. One decent night's sleep and he'd be back to normal. He hoped.

When his eyelids got heavy, he turned off the television and settled back into his pillow, arms firmly wrapped around the body that fit his perfectly.

Right before he drifted off, Parker's snores stopped abruptly, almost louder because of their absence. Seconds later, he stiffened and sat upright.

The sudden movement triggered Ivan's adrenaline, and he jumped out of bed. Flicking on the light allowed him to assess the room for threats while locating possible weapons in lieu of his gun.

"What? What's wrong?" Nothing appeared out of the ordinary—even the throbbing beat from the stereo downstairs hadn't changed much.

"I… I can't sleep here. I have to go back to my room."

Ivan gritted his teeth, biting back the sarcastic reply threatening to pop out. Not sleeping together would prevent them from getting too attached, but shit. He'd been more comfortable than he could remember being in a long fucking time.

Parker got out of bed with the same shameful look on his face, a blush heating his cheeks, and he refused to meet Ivan's eyes as he gathered up his clothes. This time, though, Ivan was able to engage some logic circuits. Last time, he'd seen this reaction as the guilty response to cheating on his boyfriend, but if that wasn't the case, what was going on?

He took a deep breath and forced himself to speak calmly. "Why can't you sleep here?"

"I just can't." The blush on Parker's face got brighter, smoothing away the sharp edges of Ivan's anger.

"Hey. You can tell me." Ivan wrapped his arms around Parker, heedless of the clothes he clutched to his chest. He stared into Parker's face, waiting for Parker to look at him.

When Parker finally lifted his eyes, the uncertainty in them made Ivan squeeze him just a little tighter. He might not be able to protect Parker from everything, but from this? Whatever reason Parker had for not wanting to sleep here, Ivan was sure he could protect him.

"What is it?" Ivan's voice dropped to a low, coaxing register.

Parker pushed out of Ivan's arms and glared at him. "Fine. If you want to know so bad, come on."

Ivan snatched up a pair of briefs and slipped them on before following Parker to his room. Between their rooms, music swelled; the party was still going.

Once inside, Ivan closed the door and locked it while Parker tossed his clothes over a chair and walked to his nightstand.

Ivan almost laughed. Surely it wasn't something to do with the limited number of sex toys, was it?

Parker pulled out the fighter pilot mask and black tubing, and Ivan's urge to laugh disappeared. Shit. That kinky sex toy? No, that wouldn't explain... no.

"I don't understand."

"It's a CPAP machine, and it keeps me breathing while I'm asleep."

"To keep you breathing?" Ivan didn't understand why Parker sounded so angry when the thought of Parker needing something to keep him breathing scared the crap out of him.

Parker lifted a shoulder. "Okay, fine. Maybe it's not quite as dramatic as that." He sank down on the bed, shoulders curled in defeat.

"Explain, please."

"I have a condition called sleep apnea. It makes me snore, and I'll stop breathing for a few seconds, several times a night. If I don't use it when I sleep, I'll wake up with migraines, and it fucks up my blood pressure."

"But you wouldn't like, stop breathing altogether, right?"

Parker twined the tubing around his fist. "Probably not. Hasn't yet, anyway."

"So, you need this. What's the problem?"

Squinting at him as though he were from another planet, Parker just waited. He waited long enough for Ivan to finally figure it out. Was he old before his time? This didn't seem so earth-shattering, but then, things were always more dramatic and angst-inducing when you were young. Still, Parker probably never had one-night stands, not here at least.

But he was too fucking exhausted to spend too much time counseling Parker, and he didn't want to lose the remnants of his post-orgasmic lassitude talking this out.

"Well, strap it on and let's get some sleep." Sleep. He might actually sleep tonight if he got to hold Parker through the night.

"I can't!"

"Why the fuck not?" Ivan stripped off his briefs and climbed into the bed on the other side of Parker.

"Neil would never stay the night because it's too loud."

Ivan sat up, muscles tense like he was ready to fight. "I thought you weren't together."

Parker's nostrils flared. "We're not. Jeez. But he's been my best friend since we were kids. Staying the night and not having sex is possible, you know."

Relaxing back into the pillows—now that he didn't have to go punch Neil—he waved at the machine. "And staying the night, no matter what your medical condition, is also possible."

Before he could determine if the suspicious glint in Parker's eyes was anything more than a trick of the light, Parker directed his gaze downward at the mask in his hands. With trembling fingers Parker performed actions which were clearly second nature.

"Come on." Ivan patted the bed, and Parker climbed in beside him. "Let's get some sleep, Darth."

Parker's eyes widened over the mask, and he reached a hand up to pull the mask down.

"Calm down. I'm joking." He wrapped an arm around Parker's waist and pulled him close. The stiff, unyielding muscles felt somewhat like trying to cuddle a surfboard, but he persevered. He pressed his nose to the side of Parker's neck and gave him a tiny kiss. All in a rush, Parker's muscles loosened, and the man in Ivan's arms became pliant. Ivan let himself relax, breathing in the sweaty musk that he'd love to fall asleep next to for the rest of his life.

PARKER danced around the kitchen, the stereo... not blasting, because Ivan was still asleep, but playing at a volume that let him sing along. Sleeping next to Ivan had been better than he'd imagined, because every time he'd imagined it, he hadn't been wearing his CPAP. Somehow, he'd lucked into meeting a great guy who was great in bed and didn't care that Parker wasn't experienced, and who didn't care about his condition.

Their sleep hadn't been completely uninterrupted. Ivan had awoken a couple of times during the night with what appeared to be some sort of nightmare, but as soon as he looked at Parker and patted him a bit, he fell back asleep.

Pulling out bowls and pancake mix, Parker began to sing along with the song. It was a bit of an oldie, but it made him think of Ivan—everything did, lately—and he knew the words. He might not be much of a cook, but pancakes he could do, and Ivan deserved a treat. Maybe they could go to the market today as Ivan had suggested earlier. Boyfriend things, although he didn't want to rush labeling their relationship. After all, Ivan had just gotten out of a marriage. Still, he couldn't wait to tell Neil that he was right. And he was so happy now, he might not even bitch Neil out for the insane fucking mess he'd left from the party. Today, nothing could ruin his good mood.

Warm arms wrapped around him from behind. Sighing, he leaned back against Ivan's chest. This was how it was supposed to be. This was what he'd been missing and wanting.

"Morning." Ivan's voice was gravelly with sleep, and the press of lips against his neck felt like home. As long as he didn't rush things, waited for Ivan to be ready for another relationship, things would be great. "What are you making?"

"Pancakes."

"Oh, yeah? I should make you sleep with me every night. "

Parker closed his eyes and manfully held back a plea for Ivan to do just that. Ivan hadn't cared about his condition, hadn't flinched or freaked out or anything, and, if this morning was any indicator, hadn't lost any of his attraction for Parker.

"Ready to eat?" That was a safe thing to say.

"Sure."

Parker dished out the pancakes that he'd made. Probably not enough to satisfy them both, but he could make more later.

Sitting across from him at the table, Parker smiled shyly at Ivan. He'd never had breakfast with a guy after spending the night together, but it was pretty fucking awesome. Was it too soon to suggest they sleep in the same room every night? Ivan might have been joking about that. They hadn't discussed anything; Ivan might not want to be exclusive. But he was so thankful he hadn't called Thom last night. Somehow, even if he'd had sex with Thom, he knew he wouldn't have woken up as happy as he did this morning. He didn't fit with Thom like he did with Ivan.

"Neil's guests left quite a mess." Ivan spoke between bites.

"Yeah, I know. I'll clean it up after breakfast. Then maybe we could go to the St. Lawrence market or something?" He waited, barely breathing. What if now that they'd slept together, Ivan didn't want to do dating stuff together? He didn't really even know if Ivan was out. Even if they did go on a "date," he'd have to be careful about how he interacted with Ivan in public.

"Why do you let him do that? He's taking advantage of you, you know."

Parker grimaced. No matter what other people thought, he wasn't all that naïve. "When we moved in here after my grandmother died, I started a new school where I didn't have any friends. No one wanted to be friends with the new kid, especially not...." He swallowed heavily. Ivan had been more accepting than he'd expected about his sleep apnea, but Parker had experienced firsthand, and multiple times, the bias gay men had against overweight guys. He'd lost most of the excess weight he'd been carrying, but he could easily gain some of it back, and he sure wasn't as toned as Ivan was.

One brow lifted while Ivan's bright blue eyes stared at him. "Especially not...." Ivan prompted.

"Especially not the new fat kid." Parker whispered the last two words, but Ivan heard him, because his eyes softened in an expression Parker hoped wasn't pity.

"Is that why there aren't any pictures of you around here? You should put up some of you and your mom." Ivan coughed like he'd swallowed wrong, then cleared his throat. "I mean, you must have some, right?"

Parker nodded.

"I bet you were a cute kid." There was no doubt in Ivan's voice, and Parker found himself able to smile again. "So, you're grateful he was nice to you? That's why you let Neil walk all over you?"

"Yep. He's been my friend throughout everything. Helped me when my mom died. I know he can be a little selfish, but he's there for me. He's a constant in my life. Besides, he's also my first."

Ivan's eyes rounded. "Your first what?"

Did he really have to spell it out? He shouldn't have mentioned it in the first place. Talking about sex, especially when it involved his own sex life, was not something he was comfortable with. "You know. My first... guy."

Somehow, he wasn't expecting the black scowl.

"Now I hate him even more."

What? "Why? Oh." The shoe dropped, and Parker couldn't stop the smile. Suddenly, a lot of Ivan's actions made a lot more sense. He'd never had anyone be jealous over him before, and he found he liked it. A lot.

"Yeah, 'oh'." Ivan smiled back at him. "You're loving that, aren't you? Any other ex-boyfriends I need to know about? Other secrets?"

Parker didn't understand why Ivan's smile morphed into an almost frightened expression, but Ivan didn't have anything to worry about.

"No ex-boyfriends. At least, none that I still talk to. But you remember Thom from school? He wanted to ask me out."

"Of course he did. He couldn't keep his eyes off your ass."

Unbelievable. Everyone knew except him. He was used to people staring, but usually because he was the fat kid. Unless someone came right out and said it, he'd never known when someone wanted him, and it just hadn't happened all that often. That he knew about.

"Usually guys are interested in Neil. I guess I'm just used to not getting any attention."

"Neil? You're joking, right?"

"No." Parker wasn't sure why Ivan was so incensed, but he did like the implication that Ivan thought he was more attractive than Neil.

"And I hate Thom, too, by the way, although... wait... you haven't slept with him, have you?"

"No."

"Okay, then, I hate him slightly less than Neil."

The sound that escaped Parker's lips was almost a giggle. Yes, he could get used to this.

"You did say secrets, though." Neil wouldn't be able to help him figure out the right course of action, and he didn't know who else to ask. He trusted Ivan not to steer him wrong.

"Um, yes, I did. Did you have something else?"

"Remember when I asked if you'd been in my room?"

Ivan paled slightly and looked a lot less happy than when Parker admitted to having sex with Neil. "Yes."

"I'm really sorry if it sounded like I didn't trust you. I do. I trust you." He did too. In fact, he trusted Ivan more than Neil for many things; one of them was to not make fun of him.

"Okay, that's good." Ivan's mouth worked a bit as though he wanted to say more, but in the end he closed his mouth and shoved his plate away, even though there were still a few pieces of pancake soaking in syrup.

"Here's the thing. I think someone was in my room." Parker reached out and squeezed Ivan's hand. "I don't think it was you. You had no reason to do this, but I found money in my closet. A lot of it."

Ivan frowned. "Money?"

"Yeah. Bundles of it, like you see in the movies, just sitting in my file box. I don't usually spend a lot of time filing." Parker directed a sheepish look toward the pile of mail in a basket in the corner. "I don't know how it got there, and I don't know what to do about it."

"You don't know how it got there."

What was up with Ivan? Parroting back his words wasn't much assistance.

"Weird, right? I have no idea what to do. Do I call the cops? Although they'd probably just laugh at me."

"How much money?" Ivan sounded like he was being strangled.

"I don't know. I just put it back where I found it. A couple thousand or so."

Ivan shoved back from the table and started to pace, rubbing a hand over his face. A cold tremble shook Parker's belly. He wasn't sure he'd ever seen Ivan so distressed, and it was freaking him out just a bit.

When Ivan halted and turned to face him, the niggle of fear turned into a full-blown clench of nausea. The scent of maple became sickening. "What's wrong? It's not your money, is it?"

"Can we talk in the living room?"

Those words never preceded anything good. Parker might not have much experience on the relationship front, but he knew enough to know that.

"Sure." With leaden feet, he followed Ivan. He sat on his customary spot on the couch, but Ivan surprised him by sitting down next to him.

"Look, I...." Ivan stared up at the ceiling, and Parker wanted to tell him just to spit it the fuck out, but he didn't want to upset Ivan any more.

"Shit, Parker, I don't... I've never had to...." Ivan's knee began moving rapidly up and down. Parker choked back a nervous giggle, because he remembered in high school someone telling him that sort of nervous twitch was the result of sexual repression. After last night, Ivan couldn't be suffering from that. Stupid thing to think about, but he wanted to focus on anything besides Ivan's agitation. Because those words sounded like breakup words. He wasn't sure how the magic pile of money had gotten them here.

No. That was his insecurity talking. If this had something to do with the fantastic sex they'd had, then Ivan was the freak here, not him.

"I'm an undercover cop."

Parker blinked. Not an insurance salesman. "Okay. I've watched cop shows before. I get that you probably don't tell everyone that." He refused to be hurt that Ivan hadn't trusted him with this information. After all, they had only known each other well under a month.

A loud pop filled the room as Ivan cracked the knuckles on his unwrapped hand. "I'm supposed to be investigating you."

"Me?" Parker didn't have anything else to say. He stood and did some pacing of his own. "Why me?"

"Drug dealing. Maybe trafficking. You're a suspected associate of Viktor Razhin, head of the Russian mafia."

"Drug dealing? Trafficking?" Parker's voice climbed into soprano registers and cracked, but he had zero control over that.

"I'm not a drug dealer! And I don't know anybody named Viktor Razhin, or even any criminals."

His eyes landed on a couple of books on the shelf, and he had to curl his hands into fists to stop himself from throwing them at Ivan. He'd never been a violent person, but this... this hurt worse than almost anything. Ivan thought he was a drug dealer.

"I know you're not. You can't be." Ivan turned pleading blue eyes on him, and he wanted desperately to believe everything wasn't a lie.

The noose around his heart loosened slightly, until a thought struck him. "But you didn't know until I asked you about that money. Because if I was a drug dealer, I'd know what that money was for."

There was no mistaking the guilty look on Ivan's face. The noose squeezed tight like a boa throttling its dinner, and Parker swallowed heavily to keep his breakfast down.

"Hey, I'm sorry. I don't know if this will help, but after I met you, I didn't want to believe what my boss told me about you."

"You had sex with me thinking I was a drug dealer." And not just sex. He'd accepted Parker, made him think about the future, had been tender with him. And it was all fake. A manufactured mirage. But why? To get him to incriminate himself? His eyes burned, and he turned away from Ivan. He'd taken so much from Parker. He didn't get to see how he'd gutted Parker with this revelation.

The couch creaked, and a fraction of a second later, Ivan's body heat radiated against his back. He wanted to lean back, get the comfort Ivan offered, but he couldn't.

"The sex wasn't part of the job. I swear. I couldn't resist you." Ivan's hand landed on his shoulder, and he twisted away.

Words he'd have loved to hear just an hour before, words no one had spoken to him with the depth of feeling Ivan infused, and words he could no longer take at face value because Ivan was a lying shit who was a great fucking actor.

"Well, you should have." Parker was proud his voice hadn't wobbled a bit. He bit the inside of his cheek hard to force the tears back. He stepped away from Ivan and turned around.

Standing strong against Ivan's pleading eyes took everything he had.

"I know this isn't an excuse, but I was doing my job. I still need to."

"That's great. And now that you know I'm not a drug dealer, you can run back to your life, Ivan Baker. Oh wait. Is that even your real name?"

A grimace twisted his lips. He was sure he'd called out Ivan's name the last time he came. He'd almost told Ivan he loved him, even though it was too soon. The thought that not even his name might be real…. His breath came shallow and fast, his vision getting spotty.

"Parker. Snap the fuck out of it! Sit down and breathe. Slowly, evenly."

Hands, hot like brands, gripped his shoulders and shoved him down on the couch. Parker did his best to comply, because he didn't want to faint like a fucking loser.

After a few moments of following Ivan's breathing instructions, he refocused his eyes on Ivan crouching between his legs.

"You okay? You were hyperventilating."

Parker nodded. Physically, yes, he was fine.

With a tentative touch, Ivan rubbed Parker's knee before sitting down beside him.

"My name is Ivan Bekker."

At least the Ivan hadn't changed. But Bekker? "Hey, that's what your ex-wife called you. It's close enough to Baker I thought I'd misheard. How did she find you?"

Ivan's head fell back against the sofa back. "She's not my ex-wife, she's my partner."

"Your partner? Like a cop partner?"

"Yep."

A brief spurt of pleasure warmed his heart before he remembered that just because the ex-wife wasn't real didn't mean they were in any position to start a relationship. Ivan *Bekker* was a lying creep who thought he was a drug dealer.

"Why did she show up here, then? Is she your backup or something?" Because she'd played the role of wronged ex-wife to perfection. She and Ivan could be Hollywood stars.

"I don't have any backup on this operation." The weariness in Ivan's voice exhausted Parker just listening to it. "My boss, Sarge, thinks there's a leak in the department. We had a sting that didn't go well, and he leapt on this chance to take Razhin down without alerting him to our actions."

"I hate to burst your bubble, but I really don't know this Razhin guy."

"Doesn't matter. There's enough evidence in your file box upstairs to connect that grow-op to you, enough to put you away for a long time."

Panic exploded in his chest. "Grow-op? What grow-op?" Holy fuckarama, Ivan was going to put him in jail? There had to be some mistake.

"How much land do you own in cottage country?"

The odd question sliced through the panic scrambling his brain. "A couple of acres or something. But it's only got about a hundred feet on Georgian Bay itself. Why?"

"Judging from the invoices in your file box, most of that land is probably full grown marijuana plants."

"Invoices? What are you talking about?" Could he be a drug dealer and not know it?

"The invoices. With the money."

Anger overpowered the fluttery panic. "You searched my room. You knew about the money, and you know about invoices I don't even know about. Are you trying to set me up?" That made more sense than anything else Ivan had said.

"I'm not. I swear. Parker, please. We need to go in. Turn this over to my colleagues."

"But won't that mean I'll get blamed for all this?" Although if his cottage property was covered with weed, he maybe deserved some of the blame. After all, he hadn't done much to ensure the property was looked after. He'd spent so much time avoiding the memories of that place… too much time, obviously.

"I'm going to do my best to make sure that doesn't happen. There's something very wrong here."

Tears welled up again, but this time he wanted Ivan to hold him and tell him everything would be okay. No matter how Ivan had lied to him and betrayed him, he still felt safe. Parker came dangerously close to opening his mouth and pleading with Ivan to protect him.

"What can we do?" That was better. Much more dignified and adult. "How did I get involved in all this?"

"We have to go in. But if this is still somehow tied to Razhin, he might get wind of me taking you in and think you're a threat. Problem is, the only people I can trust are Homicide cops."

Oh dear God. A drug kingpin might find him, Parker Wakefield, a threat. A loose end that needed to be tied up. What he wouldn't give for one of Neil's joints right fucking now. For now, he had to trust Ivan to keep him safe. After this was all over he could worry about how he'd never speak to Ivan again for all the shit he'd put him through.

"So, let's go." There were a lot of windows in this place. And all those guys at the party last night. What if one of those was Razhin or one of his… goons? Was that a word real criminals used? What if they'd bugged his place? Neil hung out with some real lowlifes. Maybe one of them had planted shit in his room. He rarely delved into that particular box.

Ivan clamped a hand on his knee. "Breathe. Calm down. I have to make a phone call first."

Parker waved his hand, indicating Ivan should get the fuck on with it. Calm down, the man said. No fucking problem. The sooner this was over, the better. Then he could go back to his boyfriendless existence. Concentrate on school and friends. Things that weren't going to slice his heart into ribbons… literally or figuratively.

IVAN glanced back at Parker before he took his cell phone out on the porch. God. He'd almost made the guy cry. He was such a fucking shit. It had been a fantastic night, and he'd had to go and ruin it. Finding out for sure Parker wasn't the criminal he'd been expecting had been a very short-lived relief because immediately after, he'd had to crush Parker's spirit. And he wasn't any closer to figuring out who was responsible.

Never expecting to use Kurt's number this soon, he quickly dialed and waited for Kurt to pick up. He didn't have a long wait.

"Kurt, it's Ivan. I need to come in." Calling Kurt first and coming in without notifying Martelli could be career ending decisions, but he couldn't think of any other way to protect Parker. Not when Martelli was so determined to take down Razhin by way of Parker. He'd never be able to live with himself if Parker ended up as collateral damage.

"Already? Are you okay? What happened?"

"I told Parker everything."

"Everything? Ivan, what the hell?"

"I believe he's not the guy I'm after, and I just needed to." Ivan drummed the fingers of his left hand against the rough brick. The muscles in his jaw flexed.

"Okay, okay. We'll work this out. Can you wait until tomorrow? Simon's out of town, and I'm still out on medical leave."

The tapping got a little faster, enough to scrape the pads of his fingers. "Sunday?" He could manage to keep it together one more day; he could endure the alternately wounded and accusing looks from Parker.

"You have to help me, Kurt. I found evidence to suggest there's a substantial grow-op in cottage country, but it's not Parker's. I'm sure of it. I can't let Parker go to jail." His voice cracked, and he coughed to try and cover it up, but the gasp on the other end told him he was unsuccessful.

"Don't worry. We'll work it all out, I promise."

Ivan snorted. That was a promise no one could make; he'd been a cop too long. But he took it in the spirit it was intended. "I'm sorry, man. I hate to drop this on you."

"No. Don't be sorry. We're friends. That's what I'm here for."

Ivan dropped his forehead to the brick, shuddering. He didn't deserve a friend like Kurt, but he'd take whatever he could get.

"Thanks."

"Hang tight. I'll let Simon know."

Ivan disconnected the call and reentered Parker's home. Maybe he could get Rick or Kurt to help him pack up his stuff after this was all over.

"Everything okay?" Parker was in the kitchen cleaning up the remains of breakfast. One of the sweetest mornings he'd ever had and all he'd have was a tainted memory.

"Yeah. We'll go into headquarters tomorrow." Problem was, now that everything was in the open, they were more exposed than ever. Maybe they weren't truly, but that's how it felt. Vulnerable. Like there was a neon sign outside proclaiming not only their suspicions but also how much money sat inside, unguarded by any traditional weapons. They could go to a hotel, but there was no guarantee he could keep Parker any safer there, and he might put a lot more innocent people at risk if Razhin's men came looking for the money before he got it to Simon.

"On a Sunday?"

"Yeah. My… liaison will be available, and even though policing is a 24/7 operation, Sundays are generally slower. We'll have a better chance of sorting this out, getting you proper protection." The more people who knew Parker was innocent, the less likely the departmental leak would be a danger to him.

"So, what do we do today? I… I suggested going to the market. Um, earlier. Before, you know." Parker directed his gaze toward the ceiling and sniffed.

God. He wanted to do that. Badly. Normal activities with Parker were a soothing balm to his tortured thoughts.

"We could still do that." Pretending that everything was okay wouldn't be easy, but it would kill a few hours. Although the exposure at the market might increase his sense of vulnerability, it would also be easier to evade any pursuers.

"No, we can't." Parker turned on him, fire in his eyes. "Maybe you're good at acting, but I'm not. And by the way, how do I even know you're a cop? You certainly haven't shown me any identification. For all I know, you're the one trying to set me up. Or maybe you're some sort of stalker."

The words and tone were like a punch. He'd expected anger and for Parker to hate him, but he hadn't thought it would happen so fast. "First off, if you're in a situation where you think you've got a crazy stalker, for God's sake, don't let him get you alone, and don't confront him. Second, I can take you to a colleague, if I need to. I don't carry ID with me undercover, but he's got some, and he can vouch for me."

Parker's eyes widened, but he made no move to escape. Good. Somewhere deep inside, he knew Ivan wasn't that guy.

"Finally, you said you thought there was a couple thousand dollars upstairs, right?"

He waited expectantly, and when Parker nodded, he continued. "So then, if that money were mine, or if I was trying to set you up, it wouldn't be in my best interests for you to know there's a hell of lot more than that up there."

A frown creased Parker's brow. "How much money is there?"

"Around a quarter of a mill."

"A quarter of a million? Dollars? No fucking way. I don't believe you."

"You've got a dangerous amount of cash in your file box."

"No. That's insane." Parker stood and ran toward the stairs. Ivan followed right on his heels.

Up in the master bedroom, Parker yanked the file box out of the closet and threw it on the bed. When he pulled out a bundle, Ivan smacked it out of his hands.

"I'll prove to you how much is there, but in case the techs can get fingerprints off this, I don't want yours all over it. Be much harder to prove you're innocent if you've fucking touched every bill."

Ivan counted the bills in one bundle. A choking sound from Parker made him look up. Face ashy and pale, Parker stared at the brown hundred-dollar bills Ivan had separated from the twenties on either end.

"I thought they were all twenties."

"You were meant to think that." The colors weren't that different, and each bundle had been carefully arranged so that the only twenties bookended the hundreds. "But even if they were all twenties, that's still around forty thousand. Didn't you notice how heavy this was? One bill equals approximately one gram. This much money probably weighs close to five pounds."

"I… no. And I never took all the money out. It, uh, freaked me out."

"Good. It should freak you out. I've seen people killed over a couple hundred dollars, but this much money ups the ante considerably."

"Shit, Ivan, I—"

Whatever Parker had been going to say was interrupted by the buzzing of his phone. He pulled it out of his pocket and glanced at the caller ID. With a weird sheepish expression, he answered.

"Hey." Parker was silent for a moment before he frowned. "Neil?"

Parker listened, his frown deepening. Until he dropped the phone, like it bit him. The phone skittered under the bed, and Ivan dove down to retrieve it. The call had been disconnected.

"What? What was it?"

"He knew." Parker stumbled back against the dresser and covered his eyes with a trembling hand.

"Knew what?" Ivan hadn't been freaked out until Parker demonstrated clear signs of fear. "Parker?"

Ivan waited while Parker scrubbed at his face. He looked up, riverbed eyes pleading for Ivan to make everything better. If he could he would.

"Neil butt dialed me. I think it's his money. He was talking to someone else, and he knew about the money, before I told him about it."

"Neil. Okay, that makes sense. He's got easy access to your stuff and.... Wait. You told him about it? When?"

Parker's gaze darted away, and pink highlighted his sharp, sharp cheekbones. "While you were out on the porch making your phone call."

"Why?"

"Why the fuck do you think? Asshole. I was freaked out, okay? And mad at you. Neil's my best friend, and he helped me through some of the worst times of my life. I hoped he'd help me through this." Parker's eyes got shiny, and Ivan wanted to kick himself.

This morning had definitely not gone as either of them would have liked. He couldn't exactly fault Parker for asking his oldest friend for advice, especially when Ivan hadn't really clued in to the fact that after Parker, Neil was the most likely suspect. He wasn't sure if it was lack of sleep or jealousy over Parker that clouded his mind to that now obvious detail, but this was one more reminder that he had fucked up royally from day one. Parker was pissed at him, might never want to speak to him after this was all over, and Ivan couldn't blame him, even though the Parker-shaped hole in his life would be more devastating than Colin's departure.

"Did you tell him I was a cop?" Had he been investigating the wrong man all along?

Parker's lips thinned as he pressed them together, but he nodded.

There was no time to acknowledge the fear and worry that simple action caused. "Have you got a duffle bag or something?

Backpack? We've got to get this out of the house and someplace safe."

Ivan flipped on the light in the closet and scanned quickly for something that might work. He couldn't leave this evidence here.

"Where are you taking it?"

"I don't know yet. But this might be the only chance of proving you're being framed. We can't let Neil get his hands on it."

"I'm sorry, but I can't... I don't know how to deal with this. You've both lied to me, and yet, I'm somehow trusting you, not the guy I've known for years."

Jeez, he couldn't have Parker back out now. Prison would be hell for him, and if Neil had anything to do with the evidence in the file box, there's no way he cared if Parker took the fall. "Look, we'll take it to Kurt or Simon. Someone who can prove they're cops. Will you believe me then?"

Parker lifted a shoulder in a half shrug. "Do you think... Neil's coming for this?" He waved a hand.

"Yes, I do." There was no point in telling Parker he'd started a countdown clock in his mind, calculating how long it had been since Parker outed him to Neil. Shitty-ass cop that he was, he didn't even know where Neil lived, so he didn't know how long it would take him to get here from his apartment. As soon as Parker and the money were somewhere safe, he'd find out. Hopefully the money would be enough to tie Neil to something so he could arrest the fucker. Or get someone not on leave to arrest the fucker.

"I think I've got an extra-large backpack in one of these boxes." Ivan sensed Parker moving away, but he continued to rummage through the closet in search of a bag.

"Where's your car? Near here?"

"Not really. I rent garage space, but it's like, a couple subway stops away."

Shit. He'd take the box as is, but a bag would be easier to transport on public transit.

"I wonder what he's doing here?" At the words, Ivan glanced up. Parker stood by the window, looking out. Abandoning his search for a bag, Ivan strode to the window. Standing on the sidewalk in front of the neighbor's house was the guy Neil had sucked off at the party. He had a buddy with him, and they were standing beside a large black SUV like they were waiting for someone, but their hyper-alertness was plain to see.

"Do you know those guys?"

"They're friends of Neil's. They were here last night. But I don't know them."

The one Ivan recognized in profile turned and faced the house, and Ivan realized he recognized him from more than the night before when Neil had been servicing him beside the house. Razhin's son.

"We gotta get out of here." Ivan upended two boxes before he found the backpack Parker mentioned.

"Yeah, you said."

Ivan tipped the contents of the file box into the backpack, and Parker squawked in protest.

"We have to leave now."

"Why? And that took hours to file. What the hell?"

"Those guys out there... well, one of them is Leo, Razhin's son, and both of them have guns." The distinctive bulges under jackets too warm for the summer told the story in an instant.

"Guns? Are you sure?" Parker bent closer to the window, and Ivan yanked him back.

"Are you trying to get shot?"

"I just can't believe this. Maybe you're not a cop. Maybe you're insane."

"Parker, you can't fucking deny the money and that Neil knew about it. And it's too damn hot out for those jackets."

The last tiny bit of defiance fled, and Ivan was almost sad to see it go. Betrayal. This wasn't the same as finding Colin in bed with someone else, but it had to be similar.

"Look." Ivan kept Parker's head near the edge of the window as Leo shifted his jacket, revealing the black handgrip of a gun. "Did you see that?"

"Oh my fucking God." Parker wheezed a bit as he tried to control the volume of his voice. "Don't you have a gun?"

"No, I don't have a gun. This isn't the movies. I'm on leave, and I'm undercover as an insurance salesman. Even if I had one, I can't have a shoot-out on a residential street." His heart pounded, and his breathing accelerated, the scenes from his last shootout as vivid as they'd only been in his nightmares. A quick glance out the window confirmed the two men were approaching. They weren't walking quickly enough to make anyone look twice, but they moved with a purpose Ivan couldn't mistake. He clenched his fingers into a tight fist, hoping to hide the tremor.

"What do we do?"

Ivan ran to the bathroom, turned on the shower, and fixed the door to lock behind him before running back into the bedroom and shutting the door. He slung the backpack over his shoulders and pressed Parker against the wall. It was unlikely the men, even should they look up, would be able to see them through the window, but he didn't want to take any chances. There was only one way to avoid a bullet in the back, and it would require stealth and timing. He had to hope he could make up for a lack of those on Parker's part.

"You move when I say, got it?"

Parker nodded but looked confused.

"We're going to go out the window and get the fuck out of here."

"Out of the window?" Parker wriggled against him. "I can't do that."

Ivan leaned back for a moment to look directly into Parker's eyes. "You must. It's the only way." They were trapped up here like cats in a tree. He'd rather go out the back, but there wasn't even a porch roof to help them down.

Another quick nod and a heavy swallow answered him. Reaching out, he curled the fingers of his good hand under the windowsill and waited. No knock or doorbell preceded the thunk of the men trying to open the door, and Ivan used the sound to cover him pushing the window up.

"Out," he whispered. Parker paled but did as instructed. Ivan followed, the pack pulling him a little off-balance. They moved quickly to the corner because Ivan hoped to use the foliage and lack of windows on that side to hide their departure. Parker paled further as he looked over the edge of the porch roof. Ivan calculated the risk. The sounds of careless men in the house grew louder. They had mere minutes to get out of sight. Ivan tossed the bag into the bushes to cushion its fall and shimmied down the porch support.

"C'mon. I'll catch you if you fall." Ivan spoke as loudly as he dared, hoping to all that was holy he wasn't going to get a bullet in the chest while he looked up, waiting for Parker.

He didn't have to wait as long as he'd expected; Parker's long body promptly clambered down with a minimum of noise. Later, he'd have to commend Parker for his ability to keep his head under stress. Shit, he was probably doing better than Ivan because he didn't know how fragile a body was. He didn't know how much blood a body had. The damage a bullet could do.

The thud of Parker's feet on the dirt of the garden shook him out of his fugue.

"Where to?"

"Follow me. Fast." Ivan grabbed the pack and ran, staying close to the houses. As long as they could get to the place he'd observed Parker from, he could get them away, free and clear. But the next few minutes were critical. If Razhin's men figured out what had happened and came outside too soon, they'd be dead.

CHAPTER
Ten

THIRTY minutes later, sweating and panting, Parker stood beside Ivan in front of a quaint little one-story home much closer to his own than he'd expected. Was this a safe house? Parker hadn't seen anyone following them, but Ivan had been too busy eluding pursuit to talk to him. Second thoughts about following Ivan blindly had come and gone. Now, he was on his fortieth or fiftieth thoughts, but at least this wasn't as scary as some places Parker could imagine… if Ivan was some sort of crazy stalker instead of a cop. He wasn't sure right now which one was more believable, but trusting Ivan seemed right and natural.

Parker touched the phone in his pocket. How easy was it to track people by their cell phones? Maybe it was only easy if it was the government after you.

Ivan pressed the doorbell, leaning on it. Under normal circumstances, such rudeness would make him swat Ivan's arm away, but tension had turned Ivan into a seething mass of nerves, and that anxiousness had more than transmitted itself to Parker. When he wasn't asking Ivan to talk to him, he kept running over what he'd seen out of the window at his house. Men with guns, possibly sent by Neil, had come to his house. Maybe not for him, but for evidence in his house. Evidence that pointed to him as some sort of drug dealer. Maybe worse. Drug lord? What did you call someone who ran a huge grow-op? He wanted so badly for Ivan to be wrong about everything. He wanted to go back to falling in love with a recently divorced insurance salesman, not running around the city with a paranoid undercover detective who was a complete stranger, despite having lived with him for two weeks.

A man with tousled auburn hair, who was even more muscular than Ivan, yanked open the door with a scowl. He'd barely spit out an angry "What?" before he recognized Ivan, and concern replaced the anger.

"Ivan? What are you doing here?" His eyes shifted. "Is this Parker?" The incredulousness in the man's tone made Parker drop his shoulders defensively. Who was this, and how did he know Parker's name?

"It's gone to shit, Kurt." Ivan glanced behind them for the millionth time. "Can't talk out here."

Kurt didn't look pleased, but at least now Parker knew he was one of Ivan's cop friends.

"Come in, then. I thought you were going in tomorrow."

When Kurt stepped out of the doorway, Ivan pushed Parker into the house in front of him. With Ivan crowding him from behind, he followed Kurt into a plain white living room. Nicely furnished, with a few colorful throw pillows and blankets, but still rather stark. Parker wasn't a clean freak by anyone's standards, but he'd never have chosen white as a color scheme for anything but a kitchen. Too hard to keep stain-free and spotless.

"Sit down." Kurt didn't sound too inviting but neither did he seem pissed off either.

Parker sat on one of the chairs. Kurt sat carefully on the couch, letting out a quiet grunt.

"Are you okay?" Parker asked.

Kurt flashed him a smile, one that sent a wave of unexpected desire through him. He wasn't as sexy as Ivan, but this was a very attractive man. Parker smiled tentatively back, hoping Kurt didn't notice the sudden rush of blood to his cheeks.

The thunk of Ivan's pack hitting the floor made Parker jump. Ivan glared at him before he sat in the other chair.

"He's fine."

"I'm fine," Kurt repeated without rancor. "Just had surgery a couple of weeks ago, and it's taking longer to recuperate than I expected. What happened?"

Ivan jabbed a thumb in Parker's direction. "I should have been investigating his friend Neil. Somehow, Neil's setting him up. I just don't know how yet."

"Okay. But what's with the urgency?" At least Kurt hadn't asked if Ivan was sure. After seeing all that money and those invoices, Parker was almost sure he'd bought all that shit himself.

"My cover got blown, and Neil found out we knew about the money. Didn't take long before Leo Razhin and a buddy showed up at the house, armed."

The truth was, Parker had fucked up. It was nice of Ivan to cover for him, but that didn't make up for all the lies. For sleeping with Parker under false pretenses, like just about every other guy—admittedly few—who'd gotten into his pants.

Kurt's eyes narrowed as he stared at Ivan. "And you came right here? Did you call anyone?"

"No."

Eyes closing, Kurt let his head fall back on the sofa. Exasperation seemed an odd reaction for Kurt, who as far as Parker could tell was only peripherally involved.

"You still got your burner phone?"

Ivan didn't answer, just pulled out the phone in question and dropped it on the coffee table.

"Call the police. Report it anonymously."

Those words were like a slap in the face, and Parker stood. "I thought you guys were the police. Why would you need to call the police?" Because they could have done that from his bedroom instead of escaping like fugitives. This whole terrifying episode could be over already.

Ivan stood and faced him, brows drawn together. "Doubting me again? I'm not the bad guy here."

"Aren't you? Aside from one weird call from Neil, all this shit started as soon as you arrived in my house! How do I know this isn't some elaborate game? Maybe you're in it together."

The eye rolling made him want to punch Ivan, but the guy had already been through a lot, even if he was a crazy fuck. Being angry and in denial was easier to deal with than the tearing pain of losing the "what might have been." He hadn't realized how deep his feelings for Ivan had become until he'd found out the Ivan he knew didn't exist and the happy ever after he'd envisioned could never come to pass. Anger was easy in comparison.

"In what together? What reason would I have for such an elaborate sham?"

Parker shrugged, and Ivan got angry. Well and truly angry. The kind of anger that, if he was a cop, probably got confessions on the spot. His fists came up, one of them still carefully wrapped from Parker's first aid, and Parker took a step back.

Horror quickly replaced Ivan's fury. "I wasn't going to hit you."

"I know." But he was maybe lying. Ivan sensed his uncertainty, because his nostrils flared and his eyes filled.

"Never. I swear. I'd never hurt you."

But he already had. Just not physically.

Ivan turned and ran out of the room, slamming the door on what was presumably the bathroom, but Parker wasn't sure. He turned to Kurt, who sat straight up, mouth hanging open.

"Shit. I had no idea it was this bad."

"What?" Parker had no fucking idea what had just happened. He dropped back into the chair.

"I'll explain in a minute. What's your address?"

He'd lost all energy for fighting. Whatever was happening wasn't putting him in danger right this minute, and that's about all he was equipped to process. He told Kurt, who immediately picked up the phone Ivan had left behind.

"Hello? Yes, I'd like to report a break-in. My neighbor's house. Two men I didn't recognize, and they had guns."

There was a pause while Kurt listened. He gave Parker's address and a decent description of Neil's friend, although he was way off on the other guy. "My name? No, I'd rather not say. But please hurry. They looked angry."

Kurt clicked off the phone and tossed it back on the table.

"What the hell is going on? Why did you do that?"

"If they're still there, which I doubt, this might keep them busy for a bit. Get them arrested and out of our hair while we figure this out. Half an hour is a long time, but maybe they won't have had a chance to thoroughly trash your place."

"Trash my place?"

"I assume the money's in there." Kurt waved a finger at the bag. Parker had almost forgotten about the money. No, not almost, he'd just tried desperately to forget about it. He tilted his head and assessed Kurt. Was that what Kurt was after? Maybe they were lying about being cops and were just after Neil's money. Maybe Neil wasn't setting him up, but was trying to keep the money safe by hiding it at Parker's.

Kurt snorted and shook his head. "Stay here. I'll be right back." The discomfort in Kurt's movements was evident, and Parker should have recognized the careful way he held himself. He'd seen more than enough trauma patients move the same way.

Parker had enough time to wonder about Ivan's disappearance before Kurt returned.

"Here. My badge and ID."

Fingering the items Kurt handed him, Parker couldn't see any reason not to believe Kurt.

"Please. Help me understand."

Kurt gripped his shoulder in an attempt to comfort him before he sat back on the couch.

"First, the phone call. Calling in anonymously means Ivan won't be exposed, and no one will expect you to be around to answer questions. The questions will come, but this gives us a bit of breathing room."

"And what's with Ivan?" He should care more about the trouble Neil had gotten him into, and he was still fucking angry at Ivan for treating him like dirt, but Ivan's upset cut at him worse than the betrayal. Deep down, Parker believed Ivan wouldn't hurt him physically, but he'd also never seen Ivan furious before.

With a glance at the hallway, from which the faint sounds of running water emanated, Kurt turned back to Parker. "What has he told you? About his real life, I mean. About how he came to be working on this investigation."

Investigating him. A flare of anger burned away some of the confusion. "Not much." Parker outlined what he'd been told. After hearing it again, he was amazed he'd fallen for it. Even though Ivan had apparently been telling the truth—that time—he must have a tremendous capacity for getting people to like him, believe him. Which made Parker's decision to sleep with him all the more suspect. Had he been manipulated from the beginning? Had Ivan had some ulterior motive, like trying to get a confession?

Kurt leaned forward and lowered his voice. "I was afraid of that. I'm worried about him. This is so...." Kurt stopped himself and peered into Parker's eyes.

"What?"

"Look, I barely know you, and if you're going to make trouble for Ivan, I will deny I ever said anything."

Make trouble for him? Parker was never going to see him again after this was over. He shouldn't care what was going on with Ivan, for precisely that reason, but he wanted—needed—to know.

"I won't. I promise."

"This investigation was highly irregular, enough so he could get fired over it, even though it's not his fault. But that's not the worst of it."

Fired? And that wasn't the worst? Parker gestured for Kurt to continue. If Ivan returned from the bathroom, he'd probably never get to hear the rest of it.

"Did you hear about that drug bust a couple of weeks ago? Ended up in a shoot-out. The press crucified the police."

"Yes, of course." He didn't watch much news, but that hadn't escaped his notice. Happened the day before Ivan moved in.

Kurt patted his shoulder. "That's when I got shot. That's when Ivan killed his first man."

Parker gasped. "Killed?"

"Yeah, one of the young enforcers, maybe a year or two younger than you. It was life or death, and I know he tried to save the kid, but couldn't. His boss grabbed him before he'd even washed the blood off and sent him after you, using administrative leave to cover the fact that this wasn't an official investigation."

"But what about... internal affairs? Didn't he have to talk to them?"

"Special Investigations Unit. Yes, he did. He was cleared pretty quick, actually."

"Then how is he... wait. He should have also had counseling, right?"

Kurt nodded. "But he's had to lie through his teeth to his therapist because he doesn't know where the departmental leak is coming from. His boss is using his counseling as an excuse to extend his leave, but he's not going to get better until he can come clean with the shrink."

Ivan had killed a man. In the line of duty. Parker slumped back into the chair. No wonder Ivan had been so jumpy around the house. So much became clear. Then, like he'd been electrocuted, Parker sat up straight. "Oh my God. He's heading toward a case of full-blown PTSD."

"Yeah, I think so too." Kurt glanced back at the hallway again. "And it's not getting any better for having been put in this situation."

Parker should have seen it. He wasn't a therapist or anything, but he'd seen the ravages of severe trauma every time he volunteered at the trauma center. Some of his anger and hurt bled away. Not all of it, but he didn't think Ivan had intended to make him fall in love. That was his own stupid fault.

"What can we do?" If it weren't for the existence of the money, he might be able to attribute this whole mess to the PTSD, but that money was painfully real.

"Find out what the hell is going on and get Ivan the help he needs. He's a great detective and a good man making the best of a bad situation. I don't want this to scar him for life."

Impulsively, Parker reached out and patted Kurt's knee. "You're a good friend. Not many would take risks like that." And he should know. Even without this, he knew Neil would never sacrifice for him.

Kurt smiled, a sad smile that told Parker there was a long story behind it. "I've been rock bottom, not long ago. It took friends and family to get me out. How could I not do the same?"

"What about Ivan's family?"

"They're close, but my guess is he hasn't given them a chance to see he's self-destructing."

Were his sisters and parents a lie, part of the cover? Parker opened his mouth to ask, but the sound of the bathroom door opening brought their discussion to an abrupt, uncomfortable end. When Ivan came back into the room, he wouldn't look Parker in the eye, but other than that, he looked composed.

"What now?" Kurt asked when Ivan scooped up his phone.

"We need to go through the papers in the bag, find out what's going on. It might be all we have. If Neil gets spooked, he'll dismantle the operation at Parker's cottage." Now that he was observing more closely, the strain of keeping it together was obvious. Ivan needed help, and fast.

"Your suspected grow-op, you mean?"

"Yeah. I'm thinking I should just go up there, scope the place out."

"No. Goddammit, Ivan. I may not be in the Drug Squad but I know damn well how much firepower the people protecting those things have. You're not going. Give me the address, and I'll call Simon. He's still got tons of friends on the RCMP, and they'll be better prepared to go in."

Parker shuddered. His previous experiences with grow-ops were from movies, but if they were even vaguely close to reality, he didn't want Ivan going there alone either. He just hoped no unsuspecting innocent tried to go hiking on his land. For God's sake. Why hadn't he taken more of an interest? Why had he let Neil deal with everything? He'd allowed this to happen.

"Who is Simon?"

Kurt cut off what he'd been going to say. "My partner on the force. He used to be with the RCMP before he transferred to the Toronto Police Services."

The Royal Canadian Mounted Police. They were federal police, but Parker got a picture in his head of a bunch of men in those traditional red uniforms trying to ride horses stealthily through a field of marijuana.

Too bad Simon wasn't Kurt's life partner. Parker was fairly certain Kurt was gay, and given how much he and Ivan seemed to have in common, including their age, he'd be a lot happier if the other attractive man was taken.

"That's actually a good idea." Ivan relaxed just a little. "Are you up to sifting through the stuff I brought with me?"

"Yeah, sure. Let's spread it out on the kitchen table, and we can go through it."

Parker wasn't sure Kurt was up for it. He moved stiffly and might be a little paler than when they'd arrived. He'd help if he could, but he'd probably just get in the way. Not that he'd even know what to look for.

As soon as Kurt disconnected his call to Simon, the two detectives pulled on latex gloves and began to spread out the documents, leaving the money in the pack on the floor.

Within moments of delving into the evidence, Kurt and Ivan seemed to forget about Parker. They did throw a few questions his way, all of which served to alarm him about the state of his apparent involvement in… whatever Neil and his buddies had been up to.

Parker pushed his chair away from the table, away from the pile of implicating documents. Ivan and Kurt shuffled and sorted through the jumble his life had become, old papers shoved aside with barely a glance, new ones inspected carefully.

A slender, dark-haired man, gorgeous and about the same age as Ivan and Kurt, appeared in the doorway. "Well, hello. Kurt, I didn't know we were having guests. Are you sure you're up to this?"

Kurt glanced up, and the joy in his expression made Parker feel like he was observing something private. Beautiful, but private. His stomach squeezed a little in envy.

"I'm fine. Strong as an ox." Kurt winked, and the beautiful man rolled his eyes. "Davy, this is Ivan. Remember I told you about him?"

Davy smiled at Ivan and shook his hand before bending over to kiss Kurt on the lips. The little tug of envy became a great swirling ball. He wanted that, so much, but at least he didn't have to worry about Ivan and Kurt. Kurt hadn't looked at Ivan the way he was looking at Davy, like the sun and the moon and the whole world were all wrapped in one dark-haired package.

"Kurt's told me so much about you. It's good to finally meet you." Davy turned to Parker and smiled. "But this can't be another one of your cop buddies, can it?"

Parker shook his head while both Kurt and Ivan answered in the negative.

Davy approached, hands outstretched. "Are you okay? You look a little frazzled."

"It's a long story, Davy. Right now, we're trying to keep Parker from getting arrested for something he didn't do."

"Oh no." Davy patted him on the head. "They'll fix things up for you. But I can see you're just here fretting. Let me grab us something to drink, and we'll go watch a movie or something in the other room. Something to take your mind off this."

Davy stumbled over the bag as he headed to the fridge. "Uh, Kurt, is this a bag full of money?"

"Yep. About two hundred thou." Kurt handed Ivan another sheet of paper.

"Dollars?" The word was strangled as Davy blanched. "Ooookay. Parker?"

Parker stood. Anything to get away from this... unreal situation.

"Hey, it'll be okay." Davy gave him a quick hug, which was over far too quickly. The comfort of another person's arms was a luxury he hadn't realized he'd been missing. But Davy was a stranger. What Parker wouldn't give to be back in his bed, with Ivan's arms tight around him.

Parker nodded. "Thanks."

Before they had a chance to leave, someone pounded on the front door. He and Davy froze while Kurt and Ivan scrabbled at their sides. Parker had seen Ivan make the same gesture a couple of times, and with sudden clarity realized they were grabbing for guns that weren't there. His mouth dried out in fear, and he stumbled back against the counter.

"Ivan Bekker. If you're in there, open the fuck up."

Ivan relaxed. "It's Trish."

"Your partner?" Both he and Kurt asked at the same time.

"Yep." He made a move to the door, but Kurt's arm snaked out to stop him.

"You sure you can trust her? What about the leak?"

"Kurt, man, I don't know. But Sarge was wrong about Parker. Maybe he's wrong about the mole too. I can't believe Trish would betray me… us… like that."

Kurt's eyes shadowed. "I'd be the first to tell you that your partner can hide things from you, but if you think we can trust her, I'll take your word for it."

The pounding and yelling continued.

Ivan let out a chuckle. "If we don't let her in, she'll break the door down."

Kurt nodded. "Fine. Let her in."

All three of them followed Ivan to the door. Parker was certain not one of them exhaled until the door opened to reveal Trish without any sort of weapon or evil companion.

"What the fuck is going on?" Trish shoved Ivan with both hands, and he fell back against the wall.

"Trish, Trish, it's okay. C'mon."

Trish glared at all of them, but let Ivan drag her into the living room.

"Talk to me, Bekker. You tell me the truth right now, or I'm asking for a transfer."

"How did you find me?"

That was Parker's first question too.

"I heard the call about the break in at your... house? His house." Trish pointed at Parker. "I went there. The place was a fucking disaster, and Leo Razhin and one of Razhin's enforcers were taken into custody. They were pissed, and they took it out on that house. No one had seen either of you, though."

Parker's vision blackened. His house was trashed? What would they have done if they'd found him and Ivan in the house? It didn't bear thinking of, and he wavered where he stood. Ivan stepped back and wrapped an arm around him.

He allowed the embrace for a moment before he shook off Ivan's arm. As much as he wanted Ivan's comfort, how could he accept it?

"I checked your apartment and your parents' place. I knew you were friends with Kurt, so I tried here next." She nodded at Kurt. "Hello, by the way. Glad you're up and about."

"Thank you."

"Who's that?" Trish pushed her chin toward Davy.

Kurt answered. "This is Davy, my partner."

Trish's eyes softened. "Nice to meet you, Davy. Sorry to barge in like this."

Davy waved away her apology. "Nice to meet you too."

She turned back to Ivan. "Seriously, are you okay? Tell me what the fuck is going on."

Parker couldn't see Ivan's face, but something Trish saw made her eyes widen, and she flung her arms around Ivan, hugging him.

Ivan hugged her back, and an unreasoning jealousy welled up inside. Trish was part of Ivan's real life, a life Parker could be no part of.

In moments, they'd laid out the situation for Trish, who punched Ivan in the shoulder for even thinking for a moment she was the leak.

"So, what's the plan?" Trish had impatiently waited for the whole story, but now she was ready to take action. Parker thought she must be exhausting to work with, but it might explain why Ivan was so laid back. Unless, of course, that hadn't been real either. He hated, absolutely hated, not knowing which bits of Ivan were the truth, or if any of them were.

Ivan led them back into the kitchen and gestured at the piles of paper on the kitchen table.

"Simon's going to let us know what happened up at Parker's cottage. Since he's not on leave, as soon as he got back into town he was going to submit the documents into evidence and run a background check on Parker, see exactly what he's on the hook for."

"Well, I can do that. Get this ball rolling right now. Take advantage of Leo's arrest."

"Somewhere in there, we're hopefully going to be able to prove Neil stole his identity and made the grow-op purchases, but even with Leo in custody, we don't have anything linking Neil to Razhin." Kurt wrapped an arm around Davy, and Parker couldn't help but notice how heavily Kurt leaned on him. The shadows under his eyes attested to his recent bout of surgery. He was either in pain or weary or both. They needed to leave before they set back Kurt's recovery too far.

"Wait, I have something." Ivan pulled his phone out and clicked into the pictures.

Peeking over everyone's shoulder, Parker saw Neil blowing Leo. Outside his fucking house.

"When the hell did you take that picture? And why?" Everyone turned to look at him. Shit. He hadn't meant to speak at all, but thinking about Ivan spying on Neil like that made him crazy.

Ivan's cheeks reddened, and he still wouldn't meet Parker's eyes. Hadn't since his episode earlier, which made Parker sick to his stomach.

"I took it when I thought he was cheating on you," Ivan mumbled.

Trish narrowed her eyes as she inspected him, but she didn't say anything before looking back at Parker's life laid out on Kurt's kitchen table.

"It's not much, but it might work. What's this?" She picked up a small, tattered piece of paper. Parker's birth certificate.

"It's Parker's older documents. Nothing relevant to what Neil's doing," Ivan said.

"I don't know about that." Trish's intent look made Parker squirm. What was so interesting about his birth certificate?

She flapped the certificate at Ivan. "Do you know who his father is?"

"No. Parker told me his dad was never around."

"That true, kid?" Trish turned intent brown eyes on him.

Parker shrugged. "Yeah. He'd been cheating on his wife. When my mom got pregnant, he gave her some money to stay away. She invested it well, and between that and what she inherited from her own parents, we never needed him."

"Didn't you ever try to find him?"

He'd worked out his feelings about that a long time ago. "No. He didn't want us, and I didn't care who the fuck he was. Why does this even matter?"

A thought struck him. "Wait. He's not part of Razhin's organization, is he?" If he was the son of a criminal, that would more easily explain why he'd fallen under suspicion.

Ivan grabbed the certificate from Trish. Blood suffused Ivan's face, and he looked even angrier than he had earlier.

"I don't fucking believe it," Ivan growled. "I don't fucking believe it."

"Hey, calm down." Trish laid a restraining hand on Ivan's forearm, but he shook her off and tucked Parker's birth certificate into his shirt pocket.

Dialing a number on his phone, Ivan headed to the front door. "Sarge, it's Bekker," he snarled into the mouthpiece. "Meet me at headquarters. Now. It's urgent."

Ivan grabbed a set of keys from a hook beside the door, ran out of the house, and got in one of the cars outside. Tires squealed as he pulled away.

"Did he just steal my car?" Davy asked.

"What was that?" Kurt snapped. "Whose name is on that certificate?"

"Sergio Martelli." Trish pulled out her car keys. "I'd better follow him. Parker, with me. I'm not letting you out of my sight."

"Take this in with you. The sooner we get it logged, the better." Kurt started to kneel to grab the bag, but Davy stopped him with a shake of his head.

"No heavy lifting. Let me do it." Davy pulled on a pair of latex gloves and shoved the paperwork into the backpack.

He still didn't understand. "Who is Sergio Martelli?" Besides the deadbeat who'd had an affair with his mother and abandoned her as soon as she discovered she was pregnant.

"Ivan's boss. Otherwise known as Sarge." Kurt sighed.

"Oh." Parker thought about that for a moment. He wasn't sure he grasped all the implications, or why exactly it mattered, but nothing was going to keep him from accompanying Trish and finding out what the hell was going on. His life had been turned upside down by a man he thought he loved and a man who'd never loved him one bit.

FOR each minute that passed while Ivan waited, he got angrier. He sat behind Martelli's desk, waiting. He wanted to see his boss's face when he entered. Ivan shuffled Martelli's papers, moved his stapler.

He considered calling again, but decided against it. Sure, he was pissed as hell, but it was a weekend, and it might take Martelli a few minutes to disengage from whatever family or campaign trail obligation he was engaged in. Bastard.

The office door opened sooner than Ivan expected, and he stood, although he remained behind the desk.

"Ivan. What's so urgent? Have you got something?"

"Yes, I've got an asshole for a boss."

Martelli's eyes widened. "What the fuck is wrong with you?"

"What's wrong with me?" Ivan swept files off the desk and rounded it. "Why the fuck didn't you tell me?"

"Tell you what?" Martelli shoved a chair aside instead of sitting.

Ivan let out a wordless howl of frustration. His next words weren't at all quiet either. "Why didn't you tell me Parker was your son?"

Martelli paled and got right up in his face. "Shut the fuck up, Bekker. That's got nothing to do with the investigation."

"Doesn't it? What else aren't you telling me? Is there truly a leak in the department?"

"It's not impossible, but I don't think so. That bust going sour was probably a coincidence. You know they don't always go smoothly."

Ivan's fingers twitched, desperate to wrap around Martelli's throat. He'd turned Ivan into a paranoid freak, jumping at shadows, based on a lie.

"Why the hell did you send me after your son?" Ivan spat out the words, so angry he was shaking. He was proud he'd managed to get those sentences out coherently.

"Lower your voice, goddammit. Look, I needed your help. I'm sorry it had to be the way it was, but I'd heard rumors that the boy was involved with Razhin. If he got arrested, my affair with his mother would come out. My wife would divorce me, and there's no way I'd get elected."

Suddenly, it all became clear. Ironic, really. Sleeping with Parker had allowed him to get the best night's rest he'd had since the shooting, and although his head still wasn't on right, he was more clearheaded than he'd been in days.

"You used me." His boss had taken advantage of his shock after the shooting to get him to agree to an investigation he never should have started in the first place. "What were you going to do if I brought you evidence of Parker's guilt? Were you going to bury it?"

"Did you bring me evidence of his guilt?"

"He's your son. Don't you care he almost got killed today? Don't you care he's been on his own since his mom died, and the guy he thought was his best friend set him up? Stole his identity?"

Martelli shrugged. "I had nothing to do with the kid. My wife threatened to leave if I didn't stop the affair and pay off Parker's mom. Besides, I've already got four kids. I didn't need another."

"You asshole." Ivan swung a fist, pain exploding as cracked knuckles met solid jaw. Gratified, he waited as Martelli staggered a bit. Once the man regained his footing, he used his other hand to slam into his boss's stomach, then whipped him against the wall.

The office shuddered, pictures and commendations sliding down the wall to shatter in a spray of glass. Blood dripped from Martelli's split lip as he curled up on the floor, arms around his belly.

A couple of uniformed cops burst through the open doorway, preceding the head of Homicide, Inspector Nadar. Just beyond, Kurt, Davy, Trish, and Parker were visible. Parker wore the same stunned, disbelieving look he'd worn since Ivan had confessed to being a detective. He hated it, hated that Parker didn't trust him anymore, but he had no right to that trust. He'd betrayed Parker, almost as badly as his father had done—to both of them.

"Enough," Nadar thundered.

"Arrest him," Martelli wheezed from the floor. "He's fired."

Nadar raised a brow. "I don't think so. Not until we get to the bottom of this. Escort them to separate interrogation rooms."

Ivan left the office, ignoring Martelli's whining.

"I'm sorry, Ivan. I had to call someone." Kurt's face was ashen.

"It's fine." He had no doubt Kurt had acted with the best intentions. He'd already resigned himself to losing his job. When he'd taken the assignment, he'd known it was a possibility, but he hadn't realized it would be because his boss was a selfish ass. Nevertheless, he'd rather not leave in disgrace while Parker was around to see him do it.

Without another glance at Parker, because he couldn't stand to see that hurt look in his eyes anymore, Ivan followed the uniformed cop to an interrogation room. He slumped in the uncomfortable plastic chair and rested his throbbing knuckles against the cool metal of the table. Asking for ice was out of the question; he didn't want to admit to any more weaknesses. Not in front of his soon to be ex-coworkers.

CHAPTER
Eleven

PARKER paced the room again. Not paced. Prowled. He'd been escorted to an interrogation room hours ago. Kurt—not Ivan, dammit—had assured him he wasn't in trouble and didn't need a lawyer, but Kurt's boss had grilled him. Wrung every detail out of him, including his personal relationship with Ivan. Inspector Nadar had known they'd had sex; Ivan had confessed to that almost immediately. Parker had been intending to protect Ivan as best he could, but apparently, he wasn't interested in Parker's protection.

With a grim expression, Nadar had left. Trish had stopped by briefly and given him something to drink. Despite being around Ivan's age, she'd had a very matronly air about her, quite a change from the spitfire he'd seen.

Now, though, he just wanted to go home. Or he wanted someone to bring Ivan to him to explain what the hell was going on. If everything they'd had was a damned lie, or whether it had all been for the job.

The door opened, and Parker turned to face the next inquisitor. But it was only Kurt. Kurt, who looked tired and drawn.

"Sit down. Have you been here this whole time?" Parker hadn't forgotten that the man was recovering from a gunshot wound and surgery.

"Yeah." Kurt shrugged and winced. He rubbed his wounded shoulder for a moment.

"Can I go? Or is someone going to tell me what's happening?"

A loud, heavy sigh was Kurt's initial reply. "Sorry. Nadar's been working his tail off, and this got resolved faster than I expected." He slumped down into one of the incredibly uncomfortable plastic chairs and gestured for Parker to join him.

This was faster? With an ear-piercing squeak of metal leg against linoleum, Parker pulled out a chair and sat on the edge. Waiting. From Kurt's expression, there could be no good to follow.

"Nadar's putting a rush on everything because this involves our own, but you should be free to go soon."

"Okay. What else?" Because that didn't tell him a damned thing.

"We've arrested Neil on several drug-related charges."

Okay, okay. That sort of made sense. For whatever reason, the cops thought Parker was responsible for Neil's crimes. "Why me? Why wasn't Ivan investigating Neil?"

Kurt looked down, and a black weight formed in Parker's stomach.

"I'm sorry, Parker. He's also been charged with identity theft and fraud. When your background check came in, we were able to figure out where all the money came from. He took out a huge mortgage on your Muskoka property. Used the money to set up the grow-op and, we suspect, pay off gambling debts to the Russians."

Kurt's words all made sense, but not in relation to his boring, sedate life. Except for the gambling debts. Neil had always been super serious about his poker. Parker licked dry lips and swallowed. "You said mortgage?"

"To the tune of five hundred thousand."

"Half a million dollars?" Spots swam in front of his eyes, and he forgot how to breathe.

"Hey. Hey. In and out. In and out." Kurt gripped his hands, almost burning his suddenly bloodless fingers. Parker followed Kurt's instructions until he wasn't in any more danger of passing the fuck out.

How could he be so stupid? Why hadn't he seen what Neil was doing? "What am I going to do? How… can I even fix this?"

"There's a support group that can give you some guidance." Kurt slid a business card to him. "If you can afford a lawyer, get one."

"I have a lawyer already." Thank God.

"Good. With Neil in custody, you've got an excellent chance of getting this cleared up, but it's going to fuck with your credit for a few months, at least. Possibly until the trial's done. Just be glad he didn't have a chance to take out any loans against your house."

Glad. No, no, glad wasn't the word he'd choose to describe his mood. In less than twenty-four hours, Parker's life had turned completely upside down. His best friend in jail for stealing his identity, his lover a complete stranger, and his father….

"What about Martelli?" Surely he was going to pay for what he'd done.

Kurt stared at him, brows furrowing. "So you really didn't know who he was? You'd never tried to find him?"

"Why would I? My mother and I did just fine without him, and if he never wanted me, why would I bother?" Leaving his mom when he'd found out she was pregnant had actually been a good thing. What he'd done to Ivan was completely unforgivable; it wouldn't be clear for some time if his selfishness had destroyed Ivan's mental health along with his career.

"He's retiring." Kurt snorted in disgust. "Nadar thought a quiet retirement in exchange for saving Ivan's job was worthwhile."

Kurt continued to explain. When his father had thought he was involved with Razhin, he'd taken advantage of Ivan's disorientation to investigate on the sly. No one had any idea what Martelli had been intending to do if Parker had been guilty, but he'd been terrified their relationship would become public if Parker ended up getting arrested and going to trial. It would have destroyed his chances for getting elected and likely would have cost him the rich wife he'd been trying to keep when he'd dumped Parker's mom in the first place. Ironically, his actions may still have had the same effect, and Parker couldn't dredge up one ounce of sympathy. So stupid.

"What about... um... am I safe? They know where I live."

"Should be. As far as we can tell, Leo knew about you, but Neil wasn't part of Razhin's group. Not yet. He'd already paid off his gambling debts and was working on the grow-op to impress them. They shouldn't care that you're testifying against Neil. But the Drug Squad has a few useful informants. We'll spread the word that you had no involvement in Neil's doings. Until then, we'll have a patrol car doing regular drive-bys. I'll leave you my number, and I'll check in on you too."

That made him feel a little safer, but why would Kurt be checking in?

"Where's Ivan?"

Kurt's gaze skittered away. "He said it was best this way. A clean break." He coughed.

"Was that all he said?"

Kurt patted his hand, like that was going to somehow make the pain better. "He said it was all part of the job."

Parker slid back in the seat like Kurt had punched him in the chest. Pain bloomed in his heart, sharp and searing. He'd been afraid Ivan would reject him, but the actual occurrence was almost as painful as losing his mother. And the shit didn't even have the decency to do it himself.

"I don't know if it helps, but you wouldn't be able to see each other anyway. A relationship would compromise the case."

"Oh, that's convenient." Nothing like getting dumped by your lover's colleague in a fucking police station after your life had just blown up in your face. He was a bigger loser now than when he'd been the friendless fat kid.

"You're both witnesses, and a defense attorney will have a field day with your... uh... interactions with Ivan."

By sheer force of will, he managed to keep his face from betraying his shock. How much detail had Ivan given his colleagues? Humiliation was the only thing that bottled up his agonized scream.

"I'm sorry, kid. Can… Is there anything I can do?"

Parker shook his head. If he opened his mouth now, the tears would fall, and that would never do.

"Call you a cab home?"

He nodded so hard his neck spasmed. Getting out of here was imperative. Leave this nightmare behind. Try to patch up the shredded remnants of his life.

IVAN stood at the window and watched Parker walk toward a cab. The streetlights glistened off the sidewalk, wet from a storm that had erupted after he'd arrived. Parker trudged like a beaten old man instead of the vibrant young student he was. It wasn't entirely Ivan's fault, but the guilt weighed him down. Of all the people who'd betrayed Parker today, he was the only one who regretted it.

The watery reflection of Kurt materialized on the glass to his right.

"He'll be okay, won't he?" He couldn't bear it if his actions put Parker into more danger than they'd already survived.

"Should be. No reason for Parker to be any more than a blip on Razhin's radar."

Kurt wouldn't lie to him, and at the moment, he couldn't trust his own reasoning.

"I was…." Ivan coughed uncomfortably. How did you admit to your friends you were losing your mind? "There was no conspiracy. No one was suspicious. No one was watching the house, were they?"

"No. They weren't. Neil was trying to interest them, but he hadn't gotten too far along with that plan."

Parker took one furtive glance over his shoulder, up toward the building, before getting into the cab.

"I think you should have talked to him." Kurt's hand was warm on his shoulder.

"I couldn't." Ivan touched the cool glass with a finger.

"He might have been willing to wait."

"Doesn't matter. I'm too fucked up, and even if he was willing to wait, we couldn't have contact until the trial was over. I couldn't ask him to wait years. Not for me. We only knew each other two weeks. He'll survive."

A gentle squeeze before Kurt's hand withdrew. "But will you?"

God. Wasn't that the question. Foolish to be in so deep so quick, but perhaps that was testament to how fucked up he'd become. He pressed his forehead to the cool glass as his eyes burned. He refused to blink until the cab disappeared from sight. The ache of missing Parker had already begun, but he might as well get used to it. He'd have to learn to live with the ache for the rest of his life.

"Where's Nadar?" Answering Kurt's rhetorical question would have been pointless.

"In his office."

Ivan nodded. He'd had hours to consider his next course of action, and all it had taken was a few moments at his desk to complete it.

"Thanks." He turned to Kurt and looked him straight in the eye. The thanks was for more than just answering his question. If it weren't for Kurt's help, he'd be under arrest right now, and definitely fired. This way he could leave on his own terms.

"Any time, Ivan."

OUTSIDE Nadar's office, Ivan halted and rapped on the door.

"Enter." Nadar's tone was brisk but not unfriendly, though the man had every right to be pissed at Ivan right now. Not only had his drama made Nadar come in on the weekend, but he'd had to get involved in a very unpleasant business.

Ivan hovered by the chair, but what he had to do wouldn't take very long. No point in getting comfortable.

"Can you please direct this to the appropriate people?" Ivan placed an unsealed envelope on the desk.

Nadar frowned and pointed at the chair. "Sit." He picked up the envelope and extracted the letter, frown deepening as he read.

Ivan preferred not to, but he owed Nadar for standing up for him and Parker. For the time being, Nadar was his superior officer. He sat.

"No," Nadar said.

"What do you mean, no?" Of all the responses, he hadn't expected that one.

"I mean, no." Nadar slipped the envelope into a desk drawer. "You are not in any condition to make this kind of decision. You've been under tremendous strain, and you've not been able to get any benefits from the prescribed therapy because of the situation you were forced into. If you quit, the city will be poorer for it, and I want you to be able to assess all your options. Go to therapy. Take some time to rest, for real this time. Then we'll see."

Ivan shook his head. "You don't understand. I was thinking about this before. Undercover wears on you, and I just can't take it anymore. Besides, coming back to a new superior, after what transpired… it's not going to be long before everyone realizes I'm to blame."

Martelli had been a popular officer, despite his constant thoughts of how his actions would affect his chances for election.

"Not your fault. At all. But I understand your concerns. You, and your partner, if she wishes to transfer, will be welcome in my department. Homicide requires very little in the way of undercover work, and the change might do you good. One month. Let's regroup in one month, and we'll see where you are and if you still feel the same way."

Was this a much needed reprieve or were they merely prolonging the agony? Still, it couldn't hurt to follow Nadar's directives. The mood swings, hair trigger temper, and nightmares needed to be addressed. He'd much rather have insurance with which to do so.

"One month." That wasn't too much to give Nadar, although he didn't have much hope he'd change his mind.

IVAN lay on his bed, staring up at the ceiling. He didn't quite recall when he'd last showered, ate, or anything. Yesterday had been a blur of interrogation and pain. Yesterday he'd said good-bye to Parker, and already the days stretched out before him, eons of loneliness. The last time he'd showered was at Parker's, a lifetime ago.

Every thought of Parker made his stomach roil with regret. Eating was completely out, and so far the only thing that helped was staring at the blank ceiling, pushing all other thoughts from his mind. Unfortunately, he couldn't stay here forever. Sanchez was expecting him later this afternoon for an emergency session.

Twisting his head, he checked out his bedside clock, then sat up in bed. There was no good reason for all his muscles to ache like he was coming down with the flu. If he didn't get up now, he wouldn't have time to pick up his phone from Rick before his appointment, and it was unlikely he'd be interested in talking to anyone afterward.

If he'd still had a landline, he'd have called Rick and asked him to drop it by, but he really shouldn't be without his phone.

After stretching his ancient, creaky muscles, Ivan pulled on some clothes and shuffled his way to the apartment's parking structure.

"IVAN, what are you doing here?" Rick's light-blond hair was tousled, and he appeared to have pulled on a pair of jeans in haste.

"Sorry, is this a bad time?" Sure it was two on a Monday afternoon, but Rick's work schedule was fluid, which had made it easy for Ivan to hook up with him more than once. On the job, Ivan's hours were seriously fucked up.

"No, it's fine. Come on in." Rick ushered him in, a frown on his face.

"I just need my phone." He wasn't going to win any awards for small talk today.

"Sure thing, honey. You got a lot of calls, but other than that, nothing unusual. I don't think. Should I still be on the lookout? What happened?"

Ivan followed him to the kitchen where Rick pulled his phone and charger off the counter.

"It's a long story." One he couldn't bear to talk about yet. "Everything's fine, now."

"Fine?" Rick pulled Ivan's phone back toward his body. "Honey, you do not look fine. Where's that sweet thing you moved in with? Shouldn't he be taking care of you?"

Ivan bit back a gasp. Thinking about Parker was like a toothache. Every time he touched it, the pain flared, sharp and hot, before it receded to a dull ache he couldn't quite ignore.

Rick's eyes filled with sympathy. The man tried not to care about people, but somehow, Ivan had slipped past his defenses. "Oh, big boy. I shouldn't have mentioned it. Where are you off to now?"

"Doctor's appointment."

One blond brow rose. "Okay, good. Because, honey, you look like boiled hell."

Ivan let out a rusty chuckle. Most people might have thought Rick's words harsh, but Ivan sensed the caring in the tone. Rick did his best to keep his interactions on a light note and made a special effort not to get romantically attached. Something about it scared the crap out of him. If Rick had ever gone through what Ivan was going through now, he didn't blame him one bit for his reluctance.

"I'm okay." Or he would be if he kept repeating the mantra.

"I'll take your word for it. For now." Rick sidled up next to him, seemingly unable to turn off the auto-flirt. "But let me know if I can cheer you up. Anytime, big boy, anytime."

Ivan's lips curled into what he hoped was a smile but likely didn't make it past a grimace. "Thanks, Rick, but…."

The flirt fell away, and Rick hugged him. "You let me know. They say the best way to get over a guy is to get into another. Or something like that."

Another rusty chuckle escaped, and Rick smiled. "I'll let you get into me whenever."

"Thanks, Rick." Ivan tucked his phone and charger into his pockets.

Time to face the shrink. Sanchez wouldn't accept his claims of "I'm fine" this time. Not after Nadar had given him the complete download. He almost asked Rick for a shot of tequila, but alcohol would only make his situation worse. With a sigh, he left. Under normal circumstances, he'd have accepted Rick's offer in a minute, but that was before he'd met Parker.

If he couldn't have Parker, his mind and libido had decided he couldn't fuck anyone else to try and forget. The complete opposite of his reaction after Colin left, and it sucked bad.

PARKER sat on the floor in the wreckage of his living room. Amazing how much could be destroyed in less than an hour. His lawyer and insurance agent had both assured him he was lucky. That it could have been worse. After all, they hadn't burned the house down. Leo and his buddy could have vandalized the entire place, but instead they'd engaged in a thorough and destructive search for the money. Perhaps if they'd been left in his house any longer—and he'd be eternally grateful to Kurt that they weren't—they might have moved on to destruction for its own sake. Structurally, the place was sound. Walls, doors, and windows were intact. However, they'd slashed every mattress, pillow, and cushion open. Broken most of his electronics. Emptied the contents of every drawer and cupboard onto the floor. Hadn't affected his clothes much, but he didn't have a single plate or glass left.

He'd given Neil a number of free passes over the years, but knowing Neil was responsible made it easy for Parker to harden his heart against his longtime friend. Neil may have been his friend at one point, but when the gambling debts put him afoul of the Russian mafia, he'd had no qualms about paying them off and starting a new venture at Parker's expense. If only Neil had asked. Parker would have helped him, but it was obvious Neil had expected him to ultimately take the fall.

Neil's debt had destroyed his credit rating, and Parker might still end up having to pay it back, although with Neil arrested, there was a good possibility he'd come through this financially unscathed. Eventually. Without Ivan to vouch for him, Parker could very well have ended up the scapegoat Neil had intended.

More alone than he'd ever been, he wanted to hate Ivan for all the hurt he'd caused, but next to Neil's perfidy, he couldn't. Ivan hadn't done any of it maliciously, not like Neil. More than anything, Parker wanted Ivan back in his life, but Ivan didn't want him. Their relationship—of sorts—was over. His lawyer had even applauded Ivan's decision, which strangely made Parker soften toward Ivan and hate his lawyer, just a bit.

The doorbell rang, breaking up Parker's depressing contemplation of his house. He hoisted himself to his feet. Probably the insurance adjuster.

Parker yanked at the unyielding door to reveal Alicia.

"Parker!" Alicia hugged him. "Missed you in class today. I have a favor to ask, so I thought I'd stop by, since you didn't answer my text."

Huh. He must have accidently turned his phone off. "Sorry. It's been a crazy weekend."

"Was it?" Alicia waggled her brows, and Parker snorted.

"Not like that." Or at least not Saturday or Sunday. He stepped back and gestured for her to enter.

"Holy shitballs, Parker. What the fuck happened?"

"It's a long story." One he wasn't ready to tell yet, although telling someone might make it a little more believable. Someday he'd tell her, but today the wound was too raw. He'd lost too much. "Basically, my house got broken into, and they trashed the place."

"Oh no! Are you okay? Did they catch the guys?"

"I'm fine." Mostly. "And yes, they caught the guys."

Normally he'd offer her a seat, but there wasn't anyplace to sit. Alicia stepped over the debris, assessing the damage.

"What was the favor?"

Alicia glanced up at him. "Oh, well, Chris and I decided to move in together, but my lease is up soon and his has a few more months. I was going to ask you if I could rent out your extra room until his lease was up. I can't move into that tiny place with him and Thom—the bathroom itself might spawn a brand-new life form—but I'll figure something else out."

The world, which had seemed so very bleak a moment ago, became a little more friendly and warm.

"No, why? You can still move in. But instead of rent, can you help me get this place back in order?"

"Are you sure?" Alicia looked around as though she'd misplaced something. "Hey, where's Ivan?"

His tiny smile fell away. "That's part of the long story. Ivan moved out."

Parker hiccupped. Tears had been fighting to break free for hours, but his last statement let them escape. Alicia let out a tiny sound of distress and pulled him into a hug.

"Please tell me Ivan didn't do this."

"No." The word came out more watery than he would have liked, but he'd never been good at being an emotionless macho man.

"Oh, good." Alicia sighed. "I liked him."

"Me too. But we're done." Parker was still pissed. Ivan had gotten him to fall in love. He'd never realized it could happen so fast, but it had; then Ivan had disappeared from his life. In a way, he was almost thankful for the distraction of his home repairs. "Will you move in? Help me?"

"Of course I'll help. Chris and Thom will help, too, I know it."

Which meant he'd have to talk to Thom, let him know he wasn't ready for any sort of dating or relationship. At least any friend of Chris's wouldn't be a dick about it, not like Neil's friends.

Alicia kissed his temple and drew back, wiping tears from his face with her hands like his mom used to do. "Let's get started now. What's the most urgent?"

Strangely, his CPAP machine had survived. "Dishes. I need dishes."

"Go wash your face, and we'll pop over to Honest Ed's. They ought to have something inexpensive."

Another ray of sunshine broke through into the bleakness of his existence. Somehow, he'd survive.

CHAPTER
Twelve

IVAN stared at the door, heart hammering in his chest. He'd made a point of never passing by Parker's house until now. He knew he wouldn't have the willpower to not go inside and beg for Parker to forgive him. It had been the right move. A clean break was the only way he'd be able to give Parker up at all.

He hadn't gone back to work yet. His one month agreement with Nadar was rapidly approaching. With proper therapy and not worrying about every word he said, he'd made a lot of progress with his PTSD. The unauthorized operation had set him back, but he was at a point where he was almost ready to go back to work, ready to transfer into Homicide.

A car horn in the street made him flinch, but at least he wasn't ducking shots for every unexpected sound. Kurt was right; this unfinished business would nag at him until he saw Parker one last time. One last time to kill the lingering hope logic hadn't been able to squelch.

He still had a key to Parker's house—kept it safe in his bedside drawer in his half-lived-in apartment—but it wouldn't be right to use it. The stuff he'd moved into Parker's house had been boxed up and delivered to Kurt's house a few days after all that shit had gone down, an unexpected consideration from Parker; sending it to his work would have broadcast to everyone what a fuckup Ivan was.

One deep breath and he knocked on the door. Footsteps pounded down the stairs, and he scarcely had a second to wonder what he'd do if Parker had a boyfriend before the door swung open.

Parker stood there, tall and gorgeous and stunned. But his shock quickly passed, and he frowned.

"Ivan. What are you doing here?"

"Hi. Parker." He should have fucking rehearsed what he was going to say, but damn it, he hadn't even been sure he'd have the balls to actually knock.

"I sent your stuff to Kurt's. I didn't have your address." The censure in those measured words almost brought him to his knees.

"I know. Thank you." No point in saying he hadn't opened the boxes, just shoved them in a closet where he wouldn't be reminded of Parker.

Parker crossed his arms and stared at him, waiting.

He cleared his throat. "Can I come in?"

Stepping aside, Parker waved him in. What would it take to make him smile? Did Ivan still have the ability to make him smile? It was the only ability he wanted. He walked into the living room and stopped short.

"You redecorated."

"I had to. The place was destroyed."

Ivan closed his eyes. God. He hadn't even thought of that. "I'm so sorry, Parker. So sorry." He should have been here to help.

"Why are you here, Ivan?"

Opening his eyes, the interior was similar enough to create warmth in his belly. Despite it all, he'd been happy here, happy with Parker.

He turned back to Parker. His eyes weren't cold—Parker wasn't capable of being cold—but he was distant. Remote. As much as he wanted to pull Parker into his arms and kiss him, he didn't have that right. Not anymore and maybe never again.

"There's been a development in the case. Neil pleaded guilty to a lesser charge and is going to testify against Leo. Not sure if we'll be able to get Razhin, but this way we don't have to go to trial." Could he salvage what they had?

"Is that the only reason you're here?"

"No." He stepped up into Parker's personal space and gripped him by the shoulders. It was all he could do to keep from kissing the man, but it was too soon. "I'm here because I've missed you. I was a complete and total shit, but the only thing I lied about was my job. I swear. I think… I think we could make something work. I lo…."

Parker's eyes widened, but Ivan couldn't tell if it was because he'd almost admitted to being in love or if it was something else. He'd never felt like this before, not even with Colin. It had been a struggle to get through every day without seeing Parker. He loved Parker, and Parker might hate him; he'd have to save his confession of love until later.

"What about, uh… are you back at work?"

Ivan's hands fell away. He should be glad Parker wasn't kicking him out, even if he hoped Parker would just fall into his arms.

He walked into the living room and stood, unsure if he should sit or not.

"Soon. I think. Nadar offered me a transfer to Homicide. Right now, I'm working on my PTSD."

"You are? Oh, I'm so glad." The touch of Parker's hand on his back was light, like a feather, but it made goose bumps rise on his nape. "Are you doing better?"

Ivan turned suddenly, Parker so close, breath warmed his cheek.

"Better, yes, but I still miss you. Can we… go out? Start dating maybe?"

"Dating?" Parker's voice was unflatteringly incredulous. "No."

Two little letters, one syllable, gutted him, left him unable to breathe.

"I want you to move back in here."

Had lack of air made him hallucinate? "Move back in?"

Parker licked his lips, and Ivan forced himself not to be distracted from Parker's words.

"I think we've moved beyond dating, don't you?"

"We've only known each other less than two months, and I was a shit. Why do you want me to move in? Don't do it because you're lonely."

Those words were a mistake. Parker's eyes flashed, and he stepped back. "I'm younger than you, and I don't have the same experience as you, but I'm not desperate for company. Alicia moved in with me right after. I love having her here, but I miss you. I miss what we had. And if that wasn't a lie, I want that back. Once Kurt opened my eyes, I should have known you were having PTSD. If you're getting help, I think we can… start again, yes, but start as a couple."

He wanted to believe. He wanted this not to be some cruel joke, but how could Parker be so certain?

"How… why?" He took a step back; Parker's proximity affected his logical thought.

"I had a month to decide what I wanted if you ever showed up, or if Kurt ever told me where you lived."

"You… kept in touch with Kurt?"

Parker lifted a shoulder in a negligent shrug. "I wanted to know how you were doing."

It couldn't be this easy, could it? He clenched his hands into fists to control the trembling. "What if we had to go to trial? It could have been years."

"I would have waited. When it's right, you just know." Parker took a step forward. "What do you say? We can wait until your lease is up, if you want."

Ivan took in a deep gulp of air. Could he do this? Could he gamble on his feelings, on them? But then he looked deep into Parker's eyes. He wanted every opportunity to see those eyes, to wake up next to Parker. Dating would be ludicrous, because he wanted to come home.

His eyes burned, and his mouth was dry, but he nodded. "I can afford to break my lease."

Parker stared at him for a moment, head tilted to the side, assessing him. Then he leapt at Ivan, lips finding Ivan's like they belonged there. Which they did.

Someone moaned—it might have been him—as their tongues dueled, frantic and desperate. Ivan slid his hands up under Parker's shirt, clutching him closer. Parker held him just as tightly, pressing their immediately aroused bodies together.

"Oh, my. Um." A woman's voice broke through their passion. If she'd waited any longer to speak, one or both of them would have been naked.

Ivan pulled his head back, Parker's dilated river stone eyes tempting him to not care if they had an audience. Almost drugged-looking, Parker turned toward their interruption. "Hey, Alicia. Ivan's home."

Home. He gave Parker a little squeeze.

"So I see."

"Hi, Alicia." He smiled tentatively, checking her expression for censure. Even if Parker forgave him, his friends might not.

"Hi, Ivan. Are you moving back in?"

He nodded. "Is that okay?"

"If it's okay with Parker."

"Oh, it's okay with me." The lustful huskiness in Parker's words heated Ivan's cheeks. Made him want to run right up to their room.

"It won't be odd living here with us?" It had been a long time since he'd had roommates. At least, ones that he wasn't sleeping with.

"Oh, I'm only here temporarily. My lease was up before Chris's was, so I moved in here until we can get a place together."

Ivan relaxed. He'd rather not put Alicia out, but he wanted to make a home with Parker more than anything.

"So... go get your stuff. Now." Parker poked him in the side. Ivan laughed. The last time he'd laughed he'd been in this house, with this man. He wasn't going to forget how that felt.

Alicia smiled at them, approval written all over her face. Good.

"Well?" Parker poked him again.

"It'll take me some time to get my stuff packed up. Are you sure?"

Parker stiffened in his arms. "Aren't you?"

Fast. So fast. But he couldn't care. He wanted every moment he could get with Parker. Life was fragile and fleeting, and he wasn't going to fuck up this relationship. Parker meant too much to him.

"I'm sure." Ivan flicked a glance toward Alicia.

"No," she said emphatically.

"What?" Parker was confused, but Ivan knew damn well what she was vetoing.

"No celebratory make-up sex until I'm far, far away. Got it?"

Blood suffused Parker's face, and Ivan had to laugh again. His boyfriend was still so innocent.

"Better buy earplugs for tonight." Ivan pinched Parker's ass and, unbelievably, his face flamed hotter.

"Well, if we're not having sex, you'd better go pack your apartment." Parker glared at both of them.

"I'm going to study upstairs. No funny business. None. Especially on the couch, because I have to sit there too sometimes."

Ivan tugged his boyfriend—be a long time before he got tired of that phrase—down onto the new couch. As soon as Alicia moved out, he was fucking Parker every which way on it. But there were a few things he needed to clear up before he dashed off to pack.

"Don't you have any more questions about Neil or what's happening with him?" Ivan had given him only the briefest of explanations.

"No. Kurt told me all about it already."

Oh, that sneaky bastard. Playing both sides, making sure Parker knew what was going on and goading Ivan into coming back.

"That's good."

Parker curled himself around Ivan and nuzzled his neck, making Ivan squirm. "Apparently there was a lot of damage to the cottage as well. As soon as they've finished dismantling and removing all the plants and the drug processing equipment, we'll have to go out there and assess the damage, figure out how much we need to fix it."

"I'm so sorry. I should have realized there'd be a lot of fallout. I've got some money in the bank." It had been earmarked to buy a condo, but he didn't need that now. He already had the car he wanted waiting in the condo parking structure.

"No. You don't have to do that. I can't take out any bank loans or anything until everything's been cleared up on my credit report, but I can take out a loan against my trust fund. I had to do that to fix things up here, and I should be able to do that to fix up the cottage."

Ivan slid over to put a couple inches between them and cupped Parker's face in his hands. "Did you mean it, that we're in this together? We're a couple, sharing a house?"

Parker nodded as much as he was able with Ivan's hands in the way. "I want to share everything with you. I want this to be ours."

"Then let me invest in our cottage. Let me pay for the repairs."

A tiny, pleased smiled turned up the corners of Parker's mouth. Just right for kissing. "Thanks."

Those lips were irresistible, and Ivan took a quick kiss before speaking. "So was that the only time you spoke to Kurt?"

A hint of pink shaded Parker's cheekbones. "No. He's been kind enough to keep me updated. About the case and…. uh… you."

"Me? He really is a sneaky bastard." But he couldn't stop grinning. The fact that Parker had cared enough to ask after him warmed him.

"You don't mind?"

Ivan let another thorough kiss answer for him.

"So if you've been in touch with Kurt, did he invite you to his housewarming tomorrow?"

"Yes. But I wasn't going to go. Mostly because my lawyer told me you were right about staying out of contact."

"If you don't have plans, did you want to go? Together?" He hadn't made it to Kurt's painting party, mostly because he hadn't been in any mood for socializing two weeks ago. Until this very moment, he hadn't been sure he wanted to go the housewarming either and pretend to be happy. Now that he was happy in truth, he wanted to show Parker off.

"Yes, I do." Parker pressed his body next to Ivan's, almost squirming in his need to get closer. The touch of Parker's lips on the underside of his jaw had him doing a bit of squirming himself.

Ivan turned his head to do a bit of nuzzling of his own. "If we go upstairs, think you can be quiet?"

"Maybe." Parker grinned.

Grabbing Parker's hand, Ivan hoisted him off the couch. "She didn't really expect us to reconcile *without* heading to the bedroom, right? She's lucky we're not stripping right here."

Parker chuckled and nodded, gaze hot as he scanned Ivan up and down.

Yes. Alicia was lucky he had enough restraint to get them upstairs, but that's all that could be expected of a man who'd been half dead for the past month.

"IVAN! And Parker? So glad you could come." Davy gave them both a hug and ushered them into the house.

Kurt stood in the living room with several people, only a couple of whom Ivan knew. Parker would know even fewer, but that was okay. They hadn't been back together even forty-eight hours. No way was Ivan letting his delectable boyfriend wander around a houseful of gay men. Well. Not everyone here was gay, but a good portion were. Not one of them would be under any illusions about who Parker was with.

"Do you know everyone?" Davy asked.

Ivan shook his head. "No, but that's okay. We'll manage."

Parker tucked up close, and Ivan threaded their fingers together. Although Parker had never come out and said anything, Ivan suspected he was nervous in groups of people he didn't know.

Kurt caught sight of them and excused himself from the group of men and women he'd been talking to. As he approached, his glance took in their entwined hands, and he smiled. "I take it things have worked out?"

Parker relaxed a bit. "He's moving in."

"Yeah? Well you already have some experience with that, don't you? Ivan knows my partner, Simon, but I don't think either of you have met his wife or my brothers."

Kurt led them into the center of the room. Parker smiled as they were introduced to Simon, Kurt's partner on the force, and his wife, Jen, as well as two of Kurt's brothers.

Their easy acceptance of Parker's presence at his side had Parker relaxing even more. For a few minutes, the conversation eddied around them, leaving them in their own oasis, just him and Parker. "You know, Kurt's got six brothers and sisters."

Parker's eyes widened. "They aren't all here, are they? This place will be packed."

"I don't know if they're all showing up tonight or not. My understanding is that the family makes a point of all being available for birthdays, weddings, and births, but other events don't have the whole crew." Ivan smiled. "My family likes the Sunday dinner tradition."

Parker paled. "Your family."

Ivan smiled and squeezed Parker's arm. "Don't you worry. They'll love you. If you're up to it, I'll take you to meet them tomorrow."

"Tomorrow?"

"Trust me. They know how miserable I've been without you. My sisters especially will adore you."

Parker pressed his lips together and nodded.

"Ivan, I didn't know you'd be here!"

Ivan broke away from Parker to greet the newcomer.

"Rick? How are you?" The lithe blond gave him a big hug and kept his arms draped around Ivan's neck. Parker wasn't pleased, but he didn't say anything. Not yet. Ivan took a step away from Rick's embrace but wasn't able to evade it entirely.

"I guess you know Kurt, right?"

"Yes, I know Kurt. We're going to be in the same department when I go back to work." Rick knew he'd been off work and that he'd been in the Drug Squad. Fortunately, he hadn't pressed for much in the way of an explanation about Ivan's erratic and mysterious behavior when he'd moved in with Parker. "How do you know Kurt?"

"Davy's one of my best friends."

Shit, the world was a really small place.

"So, my big, strong cop, are you feeling better?" Rick's words had Parker frowning.

Parker took a step closer. "He's my big, strong cop."

"Oh, ho, the boy has teeth."

"Rick, enough." He knew Rick well enough to know he wasn't actually trying to make any sort of claim, but he was testing Parker. Sometimes, Rick did shit just to get a rise out of people, but he was a good friend, one of the few Ivan had; he didn't want Rick and Parker at odds.

"I'm not a boy, and he's mine." Then again, Ivan could get used to a possessive Parker.

"Really, Rick? Aren't you a little old to be getting into a catfight with a twink?"

They all turned toward the new voice.

"Ian?" Ivan coughed uncomfortably. He hadn't expected to be surrounded by three men he'd slept with, although Ian had only been a one-night stand. More than an anonymous quickie at a club, but it hadn't developed into the semi-regular encounters he'd had with Rick.

"Ivan?"

Rick's grip around his neck tightened, and Parker glared at all three of them.

"Ivan." Parker wasn't stupid, and he was getting angry. "Have you slept with both these guys?"

Neither Rick nor Ian was happy about that revelation. Ivan finally shook Rick off and wrapped his arms around Parker. "I told you about that bad break up, remember?"

Parker nodded tightly, eyes shining. He had to fix this. "I went a little crazy afterward. Slept with a lot of guys. But Rick and I became friends."

A huff of irritation came from behind, but right now, no one mattered more than Parker.

"But not since? Wait." Parker closed his eyes and took a deep breath. "I have no right to ask that. But never again, right?"

Ivan brushed his lips over Parker's. "Not since I met you. I couldn't."

A blinding smile made Ivan wonder just how long they had to stick around to be polite. With his arm tucked around Parker's waist, they turned back to Rick and Ian, who stood toe to toe, glaring at each other. Kurt joined them, seemingly oblivious of the antagonistic undercurrents.

"Hey, I see you met my other brother, Ian," Kurt said.

"Ian's your brother?" Parker's voice was shocked.

Kurt raised a brow. "Oh. I see. Which of you were one of Ian's club conquests?"

Parker poked a finger at Ivan, while his face heated. Perhaps Kurt wasn't oblivious to the undercurrents so much as accustomed to them. Apparently, since Ivan's encounter with Kurt's brother the guy had come out of the closet. Good for him.

"And Ivan slept with Rick too." Great. Parker didn't need to spill all the secrets, did he?

Kurt nodded. "Well, that explains the glaring."

"You... you're not upset?" Ivan had never been in a position to be protective of siblings because of their lovers; his sisters had both found their significant others while Ivan was still in his mid-teens, but Kurt might feel differently.

"No. Why would I? I've always known he was a bit of slut, but I only recently found out it was guys he was banging." Kurt turned, a teasing expression on his face, but somehow, Rick and Ian had both disappeared without anyone noticing.

Kurt shook his head. "Davy'll kill them if they've left again without telling us."

Again? Ian's bitchy words about the catfight made a lot more sense.

"Hey, speaking of leaving, do you mind if we take off? Give Davy our best?"

Kurt laughed and cuffed Ivan on the shoulder. "Yeah, no problem."

On their way out, they waved at a few people, but they didn't pause. Out on the porch, Parker pulled him to stop.

"Really? No one while we were apart?"

"Really. No one since I met you. I...." It was still too soon to talk about the *L* word, wasn't it? Parker was it for him, though.

Parker's eyes softened, like he'd known what Ivan had been about to say.

"I know. Me neither. No one else ever again."

"No one else. I promise. You're all I want. Forever."

Parker traced a finger over his lips. "Forever."

KC BURN has been writing for as long as she can remember and is a sucker for happy endings (of all kinds). After moving from Toronto to Florida for her husband to take a dream job, she discovered a love of gay romance and fulfilled a dream of her own—getting published. By day she edits web content, and at night she neglects her supportive, understanding hubby and needy cat to write stories about men loving men in the past, present and future. Writing is always fun and rewarding, but writing about her guys is the most fun she's had in a long time, and she hopes you'll enjoy them as much as she does.

Visit KC at her website: http://www.kcburn.com or on Twitter: http://twitter.com/authorkcburn.

Don't miss the beginning of the story in

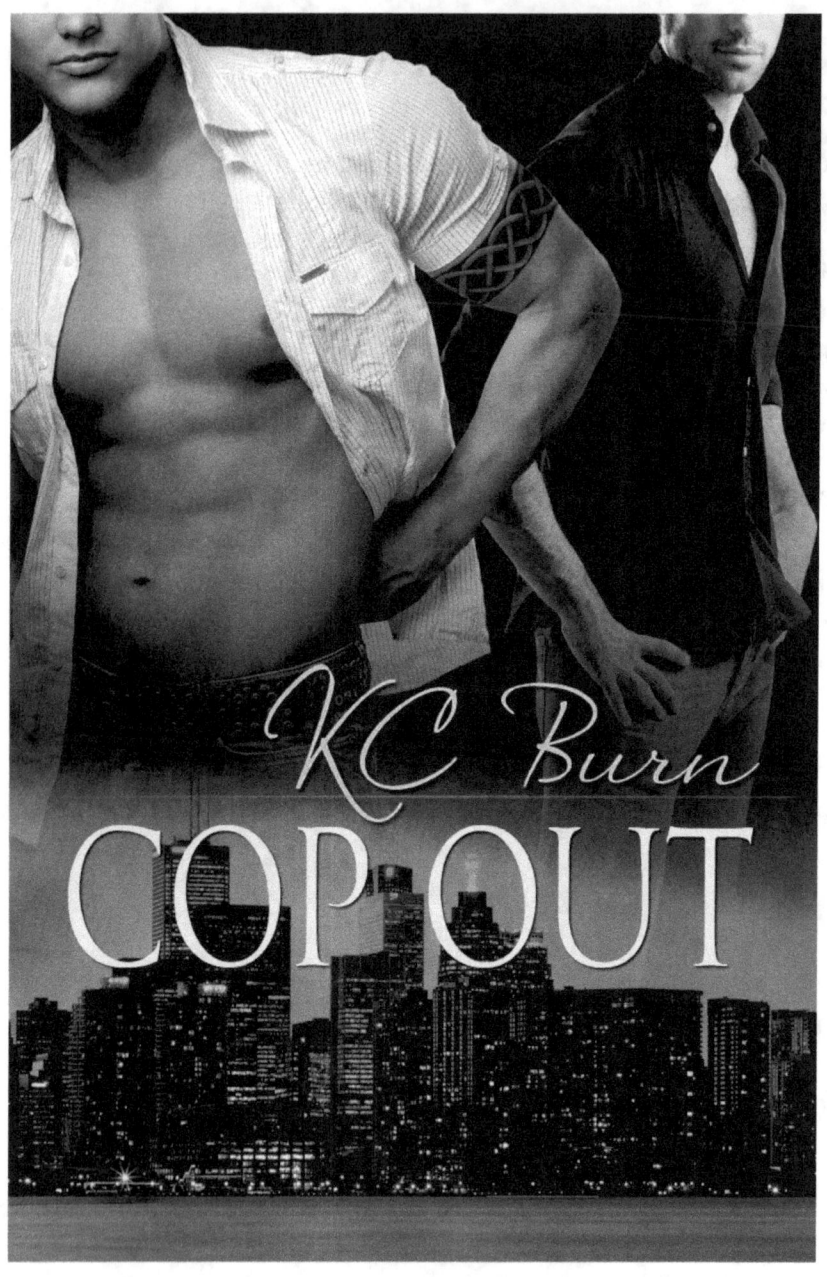

KC Burn

COP OUT

http://www.dreamspinnerpress.com

Suspense Romance from DREAMSPINNER PRESS

http://www.dreamspinnerpress.com

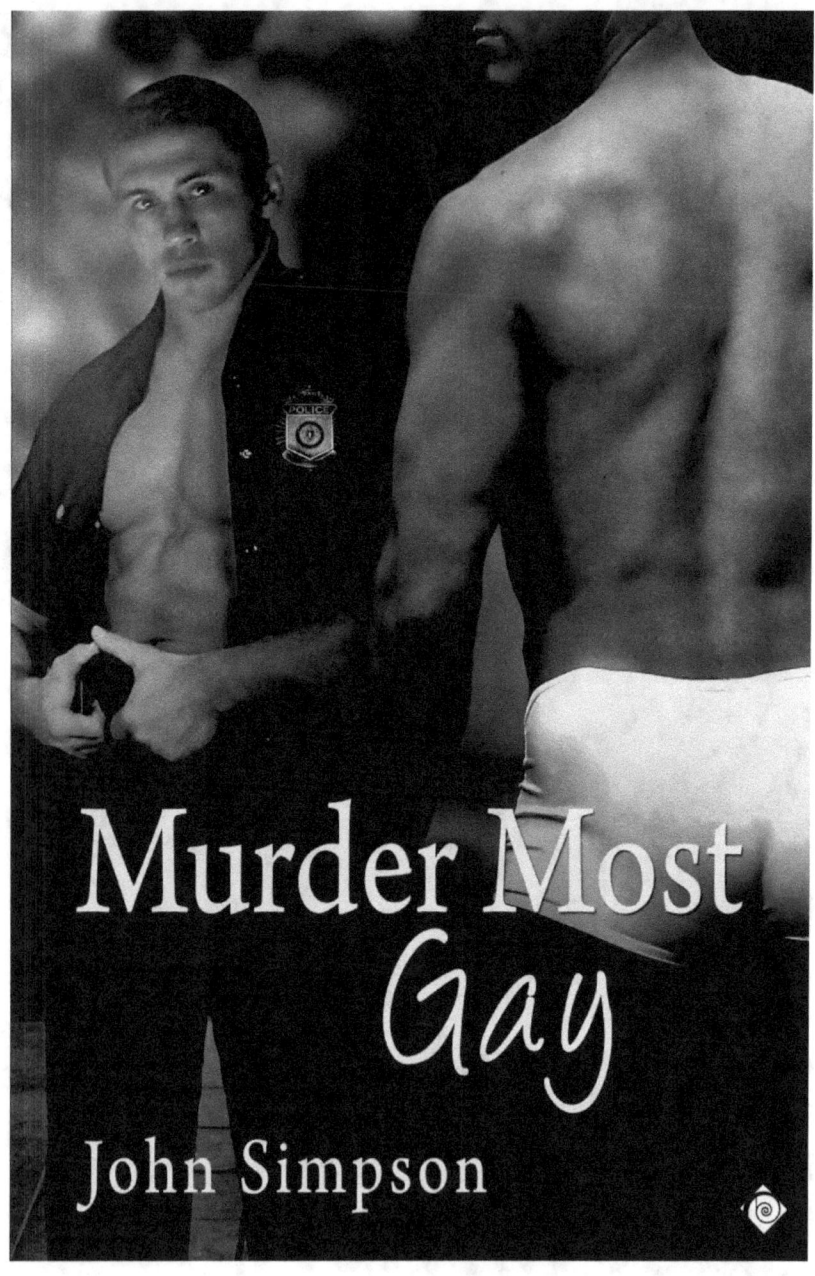

Murder Most
Gay

John Simpson

Romance from DREAMSPINNER PRESS

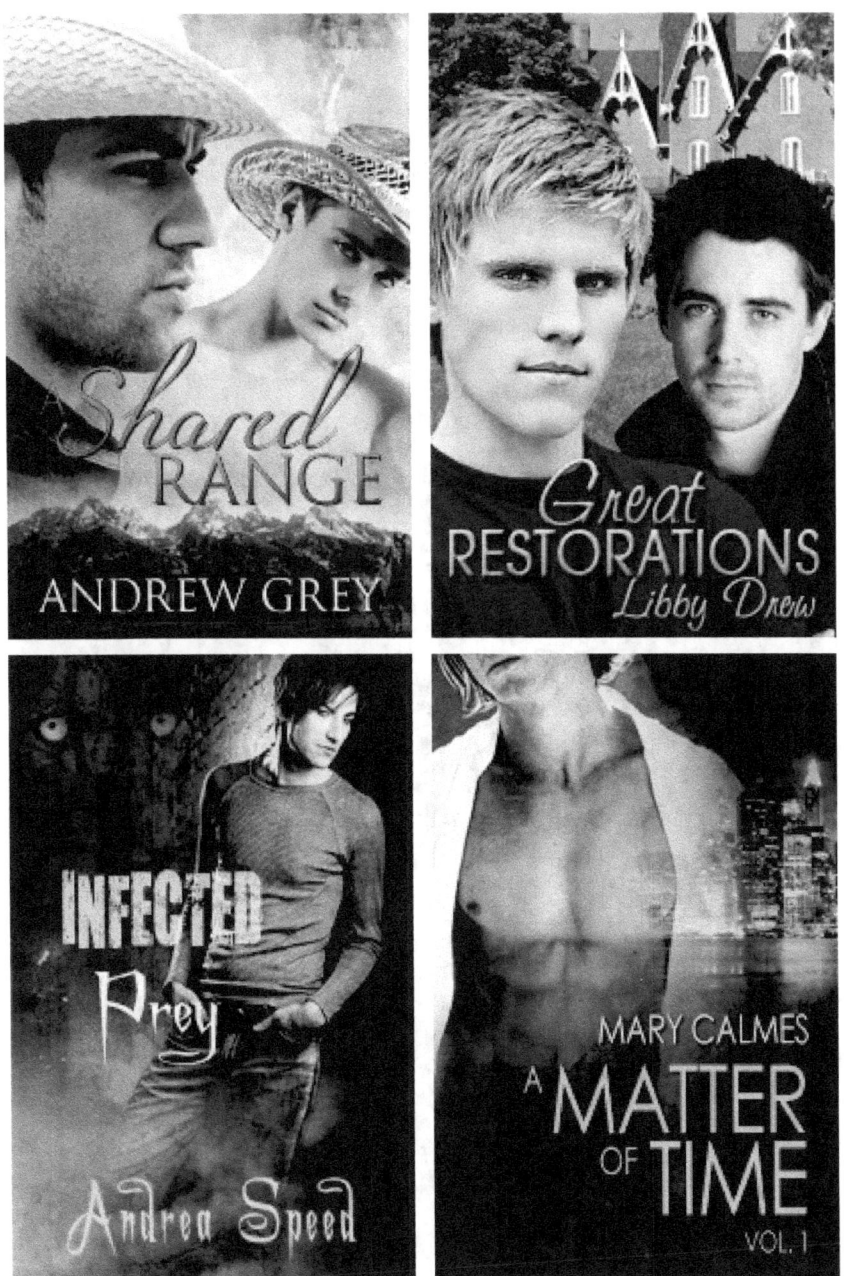

http://www.dreamspinnerpress.com

Marie Sexton

PROMISES